DEANN ELMA SCOTT

Beauty waiting in the Shadows

A Story of Love, Faith, and the Strength to Overcome

First published by Lyrics and Soul Publishing 2024

First edition

ISBN (paperback): 979-8-9921356-1-9
ISBN (hardcover): 979-8-9921356-0-2

This book was professionally typeset on Reedsy.
Find out more at reedsy.com

Contents

Preface

Every shadow hides a story, and every heartbreak holds a lesson. *Beauty Waiting in the Shadows* is more than a romance—it's a journey through love, loss, and the unwavering faith that leads us to brighter days.

Lisa's story is deeply personal, inspired by moments of pain, resilience, and the belief that God's timing is always perfect. Her journey with Don reminds us that love isn't just about finding someone; it's about fighting for what's real, even when the odds seem impossible.

This book is for anyone who's ever doubted, hoped, or dreamed of a love worth waiting for. May it remind you that even in the darkest moments, there's beauty waiting to be found.

With love,

Deann Elma Scott

Acknowledgments

Writing *Beauty Waiting in the Shadows* has been an emotional and transformative journey. My deepest gratitude goes to my sons, Lyndel, Titus, and Daniel, whose love and strength inspire me daily.

A heartfelt thanks to Flora Newton, whose keen eye and dedication to this project helped shape this book into what it is today. To Aaesha Zahra, for bringing the beauty of this story to life with a cover design that perfectly captures its essence.

To Don, thank you for inspiring this story and igniting the creative spark that made it possible.

And to my readers thank you for joining me on this journey of love, faith, and resilience. I hope this story touches your heart as deeply as it has touched mine.

Chapter 1: The Awakening

The soft morning light streamed through the window as Lisa made her way to the hotel's dining area, her heart beating faster than usual. She wasn't sure why. Perhaps it was the thought of Don—tall, dark, handsome, and full of boyish charm—that had her chest feeling tight.

She barely knew him. In fact, she didn't know much at all, except that his smile had a way of lighting up a room, and that her heart did peculiar things whenever he was near. The thought of him stayed with her all night, As she lay in bed unable to sleep. She imagined his face pressed against hers in a tight, romantic embrace, so warm, she could almost feel it. She longed to just melt in his arms and let out a long sigh that said, "eat me, digest all of me."

She let her thoughts run wild for a moment, then suddenly pulled herself together. "It could be months before any of this happens," she thought to herself. "If it ever reaches to that." She didn't want to let herself get hurt. But every time she tried to stop thinking about him, her heart betrayed her again.

"You need to calm down," she whispered to herself, but it was no use. Every time she closed her eyes, she could see Don—his smile, his gentle presence, the way he seemed to notice her in a crowded room. And every time, her chest swelled with hope, followed by the cautious whisper of doubt.

" What if she was reading too much into this? What if he is already in a committed relationship? What if he was only pursuing her as his side chick or as a trophy to add to his collection? What if nothing good could come out of this?" The uncertainty gnawed at her like a rodent in a corn field, but she couldn't deny the spark between them.

She tried to steady her thoughts as she headed to breakfast that morning, hoping she might catch a glimpse of Don sitting at his usual spot in the office. Her heart fluttered at the thought. If only she could just see him, even just for a moment, it would make her day—or maybe send her thoughts into a tailspin for another twenty-four hours.

Lingering Moments

Lisa's heart thrummed in her chest as she approached the office door, each step hesitant but deliberate. Voices floated from within, muffled yet tantalizing, and a surge of anticipation raced through her. Was he inside?

"Good morning," she said softly, her voice carrying a warmth she couldn't suppress. Peeking into the room, she offered a friendly wave to the staff. But then her eyes found him—Don.

He stood by his office computer, his figure framed perfectly in the soft light filtering through the window. Her hand lifted instinctively, as though her heart had commanded her body, and she waved at him with a smile that seemed to flow from her very soul.

Don looked up, and in that instant, it was as if the universe paused. His face lit up with a smile so radiant it felt like the first burst of sunlight after a storm. Don had that sweet boyish crease that gathers around his cheek every time he smiles - that Lisa absolutely adored. She never had the chance to tell him that, because they had not yet had a chance to talk privately. Lisa wished so much that he would take the initiative and invite her out so that they could talk. The boyish crease she adored appeared on his cheek, drawing her attention in a way that made her heart skip.

The connection between them was electric—palpable. A warmth, sweet and effervescent, blossomed in her chest and spread through her entire being. It felt as though their hearts had reached out, bypassing words, and exchanged something intimate and profound. Lisa knew, with a certainty that defied logic, that he felt it too.

Her lips parted in a quiet exhale as she turned to leave, her body moving away even as her heart begged her to stay. The moment lingered, embedding itself in her memory like a golden thread in a tapestry.

The day crawled by, each hour weighed down by the quiet hum of longing.

After lunch, Lisa found herself walking the corridor near the office again, her hands busy with dishes, her mind elsewhere.

As the elevator doors opened, her pulse quickened. There he was.

Don strolled toward her, his steps unhurried, his presence magnetic. Her breath hitched as their eyes met.

"How you doing?" he asked, his voice rich and smooth, each word carrying a melody of charm that seemed to be his alone.

Lisa felt her lips curve into a smile that she couldn't control. "Better now," she said, her voice light but carrying the weight of truth and heartful playfulness.

Don chuckled, the sound low and intimate, as if it was meant for her ears alone. He leaned in slightly, his gaze softening. "I'll come see you later, right?"

The butterflies in her chest fluttered wildly. "Yep," she replied, her cheeks warming, the anticipation sparking like fireflies in the dark.

That evening, a knock at her door sent her heart racing. Lisa hesitated, listening carefully. The steady rush of water from the shower reassured her— her roommate was still occupied.

Opening the door, she found Don standing there, his expression a mix of caution and quiet excitement. Lisa smiled, her heart soaring, then she reached for his hand, guiding him inside.

Her movements were unhurried, her fingers light against his as she led him further into the room, away from the prying eyes of the hallway. When the door clicked shut, the air between them shifted, thick with unspoken emotions.

Lisa turned to him, her eyes searching his, and without thinking, she stepped closer. Her arms circled his neck, pulling him into an embrace that felt as natural as breathing. For a moment, time seemed to hold its breath.

Don hesitated, his hands hovering as though unsure where they belonged. But Lisa guided him, her touch gentle but certain, encouraging him to let go of his restraint. His hands found her back, resting lightly at first, then moving with a reverence that sent shivers coursing through her.

Their lips met, tentative at first, then deepening into a kiss that spoke of longing and the uncharted depths of their feelings. It was a kiss that carried every unspoken word, every unacknowledged desire, and every silent hope they had yet to voice.

The warmth of his touch ignited something in her, a spark that burned brighter with each passing second. Her hands moved instinctively, pulling him closer, anchoring herself to him in a moment that felt too fleeting.

But the sound of the shower reminded them of reality. Time was not on their side.

Reluctantly, Don pulled back, his breathing uneven, his lips curving into a sheepish smile. "We've got to be careful," he whispered, his voice tinged with both regret and amusement.

Lisa nodded, her cheeks flushed, her heart still racing. "I know," she said softly, though every fiber of her being screamed for more.

At the door, Don paused, one hand resting on the handle as he turned back to look at her. Their gazes locked, and in that moment, the silence between them spoke louder than words ever could.

"Thanks," he said at last, his grin wide and unabashed, a boyish charm lighting up his face.

Lisa couldn't help but smile back, her heart brimming with a joy she couldn't contain.

As he was about to step out, she found her courage. "Don, wait," she called, her voice soft but steady.

He turned, curiosity flickering in his eyes.

"Can I have your email?" she asked. "I'm working on a project, and... I'd love to share it with you, if you don't mind."

His expression shifted, intrigued. "Of course," he said, walking back toward her desk.

Lisa opened her laptop, her fingers trembling slightly as she typed in his email address. "Promise me you'll read it," she teased, her voice light with playful insistence.

"I promise," Don replied, his smile steady.

After he left, Lisa sat down at her desk, her heart still racing. She opened the document she had started earlier that day, a project born from the emotions he stirred in her. *Beauty Waiting in the Shadows* was more than a story—it was their story, a living chronicle of their growing connection.

She reread the opening lines, imagining Don's reaction when he eventually saw it. With a playful note, she sent him the draft. To her delight, his response came quickly, filled with encouragement and curiosity.

That night, as she lay in bed, her thoughts spun with the memory of his touch, his kiss, the way he made her feel like the center of the universe.

"This feels real," she whispered to herself, her lips curving into a soft smile. "I think he loves me."

And with that thought, hope blossomed in her chest, warming her heart like sunlight breaking through the clouds.

Chapter 2: Where It All Began

The evening sun dipped lazily behind the New York skyline, casting long shadows across Lisa's hotel room. Wispy clouds gathered on the horizon, blending into the orange-gray hue of the distant cityscape. Lisa gazed out through the fully drawn curtains, the spring breeze sneaking in through a small crack in the window, carrying a lingering chill that seeped into the room.

Below her, the streets were lined with trees like solemn sentinels, their branches swaying gently in the wind, still holding the memory of winter's grip. It was a serene scene, yet Lisa felt anything but peaceful. She had left her homeland, her family, and her past behind, arriving in America on a desperate mission to find her son, Lyron. Every attempt to reunite with him had been thwarted, her hope eroding under the manipulative grip of her sister, Margaret.

She had tried everything—visiting Margaret's home with the police multiple times, only to be told that their hands were tied. Lyron was of age; there was nothing they could do unless he was willing to see her. Margaret knew this and wielded it like a weapon, keeping him isolated and beyond reach. Lisa felt utterly alone, rejected by relatives who sided with Margaret, her pleas for help met with indifference. The pain of missing her son was excruciating.

Just a year ago, Lisa had retired from her long career as a Registered Nurse and Midwife. She had envisioned a peaceful retirement—a chance to finally write, to chase the creative dreams she had put on hold for so long. But instead of tranquility, she found herself in the midst of a storm, her life uprooted by the chaos Margaret had sown in her marriage and family. Now, in a foreign country, she was left navigating a labyrinth of emotions and uncertainty.

Starting a new life in America was beginning to feel like her only option. The thought of returning home to face the painful memories she was trying to leave behind felt unbearable. "God, I don't know what to do," she muttered, her voice barely above a whisper. "Please show me the way."

She leaned against the window, watching the clouds drift lazily across the sky. A single tear rolled down her cheek, quickly followed by another. "It's so hard to believe for the best when I have no idea where my life is heading," she whispered, her heart aching with every word.

Taking a deep breath, she closed her eyes, trying to calm the turmoil inside her. Lisa had always believed in God's guidance, but in moments like this, her faith felt fragile, like a thin thread she was clinging to in the dark. Her mission to find Lyron was at the forefront of her mind, overshadowing everything else. Even the quiet longing for companionship, which had crept into her life in the form of Don, seemed distant now.

After her divorce three years ago, Lisa had locked her heart away, vowing not to let herself be hurt again. She was open to the idea of remarrying someday, but she trusted that God would send the right person when the time was right. Until then, the doors to her heart remained firmly shut. Little did she know, those doors wouldn't stay closed for long.

There were a few suitors at the hotel vying for her attention, but Lisa dismissed them all with polite indifference. Yet, love had a way of sneaking up when she least expected it. She found herself daydreaming about falling in love again. At first, she tried to brush the thoughts aside, determined not to get caught up in fantasies. But the longer she stayed in New York, the harder it was to ignore the feelings growing inside her for Don.

She didn't know much about him, only what she had pieced together from their brief conversations and the way he smiled at her when he thought no one was looking. His smile made her heart flutter, a sensation she hadn't felt in years. It terrified her, yet she couldn't help but wonder what might happen if she allowed herself to feel more.

Lisa knew Don was holding back, too. She had seen the warmth in his eyes, felt the gentle pressure of his hand when they shared fleeting moments of connection. But he never fully opened up to her. He hadn't called her, even though she had given him her number. He responded to her emails sporadically, leaving her feeling caught in a dance of uncertainty.

With a sigh, she turned away from the window, letting the curtains fall shut. The room, now dimly lit by the fading light, felt colder, almost oppressive. It wasn't just her feelings for Don that weighed on her; it was the entire situation. She had come to New York to find her son, to bring him back into her life, but every door seemed to slam shut in her face. Margaret had built a fortress around him, that Lisa feared she might never be able to break through.

As she stood there, lost in thought, her phone buzzed on the bedside table. It was her younger son calling from Canada, checking in like he always did. She smiled as she answered, grateful for the comfort of his familiar voice.

"Hey, Mom, how's everything going?" he asked, his tone gentle and concerned.

"I'm okay," Lisa replied, though her voice betrayed her exhaustion. "Just trying to figure things out."

They talked for a few minutes, the conversation a brief escape from the chaos swirling inside her. When they hung up, the silence returned, heavier than before.

She set the phone down and sat on the edge of the bed, her thoughts drifting back to Don. His smile, his quiet presence, the way he seemed to sense when she needed a moment of connection—it all played on a loop in her mind. But there was still so much she didn't know about him. Was he involved with someone else? The thought of his co-worker Myrna flashed through her mind. Were they more than just colleagues? The uncertainty gnawed at her, but she couldn't bring herself to ask.

For now, she decided to focus on what she could control: her mission to find Lyron. It was her top priority, no matter how her heart tugged her toward Don. But even as she made this resolution, she knew it wouldn't be easy. Every time their eyes met, her resolve faltered.

Crushing Disappointment at Church

The following Sunday, Lisa decided to visit a church she had been invited to earlier in the week. Her heart held a flicker of hope, fragile but persistent. Maybe, just maybe, she might find someone there who could help her reach Lyron. The service was uplifting, the music filling the sanctuary with warmth. But the real reason she had come was to speak with the pastor. She believed that the church, if anyone, would understand her pain and offer the assistance she so desperately needed.

After the service, Lisa spoke briefly with the brother who had invited her. He introduced her to the pastor, who agreed to meet with her privately in his office. As she stepped inside, her hands folded tightly on her lap, she felt a mix of nerves and anticipation. This was her last resort—she had knocked on so many doors, only to have them slammed in her face. Surely, the church would be different.

The room was filled with the soft glow of sunlight streaming through the window, casting a gentle light that seemed to reflect the hope she clung to. Lisa poured out her story, her voice thick with emotion as she described her desperate attempts to find her son. She explained how her sister, Margaret, had manipulated and isolated Lyron, creating a wall of silence that no one had been able to break through. Her words tumbled out, raw and unfiltered, as she laid bare the pain she had carried for so long.

The pastor listened quietly, his expression unreadable. As Lisa spoke, she could feel the intensity of her own emotions, the tears welling up despite her best efforts to hold them back. She had faced so much rejection already, but here, in the presence of a spiritual leader, she felt a glimmer of hope. She believed he would understand—that he would see her pain and offer a way forward.

When she finished, she looked at him, her eyes pleading for a response, for some sign of compassion. But instead of the empathy she had expected, the pastor glanced down at his watch. His expression remained distant, almost bored, as if he were already thinking about his next appointment.

"There is no way the church could help with that situation," he said flatly, rising from his chair.

Lisa's heart sank. It felt as though the ground had been pulled out from beneath her feet. "But... I was hoping someone who knows him there could speak to him," she stammered, her voice cracking with desperation. "Maybe encourage him to reach out to me. I just want to see my son, to know he's okay."

The pastor sighed, already gathering his things, his hand clutching his Bible as if it were a shield. "If the police couldn't help you, I'm afraid there's nothing the church can do," he repeated, his tone firm and dismissive. "I have three daughters, and I couldn't imagine not being able to see any of them, so I understand what you're going through. But I can't see any way in which the church could get involved."

His words struck Lisa like a wrecking ball, each one landing with a heavy, crushing force. Her chest tightened, her breath caught in her throat, and the tears she had tried so hard to suppress began to spill over, hot and unbidden. She struggled to stand, but her legs felt like lead, numb and unsteady beneath her.

As the pastor hurried off, mumbling something about a funeral he needed to attend, Lisa was left sitting there, her vision blurred by tears. The office door felt like a wall she couldn't break through, the air suddenly stifling, as if the weight of his dismissal were suffocating her.

Crying Out to God

She stumbled into the empty sanctuary, her steps uneven, her hands shaking. The soft glow of sunlight that had seemed so welcoming earlier now felt harsh and mocking. She sank into one of the back pews, the cool wood pressing against her back, a stark contrast to the burning ache in her chest. She couldn't hold it in any longer. A deep, guttural sob escaped her lips, the sound raw and filled with a pain so profound it echoed through the silent church.

Lisa bowed her head into her hands, tears streaming down her face as she let out a cry that came from the very depths of her soul. "Oh God, help me... please!" she whispered, her voice breaking on each word. It wasn't just the pain of today—it was the culmination of years of heartbreak, of fighting against an unyielding tide of indifference and rejection.

"If I can't find solace here, where else can I turn?" she questioned silently, her heart shattering with the realization. "Where else, God? I've tried everything. I've knocked on every door."

She sat there, alone in the pew, the sun streaming through the glass windows, casting colorful patterns across her tear-streaked face. It felt almost mocking, the beauty of the light against the darkness she felt inside. Her shoulders shook with silent sobs, her hands gripping the edge of the pew as if it were the only thing keeping her from collapsing completely.

The pain was relentless, clawing at her heart with every beat. But underneath it, she felt a flicker of something else—small, but there. It was a spark of resolve, of determination that refused to be extinguished. She straightened slowly, wiping the tears from her cheeks, her breath still uneven but steadier now.

"I will not give up," she whispered fiercely, her voice hoarse but filled with a new strength. "I will find my son. No matter how many doors close in my face, no matter how many times I'm turned away, I will not stop searching."

She forced herself to stand, her legs still shaky but stronger now, fueled by a sense of purpose she hadn't felt in months. The memories of her thirty-six years of marriage, ending in divorce and the alienation of her son, flashed before her eyes, threatening to pull her under. But instead of breaking her, the pain only hardened her resolve. She would not be defeated—not by a pastor's cold dismissal, and not by the countless organizations that had turned her away.

With one last look at the empty pews, Lisa made her way to the exit. The sound of the congregation enjoying lunch in the cafeteria drifted up from downstairs, but she didn't care. She didn't need their platitudes or their pity. What she needed was strength, and she found it in the quiet rawness of her pain, in her unwavering faith that God would not abandon her.

As she stepped out into the sunlight, the warmth on her face felt different. It wasn't a comfort, but a reminder. She wasn't alone. God had heard her cry, and she would trust that He had a plan, even if she couldn't see it yet.

She walked away from the church with her head held high, her heart still aching but beating with a steady, determined rhythm. This was not the end. It was just another obstacle, and she was ready to face whatever came next.

Chapter 3: Take Your Pick

The day had been a blur for Lisa, filled with routine tasks and fleeting moments of solitude. By now, she had moved past the disappointment at the church and was beginning to look forward to something more beautiful—her growing affection for Don. She kept herself busy to avoid dwelling on the confusing thoughts swirling inside her, as their interactions had taken on a more personal, delicate tone. There was something unspoken between them, something that had blossomed over time through shared smiles, fleeting touches, and the way he looked at her when he thought no one was watching.

It all started unexpectedly one day as she approached the elevator. The doors slid open, revealing two men inside with a large work cart. She hesitated, thinking there might not be enough room.

"Come on in," one of the men beckoned, making space for her in front of the cart.

"Thank you," Lisa said warmly, stepping inside just before the doors closed. She settled herself between the two men.

"I like her hair," the taller man remarked, as if speaking only to his colleague.

"Yes, it's nice," the other agreed with a nod, almost sounding rehearsed.

"Thank you," Lisa replied, flashing a smile. Her hair was styled in simple single braids—a casual, relaxed look she often wore when she didn't have any special plans. In her homeland, it was a typical, easygoing style, but here, it seemed to stand out - maybe.

The elevator ascended in silence after that, a subtle tension hanging in the air. When the bell chimed on the seventh floor, Lisa turned to exit. "Goodbye," she said with a friendly wave as she stepped off.

She didn't think much of it then—men often said nice things to her. But what she didn't know was that one of these men would soon break through the walls which she had carefully built around her heart.

A Chance Encounter with Don

A few days later, Lisa needed help transporting her bags to a storage facility. One of the men from the elevator was working as the driver that day. Despite his busy schedule, he volunteered to assist her. He stayed with her throughout the errand, offering his help with a smile. She learned his name was Don, and by then, she was starting to appreciate not only his kindness but also his presence. His attentiveness and the way he made her feel safe were beginning to leave a lasting impression.

The Laundry Errand

Later that week, Lisa needed to take care of some laundry. She hadn't planned on doing it that day, but when she saw Don on duty, she found herself hoping they might share a few moments together. When she asked if he was taking guests to the laundry, he hesitated only briefly before agreeing.

"Get ready for ten o'clock," Don said with a smile. "I'll meet you in the lobby."

Lisa felt a flutter of excitement, her spirits lifting at the prospect of spending time with him. When he knocked on her door a few minutes early, she opened it with a smile, her pulse quickening.

"You ready?" he asked, his voice gentle but eager.

"I'm ready," she replied, stepping out to join him.

After the laundry was done, Don drove them back, dropping off the other guests at the hotel's back entrance. He parked the transport and met her again, helping her carry the bag of freshly washed clothes. As they walked toward the elevator, their hands brushed lightly—an innocent touch that sent a spark through Lisa's entire body. She felt an instinctive urge to lace her fingers with his, but before she could, Don turned to her with a playful, almost shy smile.

"Here, let me take that," he said, reaching for her bag, acting as if it was accidental that his hand touched hers.

"Thank you," Lisa whispered, her voice softer than she intended. The air between them felt charged, filled with unspoken words and lingering glances. As they stepped into the elevator, the moment hung heavy with possibilities, but neither of them dared to cross that invisible line just yet.

When the elevator doors opened on the administrative floor, Don gave her a small, lingering smile. "See you later," he said quietly, and she nodded, feeling her heart swell with a mixture of longing and uncertainty.

The Elevator Surprise

The next time she went down for a meal, she scribbled her phone number on a scrap of paper and slipped it into Don's hand just as he glanced away. Then she collected her meal and headed back to her room.

Don quickly followed her, catching up just as she reached the elevator. When the doors closed and they were alone, he asked in a lowered voice, "Is this your number?"

"Yes," she replied, blushing. "I wanted to have a word with you, but you always seem so busy. I thought this would be easier."

He didn't say another word as they rode up in silence, the elevator humming softly around them. Just before they reached her floor, Don turned to her, his expression both serious and vulnerable. He leaned closer, lowering his voice. "May I have a kiss?" he asked, his eyes searching hers.

Lisa was caught off guard, her breath hitching. For a moment, she hesitated, feeling the heat rise in her cheeks. Then, without a word, she turned her face slightly, shyly offering her cheek. Don leaned in and kissed her softly.

The touch of his lips was gentle, warm, leaving a tingling sensation that lingered long after. It was a just a friendly kiss, but it felt like so much more—a promise of something deeper, something she wasn't sure she was ready for but couldn't resist.

"Thank you," he whispered, just as the elevator doors slid open.

"I'll see you later, okay?" Don said, his voice tinged with hope.

"Okay," Lisa replied, still in a daze.

A Growing Connection

The days that followed were filled with a whirlwind of emotions for Lisa. Between her ongoing search for her son and the painful situation with her sister Margaret, she found herself thinking about Don more than she cared to admit. Their brief moments together had become the highlights of her day, and she couldn't deny that she was falling for him.

Despite her growing affection, uncertainty lingered. Don was careful, almost hesitant, as if he were trying to balance his professional duties with his feelings for her. She admired his restraint but also yearned for him to take the next step.

One morning, she came down for breakfast and there he was—standing at the counter, his smile lighting up the room as soon as he saw her from a distance. It was the kind of smile that made her feel special, as if she were the only person in the world.

"I missed you," she said softly.

"I missed you too," he replied, his voice filled with warmth.

As Lisa walked back to her room, she felt lighter than air, her heart filled with hope. She didn't know where this was heading, but she was willing to follow her heart and see where it led. For now, she was content to savor these small, beautiful moments, trusting that everything would fall into place in its own time.

Chapter 4: Trouble and Uncertainty Brewing

The walls of Lisa's hotel room seemed to close in on her, their drab surfaces reflecting the turmoil brewing within. Boredom gnawed at her senses, each piece of dull furniture and the haphazard layout of the room amplifying her unease. This wasn't the luxury she had imagined when she'd envisioned her stay here; instead, it mirrored the confusion clouding her thoughts—particularly about her budding relationship with Don. Something was shifting between them, something she couldn't quite name, and it unsettled her deeply.

Outside her window, clouds gathered ominously in the sky, eclipsing the sun and casting a gray pall over the city. The cold atmosphere beyond the glass felt like a cruel parallel to her internal struggles. Inside, however, her emotions simmered, rising like a pot on the verge of boiling over. Lisa turned and twisted in bed, her thoughts circling endlessly. The affection Don had shown her was undeniable, yet her suspicions that he wasn't being entirely open with her refused to quiet down.

Was Don truly interested in her, or was she just a fleeting distraction? And what about Myrna? The thought of Myrna being more than just a co-worker—a girlfriend, or worse, a wife—clawed at her mind. Lisa didn't want to intrude on anyone's relationship. She had no intention of becoming a third wheel or stepping between two people who belonged together. But if Don and Myrna were truly committed, then why did he continue to engage her in ways that felt so intimate, so real? His actions sparked something deep inside her, stirring emotions she had long thought buried.

Now it was lunchtime, but Lisa's appetite had disappeared. She craved something else entirely—something more tangible, more meaningful. She longed for Don's presence, his touch, his affection. She could almost feel the warmth of his hands against her skin, the heat of his breath near her neck, his arms enveloping her in a tender embrace. The thought sent a shiver down her spine, and for a fleeting moment, she allowed herself to indulge in the fantasy.

But reality snapped her back like a taut rubber band. "Why hasn't he called me?" she muttered to herself, a pang of disappointment cutting through her reverie. She had given him her number, and yet he hadn't used it. The emails that once felt like a lifeline between them had stopped altogether. Doubts crept in, louder and more insistent than ever. Was Don hesitant to be honest with her? Or was there something in his life he couldn't share?

Determined to clear her head, Lisa decided to leave the room and head out for lunch. She grabbed her purse, intent on a change of scenery to shake off the oppressive thoughts weighing her down. As she stepped outside, the brisk air hit her cheeks, invigorating but still heavy with the promise of rain.

An Unwelcome Encounter

As Lisa approached the bus stop, her heart sank. Standing there was Myrna, her posture confident but her expression distant. Lisa froze for a moment, unsure of how to handle the awkwardness of the situation. Myrna glanced briefly in her direction before quickly looking away, making it clear she had no intention of engaging in conversation.

The silence stretched uncomfortably between them as Lisa waited for the bus to arrive. Every second felt like an eternity, the air heavy with unspoken tension. Lisa's unease grew as she debated whether to leave and avoid the situation entirely, but before she could decide, she saw someone approaching in the distance. Her heart skipped a beat as she recognized Don's familiar figure.

Don signaled for Myrna to cross the street to meet him. They spoke briefly, their interaction distant at first, but then Lisa saw something that made her stomach twist—a moment that could have been a kiss, or perhaps just a close gesture. Whatever it was, it cut deep. She quickly looked away, her emotions in turmoil.

"Why didn't I just stay in my room?" Lisa thought, her heart aching. She turned and walked away, needing to distance herself from the scene. She couldn't bear to watch them together any longer.

After walking a few blocks to calm her nerves, Lisa returned to the bus stop, hoping Don and Myrna had left. Thankfully, when she arrived, only a few strangers remained, and Myrna was nowhere to be seen. The next bus arrived shortly after, and Lisa boarded, relieved to finally escape the tension. But her relief was short-lived. A few stops later, Myrna got on the bus, her presence like a dark shadow that refused to leave Lisa's side.

"This is a nightmare," Lisa thought as she avoided making eye contact with Myrna. The bus ride felt endless, the tension suffocating. Lisa focused on the passing cityscape, willing herself to stay calm. When her stop finally arrived, she stepped off with a sigh of relief. Myrna remained on the bus, and Lisa took solace in finally being free of her presence.

A Bittersweet Encounter

After grabbing a bite to eat in town, Lisa returned to the hotel. She decided to stop by the office, hoping to catch a glimpse of Don, though she didn't expect much—his shift was likely over. To her surprise, there he was, sitting at his desk, alone. Her heart lifted at the sight of him.

As she approached, Don looked up and smiled, his face lighting up like the sunrise after a storm. He got up and walked toward her, closing the space between them. The office was quiet, and for a brief moment, it felt like they were in their own little world.

"Hey," he said softly, his voice warm and inviting.

"Hey," Lisa replied, her pulse quickening.

They exchanged a quick, awkward hug, their movements hesitant yet filled with longing. Lisa felt the warmth of his embrace, the comfort it brought. Before she could savor the moment, Don leaned in, brushing a soft kiss against her cheek. It was a fleeting touch, but it sent a spark through her, igniting feelings she struggled to contain.

For a moment, it felt like time had stopped, but the reality of their sur- roundings quickly pulled them back. They smiled at each other, a quiet acknowledgment of their feelings, before Don stepped back. "I'll see you later," he said, his voice laced with both promise and restraint.

Lisa nodded, her heart swelling with emotion as she watched him return to his desk. She walked back to her room, a smile playing on her lips despite the lingering uncertainty. That brief moment of connection was enough to lift her spirits, if only for a little while.

Lingering Questions

Back in her room, Lisa tossed and turned in her bed, staring up at the ceiling as her thoughts swirled like the gentle breeze rustling the curtains. The memory of Don's smile played on a loop in her mind, the warmth of it lighting up her heart like a soft, golden glow. His touch, tender and deliberate, lingered on her skin as though it had imprinted itself into her very being. For the first time in years, Lisa felt an unfamiliar but welcome sensation—hope wrapped in the possibility of love.

Yet, like shadows creeping in at twilight, doubts gnawed at the edges of her happiness.

What was the true nature of Don's relationship with Myrna? Why hadn't he reached out to her—not a call, not an email, not even one of the little notes she secretly longed for? And more pressing, where did she stand in his life?

She wanted to believe in what they shared—that spark, that undeniable connection—but the uncertainty sat heavy in her chest, like a stubborn weight she couldn't shake. Her heart yearned for clarity, for something concrete to hold on to.

Lisa tried to redirect her thoughts. She reminded herself of her mission—to reunite with her son, Lyron. That was her anchor, her reason to keep moving forward. And yet, no matter how resolutely she tried to focus on her purpose, her thoughts would slip right back to Don. It wasn't just attraction; it was something deeper, something she couldn't fully articulate.

Her gaze drifted to her nightstand where a blank notebook rested. On impulse, she reached for it, letting her emotions spill onto the page. She had slipped Don a handwritten note earlier, but the feelings expressed in it seemed to demand more. They wanted melody, rhythm, permanence.

With a soft sigh, Lisa picked up her pen, her heart guiding her words into a song—one that reflected both her longing and her worry.

All of Me for All of You

I want to give you all of me,
In exchange for all of you.
I want to melt in your arms
Like ice cream on a sunny day.
Oh baby, my lips are tingling for your kiss,
And every part of me is craving for your touch.
I can't wait to hold you near,
Just you and me, no fear.
Oh baby, I can't wait to make you mine.

As the words flowed, so did her emotions, each line a blend of vulnerability and desire. She paused, staring at the page. A small smile curved her lips, but it didn't quite reach her eyes. There was still more she needed to express—the uncertainty that lingered, the unanswered questions that tugged at her heart.

She flipped to a fresh page and began the next verse, her pen moving with purpose.

But the uncertainty, oh baby, leaves me with much longing
To know if it's me or her you admire.
Should I let you go or should I stay?
Let me know clearly your desire.
Please don't leave me waiting in vain,
My heart couldn't take the pain
Of losing you forever.
So tell me baby, what will it be?

Lisa set down her pen, reading the words she had written. They felt raw, honest—like an extension of her soul. She hummed softly, testing the melody that had formed in her mind. It wasn't perfect yet, but it was a start.

She closed the notebook, placing it on the nightstand and leaning back against her pillows. Outside, the city hummed faintly, a reminder of the life that kept moving forward, even when her own felt suspended between hope and doubt.

Lisa clasped her hands over her chest, whispering a prayer into the stillness.

"God, give me strength to navigate this. Help me to understand what I should do. And if this is the man you've sent into my life, please give me patience to let it unfold in Your time."

Her thoughts returned to Don—his kindness, his smile, the way he made her feel both giddy and grounded. Despite her doubts, Lisa couldn't deny that he had awakened something in her, something she hadn't felt in years.

And as she drifted to sleep, her heart carried the beginnings of a melody— one that she hoped would carry her closer to the answers she longed for.

Chapter 5: Adversity Unfolding

The morning light seeped through the muted gray clouds, casting a dull haze over the city. Lisa pulled her coat tighter around herself, hoping the crisp air might provide some clarity to the confusion and pain weighing heavily on her heart. Days of uncertainty had spiraled into a harsh realization: she might not be the only woman in Don's life. The love she felt for him, a love that had blossomed so naturally, now felt fragile, tainted by doubt. What once seemed sweet had begun to ferment, soured by the lingering shadow of Myrna.

There was something about Myrna, an invisible negativity that polluted the air whenever she was near. Lisa had felt it before, though Don never openly discussed Myrna or their dynamic. It was clear, though, from the way Myrna carried herself that she wasn't truly in love with Don—but she wasn't willing to let him love anyone else, either.

Lisa secured her phone in her pocket, her fingers trembling as she started walking. She didn't know where she was going; she only knew she had to move. The physical exertion might ease the turmoil inside her, the questions and doubts that gnawed at her heart.

Does Don really love me? The uncertainty tore at her, sharp and unrelenting. If his heart truly belonged to Myrna, Lisa knew she'd have to walk away, no matter how much it hurt. But the very thought of letting go left her feeling hollow, as if a part of her would disappear with him.

Tears stung her eyes as she quickened her pace. She longed for a quiet place where she could let the tears fall freely, without fear of judgment. *Why would he let me fall for him so deeply if he knew he wasn't available?* Her mind swirled with questions that had no answers. Was Don trapped in a situation he couldn't escape, or was he genuinely torn between two women? Lisa didn't know, and her respect for Don kept her from prying, even though every fiber of her being begged for clarity.

She found herself wandering into a large park. The sight of children laughing and playing brought a momentary distraction, their joy cutting through her sadness like sunlight breaking through clouds. She sat on a bench, pulling out her phone to answer a call—brief and inconsequential, but it gave her a reason to linger.

In the distance, a man played basketball alone. His tall, lean figure and focused movements reminded her of Don. *Is it him?* she wondered. The thought tugged at her heart. She longed to know him better, to understand his world beyond the walls of the hotel. But if it was Don, she didn't dare approach. The fear of seeing Myrna with him was too much to bear. She stayed put, watching as the man finished his game and left the park.

A Moment of Vulnerability

The next day, Lisa found herself in the office unexpectedly. Don was there, seated at his desk, his warm smile lighting up the room as he saw her. "How you doing?" he asked casually, his voice carrying the same tenderness that had always melted her defenses.

But Lisa's emotions were too raw to mask. "I'm not doing good," she blurted, her tone sharper than she intended. She turned quickly to finish her conversation with the new driver, adding, "I'll see you on Friday," before walking away.

Her heart sank as she replayed the moment in her mind. *Did I sound flirty? Or rude?* She hated the thought of hurting Don or making him doubt her feelings. Yet, as she caught a glimpse of his face before leaving, her heart ached. His expression was tinged with shame, as if her response had wounded him. Lisa knew how Myrna often treated him, belittling him in front of others, and the last thing she wanted was to add to his burden.

I should apologize, she thought, but the presence of other employees in the office kept her from saying more. She left, the weight of unspoken words heavy on her shoulders.

A Serendipitous Encounter

Days turned into weeks, and the distance between Lisa and Don grew. The warm connection they once shared seemed to be replaced by cold formality. Don appeared to be avoiding her, and even his colleagues' attitudes had shifted. Lisa couldn't shake the feeling that Myrna was behind it all, pulling strings to drive a wedge between them.

One morning, unable to endure the tension any longer, Lisa wrote Don a note. But days passed without an opportunity to slip it to him as she usually did. That morning, she decided to wait near the hotel entrance, hoping to catch him on his way to work. Her appointment in town could wait—seeing Don was more important.

As minutes dragged on, Lisa began to lose hope. She watched a bus pull in at the stop ahead, but something made her hesitate. She could have asked the driver to wait, but her feet remained rooted. And then, she saw him. Don was walking briskly toward her, his familiar figure filling her with a mix of relief and anxiety.

Her heart leapt, but uncertainty quickly followed. What if he ignored her? What if he walked past without a word? Unable to decide how to react, Lisa instinctively stepped behind an electrical pole, as if hiding would shield her from disappointment.

Don spotted her immediately. "Are you okay?" he asked as he reached her, his voice gentle, his concern evident.

Lisa hesitated, her emotions threatening to overwhelm her. "Not really," she admitted, her voice barely a whisper.

Without another word, Don stepped closer, his arms opening in a gesture that melted her defenses. He wrapped her in a warm, tender hug, pulling her against his chest. The steady rhythm of his heartbeat soothed her, grounding her in the moment. Lisa rested her head against him, letting herself feel safe in his embrace.

When he finally pulled back, his eyes met hers, soft and reassuring. "Are you okay now?" he asked, a small smile tugging at his lips.

Lisa nodded, a matching smile spreading across her face. "Now I am."

"Good," Don said with a chuckle, releasing her gently. "I'll see you later."

As he walked away, Lisa noticed one of the women at the bus stop smiling, as if silently approving of the tender moment she had witnessed. Lisa boarded the next bus with a lightness in her heart she hadn't felt in weeks. *He still loves me,* she thought, her smile widening. And the way he had shown it left no room for doubt.

A Stolen Moment

Later that day, as Lisa returned to the hotel, her heart skipped a beat when she saw Don again in the lobby. He was with two co-workers, their conversation casual. Lisa lingered, pretending to be preoccupied, but her eyes kept drifting to him. Don noticed her, his gaze locking with hers for a brief second before he called out, "Hold the door for me!"

"Okay," Lisa replied, her heart pounding as they approached he elevator. Once inside, the doors closed, and for a fleeting moment, it was just the two of them. The air between them was charged, the tension melting away as Don leaned closer.

Their lips met in a sweet, stolen kiss, soft and lingering. It was a moment that reignited the spark between them, a silent promise that whatever challenges lay ahead, their connection remained strong.

When the doors opened, they parted with knowing smiles, their bond feeling stronger than ever. For the first time in weeks, Lisa felt the dark cloud over her heart begin to lift. She carried that feeling with her as she stepped back into her room, ready to face whatever came next.

Chapter 6: Tension in the Air

The weekend arrived, casting a shadow over Lisa's heart that felt heavier with each passing hour. The tension between her and Don, the unresolved questions about Myrna, and the subtle but persistent undercurrents of suspicion all weighed on her mind. The warmth of Don's smile still lingered in her memories, but it was now tinged with unease, like sunshine breaking through the rain clouds.

Lisa sat in her room, staring out at the faint city lights as the evening crept in. The muted glow of the streetlights reflected her inner turmoil. She thought back to the quiet moments with Don—the way his eyes seemed to hold secrets, the way his presence calmed her even amidst her confusion. But those moments were often overshadowed by Myrna's constant, calculated presence.

An Uneasy Discovery

One afternoon, Lisa headed down to the office to retrieve supplies for her room. Don was outside, assisting a group of guests, his calm demeanor and easy smile making her heart flutter despite her inner turmoil. She collected her items and walked toward the elevator, the sound of Don's voice trailing behind her.

She felt an inexplicable urge to turn back, to steal one more glance at him before leaving. But something held her back—a quiet, persistent instinct that urged her to keep walking, do not turn back. She continued to the elevator, pressing the button and standing with her back to the hallway.

Finally, she turned—and froze. Myrna was there, following quietly behind her, her steps so soft Lisa hadn't noticed. Myrna's expression was unreadable, her movements deliberate as she stopped a few feet away. The realization hit Lisa like a jolt of electricity. *That's why I felt the need to not turn back,* she thought, her heart pounding.

In the distance, Lisa could see Don watching them with intense concern. His gaze furrowed with a discomfort that Lisa could feel even from afar. His eyes darted between Lisa and Myrna, as if silently urging Lisa to stay calm. Lisa turned back to the elevator, willing herself to remain composed. As the doors slid open, she stepped inside, avoiding Myrna's gaze altogether, and pressed the button for her floor. The doors closed, sealing her away from the tension that had followed her like an evil shadow.

Myrna's Manipulations

That evening, Lisa decided to wait outside the hotel gate, hoping for a quiet moment with Don as he left work. The cool evening air was refreshing, and she leaned against the gate, scrolling through her phone to distract herself from her racing thoughts. Don's shift was nearing its end, and she wanted nothing more than to see him, to feel the reassurance of his presence.

But as fate would have it, Myrna appeared. Lisa's heart sank. Myrna wasn't scheduled to work that day, yet here she was, walking toward Lisa with a smile that didn't feel genuine.

"Hi." Myrna said with a strange smile on her face, her tone unnatural and sinister. "Can I borrow your phone? I need to make a quick call to my friend." Myrna never communicates with Lisa normally – she never ever even makes eye contact with her, but now, she wants to borrow her phone? Lisa's suspicion meter sped to Red Alert. Something about Myrna's request felt... off, her demeanor too polished, too deliberate.

"Sorry, I don't have data service on my phone," Lisa replied, keeping her tone neutral.

"Oh, it'll just take a second," Myrna pressed, her gaze locking into Lisa's eyes with an intensity that felt propelled by another deity. Lisa felt a strange energy emanating from her, something she couldn't quite place but knew she didn't want to engage with. No wonder Don was acting so strange lately. He was under that spell too.

Lisa turned away to avoid the haunting glare in Myrna's eyes. "I'm really sorry," She said, stepping back slightly, "I cannot lend you my phone right now." Myrna hesitated, her smile slowly faltering, seems like she wanted to insist, but she soon got the message, that Lisa would not be messed with. She quickly recovered, giving a small shrug before walking off, leaving Lisa shaken but resolute. *I won't let her get to me,* Lisa thought firmly, gripping her phone tightly. *Whatever she's trying to do, it won't work on me.*

The next morning at breakfast, Myrna was there helping with the meals. As she saw Lisa she walked right up to her again, looking up into her eyes with that same evil, haunting look which felt hard to watch. She was about to say something to Lisa again but Lisa turned slightly, walking away from her. With that, she did not pursue Lisa any further.

Since then, Lisa noticed that Don was acting very strange, hiding when he saw her, sometimes, he couldn't even look at her when she approached the office. It was like Lisa's presence was too strong for his eyes. His smiles were no more. These were the times Lisa felt the urge to break things of with Don. But she soon realized that Don was dealing with something beyond his will, something oppressive that threatens to pull her under also. That's when she recognized the need to pray for his release from whatever force that kept him unable to move on with her. She must pray for the release of both him and Lyron.

The Elevator Reunion

The next day brought another encounter, one that Lisa hadn't anticipated but desperately needed. She had left the office earlier, feeling too unsettled to stay when Don had asked her to wait for him. She suspected that her former roommate—who had shown up unexpectedly near the office—might have been set up by Myrna to spy on her. Lisa couldn't risk exposing her connection with Don, so she had left, walking aimlessly through the city streets to clear her mind.

When she returned to the hotel later that evening, she saw Don walking down the corridor with a colleague. Her heart skipped, but she wasn't sure if she should approach him. Instead, she moved toward the elevator, pressing the button and waiting in the shadows, hoping he wouldn't see her.

As the elevator arrived, Don suddenly flung himself inside, startling her. She entered after him. The doors closed, and for a brief moment, it was just the two of them. The tension between them melted away, replaced by a wave of relief that washed over Lisa like a balm to her aching heart.

Don reached for her hand, his touch warm and steady. "Are you okay?" he asked softly, his eyes searching hers.

Lisa shook her head, unable to hide the weight of her emotions. "Not really," she admitted, her voice unsteady.

Don's expression softened, his concern evident. He gently pulled her into his arms, holding her close in a hug that felt like coming home. Lisa rested her head against his chest, savoring the sound of his heartbeat, the quiet strength in his embrace.

"I've missed you," he whispered, his voice filled with emotion.

Lisa looked up at him, her eyes searching his. "I've missed you too," she replied, her words barely audible.

As the elevator reached her floor, they pulled apart reluctantly, their connection stronger than ever. "I'll see you later," Don said with a smile, his tone tender.

Lisa nodded, stepping out of the elevator and turning back to catch one last glimpse of him before the doors closed. Her heart felt lighter, the doubts and tension of the day momentarily forgotten.

A Silent Resolve

As Lisa lay in bed that night, she replayed the events of the day in her mind. The stolen moments with Don, the manipulations of Myrna, the quiet strength she had found within herself—it all swirled together, a tapestry of emotions that left her both drained and determined.

She knew the road ahead wouldn't be easy. The shadow of Myrna's interference loomed large, and the uncertainty of her relationship with Don weighed heavily in the balance. But Lisa was resolute. She wouldn't let the games, the doubts, or the tension tear her apart. She would hold onto the moments that mattered, the connections that had brought light into her life even amidst the storm.

And as she drifted off to sleep, Lisa whispered a fervent prayer for Don and for a revelation of God's plan for her life, trusting that the path ahead would reveal itself in time

Chapter 7: Steering the Course

A chill hung in the air, carried not by the weather but by the subtle undercurrents of change rippling through the hotel. Conversations among senior staff carried a foreboding tone, their whispers weaving an ominous tapestry of uncertainty. Lisa could feel it, that distinct heaviness signaling upheaval. She wasn't sure what form the change would take, but she knew it would alter her course—and likely her connection with Don.

It seemed as though the springtime of joy and camaraderie that had once blossomed so freely had been overshadowed by a gathering storm. Lisa sat on the edge of her bed, staring at her reflection in the window as sunlight barely filtered through the faint, gray sky. The possibility of being transferred to a new residence loomed large in her mind. The staff had assured residents that accommodations would be arranged according to their preferences, but Lisa feared she would be separated from Don. A part of her knew Myrna would seize any opportunity to ensure their paths would never cross again.

An Uncomfortable Encounter

The following day, Lisa returned from an appointment feeling restless. Hoping for a glimpse of Don, she stopped by the office. To her disappointment, the space was unusually empty. There was no sign of Don—or Myrna.

"Did they leave early today?" Lisa wondered, her heart sinking. She grabbed her lunch and decided to take the stairs instead of the elevator, seeking a distraction from her unease.

Halfway up the first floor, the sound of approaching footsteps echoed down the narrow staircase. She stepped aside to let the person pass, only to find herself face-to-face with Myrna. Their eyes met briefly, but Myrna's gaze was cold, carrying an unspoken tension. Lisa caught her breath as Myrna brushed past her, the encounter leaving her unsettled.

"Was she on my floor?" Lisa wondered, the thought lingering like an unwelcome guest. It wouldn't have been the first time Myrna's presence felt deliberate, her actions seeming to orbit around Lisa and Don.

Don's Discomfort

The next morning, Lisa passed by the office again. This time, Don was inside, but something was desperately off. His usual confidence and warmth were gone, replaced by a slumped posture and downcast expression. He barely looked up as Lisa entered, and when their eyes met, a flicker of sadness passed between them. He seemed trapped, as if carrying a burden he couldn't share.

Lisa wanted to ask if he was okay, to offer some kind of solace, but the unspoken tension held her back. She left quietly, her heart heavy with worry. What could have happened to dim the light in Don's eyes? She made it a point to pray for him against whatever was ailing him.

In the days that followed, Don's absence became was prolonged. Lisa's suspicions began to grow. Could Myrna have orchestrated something to jeopardize his position? Lisa wouldn't put it past her. The thought gnawed at her, but she prayed for clarity, asking God to guide her through the confusion, and guide Don through whatever he was going through.

A Ray of Light

By the end of the week, Lisa's unease reached a peak. She braced herself for the possibility that Don might not return. When she entered the office the next morning, her heart skipped a beat. There he was, seated at his desk, his face lighting up with that familiar, radiant smile as he saw her.

"He's back!" Lisa thought, her spirits lifting. The sight of him, his boyish charm intact, washed away her fears. And, as if to celebrate his return, she heard Don humming a tune from the pantry. Though his choice of songs often amused her, the sound of his voice felt like a balm to her frayed nerves.

Myrna, however, was conspicuously absent. Lisa couldn't help but wonder if Myrna's schemes had backfired, leaving her out of the picture altogether. She didn't dwell on it, grateful instead for the peace that Myrna's absence brought.

The Transfer

The day of the transfer arrived, and Don was at the helm, assisting residents with their moves. Myrna's absence added a sense of relief, but the new accommodation felt like a stark contrast to their previous residence. The atmosphere was colder, the rules stricter, and the staff more guarded. Lisa couldn't shake the feeling that Don was slipping away from her again. Their stolen moments were fewer and farther between, and Don's distance felt deliberate, as though he was holding something back, almost like there was another force at play – it felt like that.

The Growing Distance

The relationship between Don and Lisa was more distant now than ever. Lisa had hoped that with Myrna no longer around, their bond would grow closer, but instead, it seemed to unravel further. Don's behavior became increasingly puzzling. He avoided her in ways that felt almost unnatural, as though something beyond them was keeping him at arm's length. Each time Lisa tried to connect with him, Don found subtle ways to move away, his actions leaving her hurt and bewildered.

She often wondered why he couldn't reach out—why he wouldn't respond to her emails or even call. He had her number, but he had never used it. He had never shared his number with her, either. Lisa weighed all of this in her mind, coming to the painful conclusion that Don didn't truly love her. Perhaps she had been nothing more than a fleeting distraction to him.

Determined to face the truth, Lisa prayed fervently, asking God to reveal what she was truly dealing with and what she should do. She didn't want to deceive herself by holding on to a love that wasn't reciprocated. "If he loved her," she thought, "he would have shown it by now. He would be feeling comfortable enough to respond to her emails or to call her."

Lisa resolved to break things off for good. She prayed for the strength to let go, knowing it would be excruciatingly hard. She decided to stop trying to reach Don altogether—no more emails, no more notes, and no more smiles exchanged in the hallway. If he wanted her, he would have to come to her.

A Silent Gesture

When Lisa met Don in the hallway with his boss later that week, she had already steeled herself to move on. Her heart ached with longing, but her resolve to break things off held firm. Don, however, seemed to sense her disconnection. As they passed each other, he stealthily offered his hand for a quick touch—a gesture they had often shared in playful secrecy, a silent acknowledgment of their bond.

Lisa hesitated, her heart battling her resolve. She knew their little game, their way of connecting without drawing attention, but this time, it felt different. Reluctantly, she brushed her fingers against his, the familiar spark reigniting in that brief, fleeting moment. Her heart betrayed her again, she thought to herself. Every time she tried to break things off, she found herself back to dreaming about him again.

A Fleeting Connection

The next day, her heart leaped when Don passed by her room. Her roommate had just stepped out, leaving them alone for the first time since the move. As he entered the room, they exchanged shy smiles before edging closer, their mutual longing palpable. He just stood there.

Lisa approached him, slowly taking his hand in hers. They looked at each other with unspoken longing, then without a word, she placed his arms around her, leaning into his embrace. Don's arms tightened around her, pulling her closer as their breaths mingled. Then their lips met, lingering as if savoring every second. And for that brief moment, the world outside ceased to exist.

Hope Rekindled

As they pulled apart, their eyes met, a silent understanding passing between them. Lisa felt a glimmer of hope, though she knew the path ahead was uncertain. She prayed for strength, trusting that God would guide them through whatever lay ahead. For now, she held onto the belief that their love, however fragile, was worth fighting for.

Chapter 8: Navigating Uncertainty

The days passed in a haze of longing and confusion for Lisa. Her heart was a tangled mess of emotions, caught between the joy of Don's touch and the growing distance she couldn't ignore. His discreet gestures—the way he squeezed her hand when no one was watching, the fleeting smiles they exchanged—were enough to keep hope alive but not enough to erase her doubts.

Her room had become both a haven and a prison, a place where she replayed every interaction with Don, dissecting his words, his silences, and his actions. She would lie awake at night, her mind flooded with thoughts of him. His kisses were like nothing she had ever experienced. They left her lips tingling with an electrified warmth that lingered long after he had gone. No one had ever made her feel the way Don did—with just a kiss, he could melt every defense she had built around her heart.

Many nights, Lisa found herself longing for his embrace, imagining his caresses, the warmth of his body pressed against hers. She ached for the day when they could be truly together, unencumbered by secrets or fears. In her daydreams, she envisioned their first night together—a moment of deep intimacy and unhurried exploration, where every touch and every kiss would speak the words they couldn't yet say.

But reality bore a stark contrast to her dreams. The distance between them seemed to grow, even as Don's gestures of affection hinted at a connection he wasn't ready to acknowledge fully. Lisa knew he was dealing with something—something that kept him from opening up completely. And though she didn't want to pressure him, she couldn't help but wonder if he would ever break free from whatever held him back.

A Glimmer of Hope

One afternoon, Lisa wandered through the hotel lobby, lost in her thoughts. She looked up just in time to see Don heading toward the office. Their eyes met, and for a moment, it felt as though the world had stopped spinning. His smile lit up his face, and Lisa felt her heart skip. She returned his smile, hoping it conveyed all the love and understanding she carried for him.

Later that evening, as the golden hues of the setting sun bathed the city, Lisa sat by her window, letting her thoughts drift. Her phone buzzed, jolting her back to reality. She picked it up, her heart racing when she saw Don's name on the screen.

"Can we talk tonight? I need to see you."

Lisa's fingers trembled as she typed her response.

"Really? Of course. I'll be waiting."

Her chest filled with a mix of anticipation and nervousness. Could this be the moment she had been longing for—the moment Don would finally let her in?

The Conversation

When Don knocked on her door that night, Lisa felt her pulse quicken. She opened the door to find him standing there, his expression both serious and gentle. He stepped inside, and for a moment, they simply stood there, gazing at each other in silence. The quiet intensity in his eyes spoke volumes, even as words failed him.

Don reached for her hand, pulling her into his arms. Lisa wrapped her arms around his waist, resting her head against his chest. The steady rhythm of his heartbeat calmed her restless thoughts. They stood there, enveloped in a moment that needed no explanation.

"I don't want to lose you," Don whispered, his voice barely audible. "I just need time."

Lisa pulled back slightly, her eyes searching his. "I'm not going anywhere," she said softly. "I just need to know that you want this as much as I do."

Don cupped her face in his hands, his thumb brushing gently across her cheek. "I do. I really do. It's just... complicated."

Lisa nodded, her heart aching with both love and frustration. "I understand," she said. "But you don't have to feel afraid with me, Don. I will never judge you. Your circumstances doesn't define who you are to me. I'll love you anyway."

Don closed his eyes, a mix of emotions washing over his face. Then, without another word, he leaned in and kissed her.

A Kiss Like No Other

Don's kiss was slow and tender, filled with all the things he couldn't bring himself to say. Lisa melted into him, savoring the moment, the sensation of his lips sending ripples of warmth through her body. This was what she had been waiting for—not just the physical connection, but the emotional vulnerability that came with it.

When they finally pulled apart, Lisa rested her forehead against his, her breath uneven but steady. "I love you, Don," she whispered.

Don smiled, that boyish crease appearing at the corners of his mouth—the smile that always made her heart flutter. Though he didn't say the words back, Lisa could feel his love in the way he held her, in the way he lingered, unwilling to let the moment end.

Dreaming of the Future

They sneaked out of her room to a quiet, secluded spot where they could talk freely. For the first time, Don opened up about his dreams. He spoke of escaping the chaos and uncertainty of their current lives, of finding a place where they could just be themselves.

"The Caribbean," he said softly, his voice tinged with longing. "I've always dreamed of going there. Maybe we could..."

He trailed off, but Lisa knew what he meant. Her lips curled into a smile as she leaned in to kiss him again. "Maybe one day," she whispered, imagining the turquoise waters and white sandy beaches, a place where they could start anew.

The seed of a dream was planted that night—a vision of a future free from the obstacles that weighed them down. It wasn't a promise, but it was enough to keep hope alive.

Lingering Longing

That night, Lisa lay in bed, her heart full yet aching with longing. Don's kiss lingered on her lips, leaving the same tingle that always kept her awake, replaying the moment over and over in her mind. She hugged her pillow tightly, imagining it was Don beside her, his arms wrapped around her as they drifted off to sleep together.

She didn't know what the future held, but for the first time in weeks, Lisa allowed herself to hope again. Whatever obstacles lay ahead, she believed they could overcome them—together.

Chapter 9: Building Trust, Brick by Brick

The weeks that followed felt like the blossoming of spring after a long, cold winter. Despite the challenges surrounding them, Don and Lisa's connection deepened in ways Lisa had only dreamed of. Don's goofy, playful side gradually began to emerge as they became more comfortable with each other, and Lisa adored every minute of it. His boyish antics often brought a smile to her face, and she savored the lightheartedness he brought into her life.

One evening, Don appeared outside her door with a mischievous grin. "Guess what?" he asked, his voice brimming with excitement.

"What?" Lisa replied, her curiosity piqued.

Don revealed a small, hand-carved wooden flower he had picked up from a street vendor. "I saw this and thought of you," he said with a dramatic flourish, presenting it to her as if it were a priceless treasure.

Lisa burst out laughing, her heart swelling with affection. "You're ridiculous," she said, but her smile betrayed how much the gesture meant to her.

Don's playful energy often softened the weight of the unspoken things between them. His antics were a reminder that love didn't always have to be heavy; it could be light and joyful, a reprieve from the complexities of life.

The Small Things That Matter

Don had a way of showing his love in the simplest gestures. He often surprised Lisa with little treats—an extra packet of sugar for her coffee, a folded napkin shaped into a heart, or a goofy face that made her laugh when she least expected it. Lisa treasured these moments, knowing that they came from a place of genuine care.

One afternoon, as they passed each other in the hallway, Don brushed his hand lightly against hers. It was a fleeting touch, but it sent tingles all over her body. He winked at her, his eyes sparkling with mischief, before disappearing around the corner.

Lisa stood there for a moment, smiling to herself. He always found ways to brighten her day, even in the smallest of ways.

Cooking Up Connection

By then, Lisa had settled into her new Airbnb, a cozy place with a small kitchen that allowed her to indulge in one of her favorite pastimes—cooking. She invited Don over for dinner, eager to share a taste of her Caribbean heritage with him.

The aroma of coconut rice with pigeon peas, stewed chicken, and fried ripe plantains filled the room as Don arrived. His eyes lit up when he saw the spread on the table.

"This smells amazing," he said, sitting down with anticipation.

Lisa poured him a glass of freshly made passion fruit juice mixed with lemon, watching with delight as he took his first sip. "Wow," he said, his eyes widening. "This is better than anything I've ever tasted. You're going to spoil me."

Lisa laughed, feeling a warmth in her chest that had nothing to do with the food. "Wait until you try the dessert," she teased, already planning to introduce him to her favorite treats from home.

As they ate, Don's playful side shone through. He pretended to analyze the food like a critic on a cooking show, using exaggerated hand gestures and dramatic expressions. Lisa couldn't stop laughing, and for the first time in weeks, the tension between them seemed to fade away completely.

"You're ridiculous," she said, shaking her head as she watched him savor the last bite of his meal.

"Ridiculously in love with this food," he quipped, grinning at her.

Lisa rolled her eyes but couldn't help smiling.

A Moment of Vulnerability

After dinner, as they cleaned up together, Don wrapped his arms around her from behind, resting his chin on her shoulder. "You know," he began, his voice soft, "I'm not good at saying how I feel, but I want you to know...I care about you. More than I've ever cared about anyone."

Lisa turned to face him, her heart swelling at his words. She cupped his face in her hands, her eyes searching his. "You don't have to say everything, Don," she said. "I see it in the way you look at me, in the things you do. And I care about you too. More than you know."

Don smiled, that boyish crease forming at the corners of his mouth—the smile that always melted Lisa's heart. He leaned in and kissed her, slow and tender, a kiss that left her lips tingling and her heart singing.

Lisa closed her eyes, savoring the moment. No one had ever made her feel so special, so desired. His kisses were a language of their own, speaking words he couldn't yet say.

Building Dreams Together

After dinner, they sat together on the couch, talking about everything and nothing. Don opened up more than Lisa had ever seen before, sharing stories about his childhood, his dreams, and the things that scared him.

"I've always wanted to visit the Caribbean," he admitted, his voice filled with longing. "I think it's the closest thing to paradise on earth."

Lisa smiled, imagining the two of them walking hand in hand along the shores of Grand Anse beach, the waves lapping at their feet. "Maybe one day," she said softly, her voice filled with hope.

"Yeah," Don replied, a faraway look in his eyes. "One day."

A Promising Future

As the night drew to a close, Don stood by the door, hesitating as if he didn't want to leave. He took Lisa into his arms one last time, pressing a soft kiss to her forehead.

"Thank you for tonight," he said. "It was perfect."

Lisa smiled, her heart full. "Anytime," she replied. "And Don? I'm here for you. Always."

He nodded, his eyes lingering on hers before he finally turned to leave.

As Lisa closed the door behind him, she leaned against it, her heart racing. She knew their journey was far from over, but for the first time in a long time, she felt a sense of peace. They were building something together—something real, something worth fighting for.

And as she crawled into bed that night, her lips still tingling from his kisses, Lisa allowed herself to dream of the future they could have together. It wouldn't be easy, but with every passing day, she felt more certain that it would be worth it.

Chapter 10: The Walls Begin to Crumble

The weeks that followed were filled with an air of quiet anticipation. Lisa and Don had grown closer in ways she had longed for, yet the shadow of Don's unspoken struggles lingered. She sensed he was trying, slowly opening himself up, but the burden he carried was still palpable. Lisa respected his pace and the walls he had built to protect himself. She understood that trust wasn't built overnight; it was laid brick by brick, with time and patience.

One crisp evening, Lisa found herself on the balcony, the city lights twinkling below as she sipped on a warm cup of tea. Her mind wandered to Don, as it often did these days. Despite the uncertainty, she couldn't ignore the deep connection they shared. He had a way of making her feel seen, cherished, even in his quiet, understated way.

Her phone buzzed, interrupting her thoughts. It was a message from Don: *"Can I see you tonight?"*

Lisa smiled, her heart fluttering. She quickly typed back:

"Of course. My place?"

"7 o'clock."

Her excitement was tempered with a hint of nervousness. There was something different about Don lately, a quiet intensity in his presence. Tonight felt significant, as if something important was on the horizon.

Opening Up

When Don arrived, Lisa could see the weight in his eyes. He stepped inside, his movements slower than usual, as though carrying an invisible burden.

"Hey," Lisa greeted him softly, stepping forward to wrap her arms around him. He held her tightly, his embrace lingering longer than usual.

"Hey," he murmured back, his voice tinged with something unspoken.

They sat down on the couch, the silence stretching between them. Lisa didn't push; she let Don gather his thoughts, knowing how hard it was for him to open up.

After a few moments, he finally spoke. "There's something I've been meaning to tell you," he began, his voice low and steady. "Something I should have told you a long time ago."

Lisa placed her hand on his, giving it a reassuring squeeze. "Take your time," she said gently.

Don sighed, his gaze fixed on the floor. "It's about Myrna," he admitted, his tone heavy with emotion. "And why things between us have been so... complicated."

Lisa's breath caught, but she stayed calm, her face composed. She had always suspected there was more to Don's relationship with Myrna but hearing him say it out loud made her chest tighten.

"She and I... we were involved," he continued, his words measured and deliberate. "It was a mistake, right from the start. She had this way of making me feel... small. Like I wasn't enough unless I did things her way. And for a long time, I let her control me."

Lisa's heart ached for him. She could see the pain etched on his face, the shame that weighed him down.

"When I met you," he said, his eyes finally meeting hers, "I realized how much I'd been missing. How much I'd given up. But by then, I didn't know how to break free. She had her hooks in deep, and every time I thought I was out, she pulled me back in."

Lisa reached out, cupping his face in her hands. "Don, you don't have to explain everything right now. Just know that I'm here for you. You're stronger than you think, and you don't have to let her control you anymore."

Don closed his eyes, leaning into her touch. "I don't want to hurt you," he whispered. "I don't want to drag you into my mess."

"You're not dragging me into anything," Lisa replied firmly. "This is my choice. I care about you, Don. And I believe in you."

A Moment of Hope

Don's gaze softened, and for the first time, Lisa saw a glimmer of hope in his expression. He leaned in, pressing his forehead against hers, his breath warm against her skin.

"I'll try," he said, his voice thick with emotion. "I'll try to let you in."

Lisa smiled, her heart swelling. It wasn't a full promise, but it was a start.

They spent the rest of the evening in quiet companionship. Don's hand never left hers, and Lisa could feel the weight of his words lingering in the air. As they sat together, she could sense the walls between them beginning to crumble, brick by brick.

A Dream of Freedom

After Don left, Lisa sat by the window, the city skyline glowing softly in the distance. Her mind wandered to the future—a future she could now see more clearly.

She imagined taking Don back to Grenada, showing him the places that held pieces of her heart. She pictured them walking along the Grand Anse beach, the warm sand beneath their feet, the turquoise waters stretching endlessly before them. She thought about the countryside, where they could pick fresh fruits straight from the trees, drinking coconut water and savoring the sweetness of ripe sugar apples and sapodillas.

It was a dream that felt closer now, though still just out of reach. But Lisa was patient. She knew that love wasn't a sprint; it was a marathon, and she was ready to run it with Don, step by step.

Building Something Beautiful

The next morning, Lisa woke with a sense of hope she hadn't felt in weeks. She knew the journey ahead wouldn't be easy, but for the first time, she felt certain that it would be worth it.

Don had begun to let her in, and she would honor that trust by standing by his side, no matter what. Together, they would build something beautiful—a love that could withstand the storms of the past and grow stronger with every challenge they faced.

And as Lisa looked out at the morning light filtering through her window, she allowed herself to dream of the life they could have, a life filled with love, laughter, and the freedom to be fully themselves.

Chapter 11: Strength in Vulnerability

The weeks that followed Don's heartfelt confession brought a profound shift in their relationship. It wasn't an overnight transformation, but Lisa could see the subtle changes in Don—the way his walls began to crack, the way his presence in her life felt more intentional, more certain.

Lisa cherished the ways Don was learning to open up. His actions spoke volumes, even when words eluded him. Whether it was the way he would show up at her door with a quiet smile and a bag of her favorite snacks or the way he would rest his hand on hers, squeezing gently, as if to say, *I'm here,* Don's gestures carried the weight of his emotions.

One evening, as they sat together on Lisa's couch, sipping warm cinnamon tea, the air between them felt charged with unspoken thoughts. Don reached for her hand, his fingers tracing delicate patterns on her palm.

Lisa turned to him, sensing that he wanted to say something. "What's on your mind?" she asked softly, her voice inviting yet patient.

Don took a deep breath, his gaze dropping to their intertwined fingers. "I've been thinking," he began, his voice low and hesitant. "About what you said before... about my past not defining my future."

Lisa's heart lifted, hope blooming in her chest. She knew how hard it was for him to confront his fears and doubts, and the fact that he was willing to share even this small piece of his struggle meant the world to her.

"And?" she prompted gently, giving his hand a reassuring squeeze.

"I've always been scared," Don admitted, his voice carrying the weight of years of self-doubt. "Scared that if I let you see all of me—the mess, the mistakes—you'd walk away." He paused, his thumb brushing over the back of her hand. "I've never been good with words, Lisa. I've always admired how you can just... say what's in your heart. I don't know how to do that."

Lisa's heart ached at his vulnerability. She squeezed his hand, her voice steady but filled with warmth. "Don, you don't have to be perfect. You don't have to say all the right things or do everything perfectly. I'm not looking for perfection. I'm looking for *you* - flaws and all. It is our flaws that make us all unique you know."

Don finally looked up, his dark eyes meeting hers with a mixture of uncertainty and longing. "You really mean that?" he asked, his voice barely above a whisper.

"I do," Lisa said firmly, her thumb brushing over his knuckles. "Your past doesn't define you. It's what you choose to be now, in the present, that matters. And I see the man you're choosing to be. That's enough for me."

Don's lips curved into a small, tentative smile. "I'm trying," he said, his voice rough but sincere.

"That's all I ask," Lisa replied, her heart swelling with affection.

A Song Inspired by Love

The next morning, Lisa woke with Don on her mind: The words *"I'm altogether broke and broken,"* came to her mind as she woke out of sleep. The phrase struck a chord deep within her, and as she sipped her morning coffee, inspiration began to flow. She grabbed her laptop, and before long, the lyrics of the entire song poured out onto the screen.

"I'm altogether broke and broken
Take the pieces of my life Lord
Put them together and make me a whole
Embellish me with your grace, make me sparkle once more

It was raw and heartfelt, a reflection of repentance and turning life around. She whispered a prayer for Don, that he would let God into his life, her own desire to lift him up. Within half an hour, the song was complete—a poignant melody about healing, forgiveness, and turning life around.

She imagined Don singing it for her album, his deep, rich voice bringing the words to life. The thought made her smile, a spark of excitement lighting up her heart.

Quiet Evenings and Honest Conversations

Their evenings together became a cherished routine. Don would show up after work, sometimes with a small treat for Lisa or a story about his day, and they would settle into the comfort of each other's presence.

One night, Don arrived looking particularly worn out. His shoulders slumped as he entered, his usual lightheartedness replaced by a quiet heaviness.

"Tough day?" Lisa asked as she wrapped her arms around him in a warm hug.

Don nodded, leaning into her embrace. "You have no idea," he muttered, his voice tinged with frustration.

"Come on," Lisa said gently, guiding him to the couch. "Let's sit down. You can tell me about it if you want, or we can just relax."

As they sat side by side, Lisa ran her fingers through Don's hair, her touch soothing. He closed his eyes, letting out a heavy sigh. "It's just... everything feels like too much sometimes," he admitted, his voice barely audible.

"You're here now," Lisa said softly. "You don't have to carry it all alone. Let me help."

Don opened his eyes, turning to look at her. His expression was one of gratitude mixed with something deeper—a recognition of the unwavering support she offered him.

"I've been thinking about us," he said quietly, his gaze steady.

Lisa's breath caught, her heart racing. "What about us?"

"I want us to have something real," Don said, his voice filled with determination. "I want to leave all of this behind and just... be with you."

Lisa felt tears prickling at the corners of her eyes. She had dreamed of this moment, and now that it was here, it felt almost too good to be true.

"The Caribbean," Don continued, a small smile playing on his lips. "I can't stop thinking about it. About us, on a beach somewhere, no distractions, no one pulling us apart. Just peace."

Lisa's heart swelled with love. She leaned in, cupping his face in her hands.

"That sounds perfect," she whispered.

Don smiled, his hands covering hers. "I'm going to make it happen," he promised, his voice steady and sure.

A Future Together

As they held each other close, Lisa felt a sense of hope she hadn't experienced in years. The promise of a fresh start in the Caribbean loomed on the horizon—a symbol of the life they were building together, brick by brick.

And in that moment, as they sat together in the quiet of her apartment, Lisa knew that their journey was just beginning. With Don by her side, she was ready to face whatever challenges lay ahead, knowing that their love would see them through.

Chapter 12: Shifting Priorities

The days after Don's heartfelt declaration were filled with a new kind of energy for Lisa. The dream of walking hand-in-hand with Don along the golden beaches of the Caribbean seemed closer now than ever. But as much as she wanted to indulge in thoughts of turquoise waters and warm, moonlit nights, a deeper ache pulled at her—Lyron.

Her son's absence lingered in her thoughts, a constant shadow in the glow of her newfound happiness. She couldn't ignore the unanswered questions that came with every passing day. Was he okay? Did he miss her? And most pressing, would she ever be able to free him from Margaret's manipulative grip?

That afternoon, Lisa sat at her small kitchen table, her laptop open to images of Grenada. The vibrant photos of the island filled her screen, showcasing waterfalls she longed to show Don, lush greenery she wanted them to hike through, and the serene waters where she pictured them sitting quietly together. Yet, her heart was too restless to enjoy the view.

Her hand hovered over the trackpad as she closed the browser. A deep breath steadied her, and she opened a new search tab, typing in *help for estranged parents.* The results poured in—support groups, advice columns, and legal services—most of which she'd read through before. But desperation pushed her to try again.

The doorbell rang, breaking her focus. Lisa opened the door to Don's familiar face, his warm smile a balm to her anxious thoughts.

"Hey," he greeted, leaning in to kiss her softly.

Lisa stepped aside to let him in, wrapping her arms around him. "You always know when I need you," she said, her voice muffled against his chest.

Don pulled back slightly, studying her face. "What's on your mind?"

"It's Lyron," Lisa admitted, leading him to the couch. She sat down, her hands twisting in her lap. "I can't shake the feeling that I'm running out of time to reach him. Margaret has kept him isolated for so long... I'm afraid of what he might think of me now."

Don nodded, his expression thoughtful. "You've been carrying this alone for too long," he said gently. "We'll figure it out together."

Lisa's lips trembled with emotion as she reached for his hand. "I just don't know how. Margaret has blocked every attempt I've made to contact him."

Don squeezed her hand reassuringly. "What about a private investigator?"

Lisa's eyes widened slightly, considering the idea. "You think that could work?"

"It's worth a try," Don said. "Someone who can find out where he is and give you a chance to approach him without interference."

The thought filled Lisa with a cautious hope. "Maybe... maybe that's what I need," she said softly.

"Let me help," Don said, his voice firm. "We'll figure this out, Lisa. Lyron is your son, and he deserves to know how much you love him."

Lisa's eyes welled with gratitude. She leaned against Don, letting his quiet strength soothe her.

The Plan

The next morning, Lisa called a recommended investigator and explained her situation. It was emotionally draining to recount the years of estrangement, Margaret's manipulative tactics, and the pain of losing her son. But by the end of the call, Lisa felt a renewed sense of purpose. The investigator assured her they would begin immediately and keep her updated.

As the days passed, Lisa and Don fell into a routine of hopeful waiting, punctuated by moments of tenderness that reassured Lisa she wasn't alone in her journey.

Don's small gestures meant everything—surprising her with flowers, teasing her to lighten the mood, or simply sitting with her in comfortable silence. One evening, he prepared dinner for her, his playful commentary keeping her laughing even as her thoughts drifted to Lyron.

"You're burning the garlic," Lisa pointed out, trying to stifle a laugh.

Don smirked, waving the spatula dramatically. "It's not burnt; it's *flavorful.* Trust me, you'll love it."

Lisa laughed, her heart lightened for the first time in days.

Hope and Doubt

Two weeks later, Lisa received an update from the investigator. Lyron had been located—he was working in a small grocery store not far from Margaret's home. The news sent Lisa into a spiral of emotions. Relief mingled with anxiety as she grappled with what the next steps should be.

That evening, Lisa shared the news with Don as they sat on the couch, the weight of the revelation heavy between them.

"So, what now?" Don asked, his voice steady but concerned.

Lisa stared at her hands, her voice trembling. "I don't know. What if he doesn't want to see me? What if Margaret's poisonous notions of me has already tainted his mind against me?"

Don tilted her chin up, his eyes locking onto hers. "You're his mother, Lisa. No one can take that away from you. He may have doubts, but deep down, he knows who you are. You have to believe that."

Lisa nodded, tears brimming in her eyes. "I just want him to know how much I love him."

"He will," Don said firmly. "We'll figure out the best way to reach him. This isn't the end."

The Battle Continues

But as Lisa moved forward, the obstacles grew. Margaret seemed to sense Lisa's determination and tightened her grip on Lyron, making any direct contact nearly impossible. Weeks turned into months, and despite the investigator's efforts, every approach to Lyron was blocked by Margaret's interference.

The strain weighed heavily on Lisa, and there were nights when she cried herself to sleep, wondering if she would ever see her son again.

Through it all, Don remained her anchor, his love and support unwavering. He encouraged her to keep fighting, to hold onto hope even when the odds felt stacked against her.

"You're stronger than you think," he told her one night as they lay in bed, his arms wrapped tightly around her. "And I'm here for you, no matter how long this takes."

Lisa clung to his words, drawing strength from his belief in her. She resolved to keep pushing forward, no matter how difficult the journey became.

A Flicker of Light

One day, the investigator called with unexpected news. A television network had taken an interest in Lisa's story after hearing about her struggles through the investigator's contacts. They wanted to feature her journey on a popular daytime show, highlighting the pain of estrangement and the hope of reconciliation.

Lisa hesitated. Could this be the way to reach Lyron? The idea of sharing her story on such a public platform was daunting, but it could also be the breakthrough she needed.

Don took her hand, his eyes filled with encouragement. "This could be it, Lisa. The chance you've been waiting for."

Lisa nodded slowly, her heart pounding with both fear and hope. "If it means reaching Lyron, I'll think about it," she said. But, in honest, Lisa did not feel the strength to follow through with this idea yet, maybe at a later time. She will let the investigator do his investigation for now.

With Don by her side, Lisa prepared for the next chapter in her journey—a step into the unknown that could bring her closer to her son or test her resolve in ways she had never imagined.

Chapter 13: Shifting Priorities

The days leading up to Lisa's anticipated reunion with Lyron were a whirlwind of emotions. Her heart alternated between hope and fear as she clung to the possibility of finally reconnecting with her son. Yet, Margaret's grip still loomed heavy over them like a shadow, a constant reminder that this moment wasn't guaranteed.

Lisa spent her days pacing her apartment, her thoughts consumed by memories of Lyron. She replayed moments from his childhood—his laughter, his curiosity, the way he used to come running to her with every scraped knee and small triumphs; and as he grew older, his generosity and selflessness towards others were increasingly evident. Those memories had been her anchor, but now they felt bittersweet, tinged with the pain of their separation.

Don's presence during those days was a lifeline. He showed up every evening, bringing small comforts: a meal from her favorite restaurant, a bouquet of her favorite flowers, or simply his steady, reassuring presence. He knew better than to try to distract her completely; instead, he became her sounding board, listening patiently as she poured out her fears and hopes.

"You'll see him," Don said one evening as they sat on the couch. His voice was soft but firm, a beacon of confidence. "You've come this far, Lisa. Nothing's going to stop you now."

Lisa wanted to believe him, but the gnawing fear of Margaret's interference was always there. "What if she's poisoned his mind completely?" she whispered, her voice trembling. "What if he doesn't want to see me?"

Don reached out, taking her hand in his and holding it tightly. "Then you'll show him the truth," he said simply. "You'll remind him who you are, and that your love for him has never changed. That's all you can do, Lisa. The rest... you have to leave to God."

His words brought a small measure of comfort, and Lisa leaned into him, letting his warmth steady her racing heart.

The Park Meeting

When the day of the planned meeting arrived, Lisa felt a mix of nervous anticipation and dread. She stood in front of her mirror, smoothing her hair for the hundredth time, trying to steady her hands. Don had insisted on driving her to the park, and as they pulled into the parking lot, he reached over and gave her hand a reassuring squeeze.

"You've got this," he said, his voice steady and filled with belief.

Lisa nodded, swallowing the lump in her throat as she stepped out of the car.

The park was alive with the sounds of laughter and conversation. Children played on the swings, and families strolled along the paths. Lisa's eyes scanned the area, her heart pounding as she searched for her son. The private investigator had assured her that Lyron would be there, but as the minutes ticked by, her nerves began to fray.

Finally, her phone buzzed. She snatched it up, her hands shaking as she read the message from the investigator.

Change of plans. Lyron left the area—Margaret called him back unexpectedly.

Lisa's heart sank. She reread the message, hoping she had misunderstood, but the words stayed the same. The opportunity she had been waiting for had slipped through her fingers – just like that!

"No," she whispered under her breath, her voice cracking. She felt her knees buckle slightly, and she reached out to steady herself on a nearby bench.

Don appeared at her side in an instant, his hand on her shoulder. "Lisa, what happened?" he asked, his voice laced with concern.

Lisa handed him her phone, unable to speak. Don's jaw tightened as he read the message, and he let out a frustrated sigh.

"That woman," he muttered under his breath. "She just won't let go, will she?"

Lisa shook her head, tears streaming down her face. "I was so close, Don. I could've seen him... I could've held him."

Don knelt in front of her, his hands gently gripping hers. "This isn't the end, Lisa," he said firmly. "You'll get another chance. Margaret might have delayed this, but she can't keep you apart forever. We'll find another way."

The Weight of Waiting

Back at her apartment, Lisa sat at the kitchen table, staring at the investigator's update on her phone. Margaret's control over Lyron was suffocating, and Lisa felt like every step forward was met with an even bigger obstacle.

Don was busy in the kitchen, making tea, his way of comforting her when words didn't seem enough. When he returned, he set the mug in front of her and sat down, his presence grounding her.

"We need to think strategically," he said, his tone thoughtful. "This isn't just about seeing Lyron—it's about breaking Margaret's hold on him. That's the real fight."

Lisa nodded, though her heart ached at the thought of more waiting. "I don't even know if he wants to see me," she said quietly. "What if I'm just... chasing something that's not there anymore?"

Don reached out, his hand covering hers. "You're his mother, Lisa. That bond doesn't just disappear like that. No matter what Margaret's told him, deep down, he knows who you are. You just have to hold on to that."

Lisa smiled weakly, grateful for his unwavering faith in her. "You always know what to say," she murmured.

A New Plan

In the days that followed, Lisa refocused her efforts. She worked closely with the investigator, exploring new strategies to reconnect with Lyron. Margaret's interference made direct contact nearly impossible, but Lisa refused to give up.

One evening, as she sat with Don, she shared an idea that had been forming in her mind.

"I was thinking about writing something for him," she said hesitantly. "A letter, or maybe a story. Something that shows him how much I love him, even if I can't say it to his face right now."

Don smiled, his dark eyes soft with admiration. "I think that's a beautiful idea," he said. "And I know it'll mean the world to him when he reads it."

Encouraged by his support, Lisa began pouring her heart onto the page. She wrote about their memories together, the lessons she had tried to teach him, and the unwavering love she had for him. As she wrote, her pain transformed into determination, each word a step closer to the son she longed to hold again.

Renewed Hope

One morning, the investigator called with a glimmer of hope. "We're working on another opportunity," they said. "It'll take some time, but we'll get there."

Lisa clung to those words, her heart swelling with renewed determination. She knew the road ahead would be long, but she also knew she wasn't walking it alone.

That evening, as she sat on the couch with Don, his arm wrapped around her shoulders, Lisa felt a sense of peace.

"Thank you," she said softly, turning to look at him.

"For what?" Don asked, his playful smile returning.

"For being here," Lisa replied. "For believing in me, even when I'm ready to give up."

Don leaned in, pressing a tender kiss to her forehead. "I'm not going anywhere," he said. "We'll get through this together. I promise."

As they sat together, the weight of the day slowly lifted, replaced by the promise of a brighter future. Lisa knew the fight to reconnect with Lyron wasn't over, but with Don by her side, she felt ready to face whatever challenges lay ahead.

Chapter 14: Strength in Vulnerability

The weeks that followed Don's heartfelt confession were transformative, though subtle. It wasn't an instant metamorphosis, but Lisa saw the quiet shifts in him—the way he lingered longer when they talked, the gentleness in his gestures, the intentionality behind every interaction.

Don's actions often spoke louder than words. On some evenings, he'd show up at her door with a bag of her favorite snacks, his smile soft and tentative, as though testing the waters of a deeper connection. At other times, it was the quiet way he'd rest his hand on hers, his fingers brushing gently against her skin, sending a wave of warmth coursing through her.

One evening, as they sat on Lisa's couch, sipping cinnamon tea, the air between them was thick with unspoken emotions. Don reached for her hand, his touch hesitant yet deliberate, tracing light patterns on her palm. Lisa's heart quickened, sensing he wanted to say something.

"What's on your mind?" she asked softly, her voice a blend of patience and invitation.

Don's gaze dropped to their intertwined fingers. "I've been thinking," he began, his voice low and unsure. "About what you said... about my past not defining my future."

Her breath caught. Those words had clearly struck a chord, and now he was trying to process their weight.

"And?" she prompted gently, squeezing his hand in reassurance.

Don exhaled, the sound heavy with years of self-doubt. "I've always been scared," he admitted, his voice tinged with vulnerability. "Scared that if I let you see all of me—the mess, the mistakes—you'd walk away."

Lisa's heart ached for him, the rawness of his words hitting her deeply. "Don..." she began, her voice steady, though her chest felt tight with emotion. "You don't have to be perfect. You don't have to say all the right things or be everything at once. I'm not looking for perfection. I'm looking for you—flaws and all."

Don's dark eyes met hers, uncertainty flickering in his gaze. "You mean that?" he asked, his voice barely above a whisper.

"I do," Lisa said firmly, her thumb brushing over his knuckles. "Your past doesn't define you. It's the choices you make now that matter. And I see the man you're choosing to be. That's enough for me."

For the first time, Don's lips curved into a small, tentative smile. "I'm trying," he said, his voice rough but sincere.

Lisa's own smile widened, her heart swelling with affection. "That's all I ask."

In that moment, the connection between them deepened, a quiet understanding solidifying their bond.

New Scene: Flashback to Don's Past

As Don sat with Lisa, her words lingered in his mind, stirring memories he had long buried. He thought back to a moment years ago—a moment that had shaped his fears.

He was standing outside a small coffee shop, rain drizzling around him as he held a bouquet of wilted flowers. Inside, he saw the woman he had once loved, sitting with someone else. The betrayal had been sharp, cutting through him like a blade. He had walked away that day, vowing never to let anyone see his vulnerability again.

Now, sitting beside Lisa, her warmth and understanding threatened to dismantle those walls he had so carefully built. It terrified him, but it also offered a glimmer of hope—a chance to rewrite his story.

A Song Inspired by Love

The next morning, Lisa woke with Don heavy on her mind. The words came to her almost as if whispered by her soul: *"I'm altogether broke and broken."*

The phrase echoed within her, resonating with the vulnerability Don had shared. She grabbed her laptop, the melody forming in her mind as she began typing furiously.

"Take the pieces of my life, Lord,

Put them together and make me whole.

Embellish me with Your grace,

Make me sparkle once more..."

The lyrics poured out, raw and unfiltered. Each line was a reflection of not only Don's struggles but her own prayers for healing—for him, for herself, for them together.

She imagined Don singing the song for her album, his deep, resonant voice breathing life into the words. The thought made her smile, her heart swelling with excitement.

Shifting Priorities

The days after Don's quiet declaration filled Lisa with both hope and unease. The dream of walking hand-in-hand with him along the golden beaches of Grenada felt closer than ever, but a shadow loomed over her happiness: Lyron.

His absence was a constant ache, a wound that refused to heal. Memories of him as a child—his laughter, his unending questions, the way he used to hold her hand tightly—flooded her mind. Those moments were her anchor, but they also reminded her of what she had lost.

One afternoon, as Lisa sat scrolling through photos of Grenada on her laptop, her chest tightened with longing. Waterfalls, lush green hills, and vibrant markets filled her screen, each image a reminder of the home she wanted to share with Don. Yet her thoughts kept circling back to Lyron.

Would he ever be back in her life again? Did he even think of her anymore?

Flashback: Lisa's Last Moments with Lyron

Lisa's mind drifted to the last time she had seen Lyron. He had been standing on the porch, his backpack slung over one shoulder, his face stoic but his eyes betraying a mix of anger and sadness.

"Don't go," she had pleaded, her voice breaking. "We can work this out."

Lyron had shaken his head. "I need space, Mom," he had said, his voice firm but not unkind. "Margaret says you don't understand me. Maybe she's right."

Those words had shattered her, and as he walked away, Lisa had felt a part of herself leave with him.

Present Day: A New Resolve

The flashback spurred something in Lisa—a determination she hadn't felt in months. Closing her laptop, she reached for her phone and dialed the investigator's number.

"Let's try again," she said, her voice steady. "I won't give up on him."

Lisa's determination to reconnect with Lyron led her and Don to brainstorm new ways to reach him. They spent evenings researching, talking, and praying together.

One night, as they sat on the couch, Don suggested, "What if you write him a letter? Something heartfelt—something only you could say."

Lisa's eyes lit up at the idea. "A letter..." she murmured. "Or maybe even a story—something that shows him how much I love him without scaring him away."

Don smiled, his admiration for her evident. "I think he'd read it. And I know it would mean the world to him."

With Don's encouragement, Lisa poured her heart onto the page, crafting a story that wove memories, love, and hope into a narrative meant for Lyron's eyes alone.

Chapter 15: A Mother's Fight

The days following Lisa's failed attempt to connect with Lyron were fraught with a mix of determination and heartbreak. The private investigator's efforts to arrange a meeting had been thwarted at the last minute, likely due to Margaret's watchful and controlling nature. It was as if Margaret had a sixth sense when it came to Lisa, always finding ways to block her from reaching Lyron.

Lisa sat on her couch, staring at her phone, the investigator's words echoing in her mind. *"We'll need more time. Margaret seems to have caught wind of the plan."*

Time. It was a word that felt both cruel and necessary. How much more of it would she need to reclaim the relationship she had lost with her son?

Don arrived that evening, carrying a small bag of takeout. The scent of Chinese food filled the room as he set it on the coffee table, his presence grounding Lisa's fraying emotions. He sat down beside her, taking her hand in his.

"What's going on, Lisa?" he asked gently.

She sighed, leaning into him. "It didn't work. Margaret blocked me again. I don't know how, but she always finds a way."

Don's brow furrowed, and he drew her closer. "She can't keep him from you forever. You'll get through to him eventually. You just have to keep trying.. and praying."

"I know," Lisa said softly, though her heart felt heavy. "But every time I get close, something happens. It's like she has a web spun so tightly around him, I can't break through."

Don didn't say anything, but his hand tightened around hers, offering silent support.

Holding Onto Hope

The next day, Lisa decided to pour her emotions into her writing. Sitting at her desk, she opened her laptop and began drafting a letter to Lyron—one she hoped to give him one day when the time was right.

She wrote about the day he was born, how she had held him for the first time and promised to always protect him. She wrote about the memories they had shared—his favorite meals, the way he used to laugh when she tickled him, the bedtime stories they had read together, and about how much she had appreciated the last Mothers' Day gift he had given her.

Tears blurred her vision as she typed, but she didn't stop. She wrote about her pain, her longing, and her unwavering love for him. When she finally closed her laptop, she felt a strange sense of relief, as if the words had lifted a weight from her chest.

Later that evening, Don found her sitting on the balcony, staring out at the city lights. He joined her, bringing two mugs of hot cocoa.

"Writing again?" he asked, his tone light but curious.

Lisa nodded, taking a sip of the cocoa. "I wrote a letter to Lyron. I don't know if he'll ever read it, but... it helped."

Don smiled softly, reaching over to tuck a strand of hair behind her ear. "You're an amazing mom, you know that? You've been through so much, and you're still fighting for him. That takes strength. It takes fortitude, and you've got both."

Lisa's eyes mellowed at his words. "Sometimes I feel like I'm not doing enough," she admitted. "Like I've already lost him."

"You haven't lost him," Don said firmly. "He's out there, and he's your son. That bond doesn't just disappear. It's in him, even if he doesn't realize it yet. And when the time is right, he'll come back to you."

"You think so?" Lisa asked, trying to believe against her discouragement.

"I know so." Don replied.

Lisa leaned into him, her heart swelling with gratitude. Don's steady presence was a balm to her wounded spirit, a reminder that she wasn't alone in this fight.

Moments of Connection

While Lisa continued to navigate the emotional turmoil of her attempts to reach Lyron, her relationship with Don blossomed in small but meaningful ways.

One evening, as they cooked dinner together, Don's playful side emerged. He tossed a small piece of onion in Lisa's direction, grinning mischievously.

"Don!" Lisa exclaimed, laughing as she picked up a spoon and playfully swatted at him.

"You can't just throw food at the chef," Don teased, holding up his hands in mock surrender.

"You're not the chef," Lisa countered, smirking. "I'm the chef. You're the assistant."

"Assistant, huh?" Don said, stepping closer. "I'll have you know I'm a very skilled sous-chef."

"Oh, really?" Lisa said, raising an eyebrow.

"Really," Don replied, leaning in to steal a kiss.

Lisa laughed, her worries momentarily forgotten as she melted into the moment. These playful interactions had become a cornerstone of their relationship, a way to find joy even in the midst of life's challenges.

Planning for the Future

As the weeks went on, Lisa and Don began talking more about their plans for the future. The idea of escaping to the Caribbean had become a shared dream, a light at the end of the tunnel.

One evening, as they sat together on the couch, Don pulled out a notebook filled with sketches and notes.

"What's this?" Lisa asked, flipping through the pages.

"Just some ideas," Don said casually. "Places we could go, things we could do. I've been looking into Grenada—did you know they have chocolate tours? And waterfalls?"

Lisa's heart warmed at his thoughtfulness. "You've been doing research, haven't you?"

"Of course," Don said, smiling. "I want to know everything about your world. And I want us to have something to look forward to."

Lisa leaned into him, touched by his words. "Thank you, Don. For everything."

Don kissed her softly, his hand resting on her cheek. "We're in this together, Lisa. Always."

Strength in Love

Though Lisa's journey to reconnect with Lyron remained fraught with challenges, her bond with Don gave her the strength to keep going. Together, they faced each obstacle with determination and hope, knowing that their love was a foundation strong enough to weather any storm.

And as Lisa drifted off to sleep that night, wrapped in Don's arms, she felt a renewed sense of purpose. Lyron was still out there, waiting to be found. And one day, when the time was right, she knew they would be reunited. Until then, she would hold onto the love and support that surrounded her, trusting that the path ahead would lead her exactly where she needed to be.

Chapter 16: Discovering Lisa's World – A Romance Made in Paradise

Grenada was more than a destination for Lisa; it was her sanctuary, a land alive with memories, where every grain of sand and every scent of nutmeg carried a story. Sharing this part of her life with Don wasn't just a trip—it was a gift, a glimpse into her soul.

The flight to the island had been uneventful, but as the plane descended, Lisa's excitement grew palpable. Below them stretched the emerald-green hills, vibrant villages, and turquoise waters that made up her beloved Grenada.

Don looked out the window, his jaw slack with awe. "Wow," he murmured, unable to tear his gaze away. "It's like stepping into a postcard."

Lisa grinned, her heart swelling with pride. "And wait until you experience it up close. Welcome to my world, Sweetheart!"

The balmy Caribbean air embraced them as they stepped off the plane. Don inhaled deeply, a smile spreading across his face. "This air... it's so fresh. I could get used to this."

Lisa chuckled. "Just wait, honey. The air is only the beginning."

A Warm Welcome

Their first stop was Lisa's home in Grand Anse, tucked into a peaceful neighborhood. As their taxi pulled up, David stood waiting on the porch, his broad smile lighting up his face.

"Mom!" he called, bounding down the steps.

Lisa stepped out of the taxi, arms open wide. "David!" she cried, pulling him into a tight embrace.

They held each other for a long moment, the years of separation melting away. When they finally parted, David turned to Don, his expression warm.

"You must be Don," he said, offering a firm handshake. "Welcome to Grenada."

Don smiled, shaking David's hand. "Thanks, David. It's great to finally meet you."

Inside, Lisa's brother Bain greeted them with a gift basket of fresh fruits from his garden—mangoes, sugar apples, avocados, and a sweet-smelling bunch of ripening bananas. Bain's quiet demeanor was offset by the warmth in his eyes as he shook Don's hand.

"I see what she sees in you," Bain said simply, his words carrying the weight of his approval.

Don nodded, visibly touched. "Thank you. That means a lot."

Immersed in Island Life

Over the next few days, Lisa took Don on a whirlwind tour of her Grenadian life. They visited the bustling spice market in St. George's, where the air was thick with the scent of cinnamon, nutmeg, and cloves. Vendors called out cheerfully, offering fresh cocoa balls and candied tamarind.

"This is incredible," Don said, marveling at the vibrant colors and aromas. He held up a piece of nutmeg pod, inhaling its spicy fragrance. "Why does everything smell better here?"

Lisa laughed. "Because it's Grenadian. It's not called 'Isle of Spice' for nothing you know."

They explored her childhood haunts—the secluded beach where she had spent countless afternoons as a girl, the old church where she had sung in the choir, and the winding paths through the rainforest where she had once picked mangoes with her brothers.

One evening, as they strolled along Grand Anse Beach, Don paused, letting the waves lap at his feet. The sun dipped low on the horizon, casting the sky in shades of gold and lavender.

"This place," he said, his voice filled with wonder. "It's magical. I can see why you love it so much."

Lisa smiled, her heart full. "It's home. And now, it's part of us."

A Culinary Bond

David, true to Lisa's word, was a master in the kitchen. He prepared a feast of Grenadian favorites—stewed chicken, coconut rice, steamed provisions, and fried plantains. Don was captivated by every bite, savoring the rich flavors.

"This is unreal," Don said, reaching for a second helping. "David, you're a genius."

David grinned. "Mom taught me well."

Lisa beamed with pride, her eyes twinkling as she watched Don and David bond over their shared appreciation for good food.

Don turned to Lisa, his voice playful. "So, when are you teaching me how to make this? I need to impress you when we get back to New York."

Lisa laughed. "I'll consider it. But first, you have to try cooking callaloo bhagi without burning it."

Falling in Love with Grenada

Don's enthusiasm for Grenada grew with each passing day. He marveled at the island's lush landscapes, its vibrant culture, and the warmth of its people. Bain took him fishing one morning, teaching him how to cast a net, and Don returned with a newfound appreciation for the simple joys of island life.

One afternoon, as they hiked to Annandale Falls, Don turned to Lisa, his face glowing with happiness. "You know," he said, "this trip is way too short. Next time, I'm arranging for a longer vacation. I want to see everything—every beach, every trail, every hidden gem."

Lisa laughed, her heart soaring. "I'd love that, Don. I'd love to show you everything."

Lingering Thoughts

As their trip came to an end, Lisa couldn't ignore the thoughts of Lyron and Margaret that lingered in the back of her mind. While Grenada had offered a sense of peace, it also reminded her of the unfinished business waiting for her back in New York; the missing link to complete her joy of being back home.

One evening, as they sat on the veranda of their resort, Lisa voiced her concerns. "I've been thinking about Lyron," she said softly. "And Margaret. I can't let this go on, Don. I need to find a way to reach him."

Don took her hand, his expression serious but supportive. "We'll figure it out, Lisa. Together."

She nodded, grateful for his unwavering support. "Thank you. For being here, for loving me through all of this."

Don leaned in, pressing a soft kiss to her lips. "Always," he murmured.

A Promise to Return

As they boarded the plane back to New York, Don looked out the window, a wistful smile on his face. "I'm going to miss this place," he said. "But I promise you, Lisa, we're coming back. And next time, it won't be a quick trip like this one. We'll stay long enough to truly soak it all in."

Lisa's heart fluttered with love and gratitude. "I'd love that, Don. And when we come back, I'll show you even more of my world."

Grenada had deepened their bond, strengthening their love in ways neither of them had expected. It wasn't just a trip; it was a journey into Lisa's heart, a discovery of the life she had built and the dreams she still carried.

And as they flew back to New York, Lisa felt a renewed sense of hope—for Lyron, for her future with Don, and for the beautiful life that lay ahead.

Chapter 17: Returning to Face the Past

The flight from Grenada back to New York felt heavy, like a bridge between two worlds. The serenity of Grenada, the joy of showing Don her roots, and the promise of their deepening connection lingered in Lisa's heart, but the reality waiting for her in New York pulled at her spirit.

Lyron was always at the center of her thoughts. The days of paradise had temporarily dulled the ache, but now, as the plane touched down at JFK, the weight of her unfinished mission pressed against her. She had hoped for inspiration, a clear path to her son, but clarity eluded her. Margaret's shadow loomed large, and every attempt to break through to Lyron seemed futile.

Don noticed her quiet demeanor as they exited the airport. He wrapped an arm around her shoulder, his touch a silent assurance. "You okay?" he asked softly.

Lisa nodded, but her heart felt far from settled. "I'm trying to be," she said, her voice tinged with frustration.

"You'll figure it out," Don said with quiet conviction. "And when you do, I'll be right here with you."

The Weight of Isolation

Back at her Airbnb, Lisa sat by the window, staring out at the city that had become both a refuge and a source of pain. The vibrant lights and ceaseless noise were a sharp contrast to Grenada's calm, reminding her of everything unresolved.

She had spent years trying to reach Lyron, but Margaret's manipulations had poisoned every avenue. Letters were returned unopened, phone calls blocked, and even attempts to connect through mutual family members had failed. It was as if Margaret had built an impenetrable fortress around Lyron, one designed to isolate him completely from his mother and brothers.

Lisa picked up her phone, her finger hovering over the contact list. She considered calling one of the relatives who lived in New York, someone who might help bridge the gap to Lyron. But her gut twisted with doubt. Most of her relatives had distanced themselves, unwilling to get involved in the family drama. Margaret's lies had painted Lisa as the villain, and the few who had initially been supportive were now wary of taking sides.

Still, she had to try.

She dialed the number of her cousin Marcia, a woman she had once been close to but who had grown distant over the years. The phone rang several times before Marcia answered.

"Hello?"

"Hi, Marcia. It's Lisa," she said, trying to keep her voice steady.

There was a pause on the other end, long enough for Lisa to brace herself. "Oh. Lisa. It's been a while."

"I know," Lisa said quickly. "I'm sorry to call out of the blue, but I need your help. It's about Lyron."

Another pause, this one heavier. "Lisa, I don't know..."

"Please, Marcia," Lisa pleaded. "I just need to know if you've heard from him. Anything at all. I don't even know where to start anymore."

Marcia sighed, and Lisa could hear the reluctance in her voice. "Look, Lisa, I don't want to get involved. Margaret... she's made it very clear that Lyron is an adult, and he doesn't want to see you. She says he's doing fine, and honestly, I think it's best to leave it alone."

Lisa's chest tightened. "Marcia, you know Margaret. You know how she manipulates people. Lyron doesn't even have a choice in this. Please, I'm begging you."

"I'm sorry," Marcia said, her tone final. "I can't help you."

The line went dead, leaving Lisa staring at her phone, tears welling in her eyes, her heart folding in pain. Why did she even think that Marcia would help?

Leaning on Don

When Don returned that evening, he found Lisa sitting on the couch, her hands clasped tightly in her lap. He immediately noticed the tension in her posture, the pain etched across her face.

"Lisa?" he said, sitting beside her. "What happened?"

She hesitated, unsure of how to put her feelings into words. "I called Marcia," she finally admitted. "I thought maybe she could help me reach Lyron. But she wouldn't even try. She believes Margaret's lies too."

Don frowned, his hand moving to hers. "I'm sorry, Lisa. That's not fair to you."

Lisa shook her head, frustration bubbling to the surface. "It's like Margaret has everyone under her spell. They believe everything she says, no one questions anything, no matter how outrageous it is. And Lyron... I don't even know what he thinks anymore."

Don's grip tightened on her hand. "You're not alone in this. We'll figure something out. Maybe it'll take time, but you'll get through to him eventually."

"I don't know how," Lisa whispered, her voice trembling. "Every door feels closed. I'm running out of ideas."

Don leaned in, his forehead resting against hers. "You're stronger than you think. And you're not giving up—not on Lyron, not on yourself. One way or another, you'll find a way."

His words were a balm to her soul, and for a moment, Lisa allowed herself to believe him.

Holding On To Hope

As the days passed, Lisa threw herself into prayer and reflection. She turned to her faith, seeking guidance in the silence of her evenings. Her journal became her confidant, filled with letters to Lyron that she hoped to share with him one day.

Don continued to support her in his quiet, steady way. He didn't push her to talk when she wasn't ready, but he was always there—a comforting presence that reminded her she wasn't alone.

One night, as they sat together on the couch, Lisa turned to him, her voice soft. "Do you think I'm wasting my time, Don? Chasing something that might never happen?"

He looked at her, his eyes full of sincerity. "No. You're fighting for your son. That's never a waste of time."

Lisa nodded, his words settling over her like a warm blanket. "Thank you," she whispered.

"For what?"

"For believing in me. For being here."

Don smiled, drawing her closer. "Always."

As they sat in the quiet of the room, Lisa felt a renewed sense of determination. She didn't know how or when she would reach Lyron, but she refused to give up. Margaret's lies might have built walls around her son, but Lisa would keep searching for a way through.

For now, all she could do was hold onto hope and trust that one day, Lyron would see the truth—and that when that day came, she would be ready.

Chapter 18: A Storm in Waiting

The crisp air of New York felt heavier as Lisa settled back into the rhythms of her life after Grenada. The sweet tranquility of her homeland lingered in her heart, but reality had a way of asserting itself with relentless persistence. Lyron was still out of reach, and Margaret's shadow loomed larger than ever. Every attempt to connect to him had been met with silence, or worse, indirect resistance from family members who had absorbed Margaret's web of lies.

Lisa felt as though she was wading through quicksand, each step forward seeming to drag her deeper into uncertainty. She prayed often, asking for wisdom, for clarity, for a breakthrough. But the answers felt elusive, the silence deafening.

A Fractured Circle

One evening, Lisa decided to reach out to her cousin Marcia again, despite the last discouraging attempt. Marcia had always been a diplomatic figure in the family, someone who could bridge divides. Lisa hoped against hope that she might reconsider her reluctance to help.

The phone rang three times before Marcia picked up, her tone guarded.

"Hi, Lisa," she said, her voice lacking the warmth Lisa had once known.

"Hi, Marcia. I was hoping we could talk," Lisa began, her voice calm yet firm.

Marcia hesitated. "About Lyron?"

"Yes," Lisa admitted. "I know Margaret has told everyone her version of things, but I just want a chance to explain. Lyron deserves to hear the truth."

Marcia sighed heavily. "Lisa, you know how Margaret is. She doesn't let go of grudges easily. She's told everyone that Lyron doesn't want to see you, and honestly…I'm not sure it's wise to stir things up."

"Stir things up?" Lisa repeated, her frustration bubbling beneath her calm exterior. "Marcia, this isn't about Margaret. It's about my son. She's kept him away from me for years, and the rest of the family has let her."

"Lisa, I understand how you feel, but Margaret has a way of…making life difficult for people who cross her. I don't want to get involved in something that could blow back on me."

Lisa's grip on the phone tightened. "Marcia, this isn't just about you. It's about helping Lyron see the truth before it's too late."

"I'm sorry, Lisa," Marcia said, her voice tinged with regret. "I can't help you."

The line went dead, leaving Lisa staring at her phone, her heart broken with disappointment.

Leaning on Don

That evening, Don returned to find Lisa sitting by the window, her shoulders slumped. He immediately sensed her anguish and joined her, wrapping an arm around her shoulders.

"Bad day?" he asked gently.

Lisa nodded, leaning into his embrace. "I tried to talk to Marcia again. She's too scared of Margaret to help. It feels like every door I try to open is slammed shut before I can even step through."

Don kissed her temple, his touch grounding her. "I'm sorry, Lisa. I know how hard this is for you."

"It's not just hard, Don. It's exhausting. I'm running out of options, and every time I think I've made progress, Margaret's lies close the door again. I don't even know where to start anymore."

Don turned her to face him, his expression steady and reassuring. "You're not alone in this. You have me, and you have God. Even when it feels like there's no way forward, there's always a way."

Lisa felt tears prick her eyes. "Thank you, Don. I don't know what I'd do without you."

"You don't have to," he said simply.

An Unlikely Ally

A few days later, Lisa received an unexpected call from an old church acquaintance, Janet, who had moved to New York years ago. Janet had heard about Lisa's situation through mutual connections and reached out to offer her support.

"I know it's been a long time, Lisa," Janet said, her voice warm and genuine. "But I want you to know I'm here if you need someone to talk to—or if there's anything I can do to help."

Lisa hesitated, unsure of whether to trust Janet. But something about her tone felt sincere, and Lisa's desperation outweighed her caution.

"Thank you, Janet," Lisa said. "Actually, there is something. Have you heard anything about Lyron? Anything at all?"

Janet paused. "I haven't seen him, but I know some people who might be able to help. It won't be easy—Margaret's influence runs deep—but I'll see what I can do."

For the first time in weeks, Lisa felt a flicker of hope. "Thank you, Janet. That means more to me than you know."

A Quiet Determination

As Lisa waited for news from Janet, she focused on building her strength. She spent more time in prayer and journaling, pouring out her fears and frustrations onto the pages. She wrote letters to Lyron, letters she hoped to give him one day, filled with memories of their time together and the love she still carried for him.

Don remained her rock, offering quiet support and encouraging her to keep fighting. He admired her resilience, her unwavering commitment to her son, even when the odds seemed stacked against her. The investigator's work had not yielded the kind of results Lisa had hoped for, but she was not prepared to give up hope, ever.

One evening, as they sat together, Don turned to her, his expression thoughtful. "Lisa, I've been thinking about Margaret."

Lisa raised an eyebrow. "What about her?"

"I think it's time to gather some evidence," Don said. "Something that proves her lies and manipulations. If you can show Lyron the truth, it might help him see through her."

Lisa considered his words, a spark of determination igniting within her. "You're right. If I can prove what she's done, it might make all the difference."

Together, they began to brainstorm, piecing together a plan to uncover the truth about Margaret's schemes. It wouldn't be easy, but Lisa knew that with Don by her side, she could face whatever challenges lay ahead.

Strength in Faith

As Lisa lay in bed that night, her thoughts turned to the future. The path to Lyron seemed impossibly long, but she reminded herself that God's timing was perfect. She didn't have all the answers, but she had faith, and that was enough.

With Don's steady presence and the possibility of an ally in Janet, Lisa felt a renewed sense of purpose. She would continue to fight for her son, to break through the walls Margaret had built, and to show Lyron the depth of her love.

And though the journey was far from over, Lisa knew that she was not alone—and that, in time, bridges could be rebuilt, even across the deepest divides.

Chapter 19: A Breath of Fresh Air

The weight of unanswered prayers and unresolved battles loomed large in Lisa's heart, but the quiet resilience within her refused to let despair win. She had always found comfort in small joys, in fleeting moments of laughter and love, and today, she felt a pull to rediscover that part of herself.

Don had sensed her need for a reprieve. Though he rarely spoke of it, he was attuned to the subtleties of her emotions—the way her shoulders slumped under the burden she carried, the faraway look in her eyes when she thought about Lyron. He decided it was time for a distraction, something to remind Lisa of the beauty in her life, despite its challenges.

"Get dressed," Don said one morning, leaning against the doorframe of Lisa's Airbnb with an unmistakable twinkle in his eyes.

Lisa glanced up from her laptop, confused. "What do you mean, 'get dressed'? I am dressed."

Don chuckled, shaking his head. "Not like that. Put on something comfortable, but cute. We're going out."

Lisa raised an eyebrow, intrigued but wary. "Where are we going?"

"That," Don said with a playful smirk, "is a surprise. Just trust me."

Lisa sighed dramatically, though a smile tugged at the corners of her lips. "Fine. Give me fifteen minutes."

A Day to Remember

When Lisa emerged, wearing a simple but flattering floral dress, Don's breath caught. He didn't say anything—he rarely did—but the warmth in his gaze was enough to make her cheeks flush.

"You look perfect," he said softly, offering his arm.

They walked out into the brisk New York morning, and Don led her to a car waiting nearby. The ride was filled with lighthearted banter, Lisa attempting to guess their destination while Don deflected with exaggerated evasiveness.

When they finally arrived, Lisa's eyes widened in surprise. Before them stretched the vast expanse of Central Park, its trees painted in the fiery hues of autumn.

"Central Park?" Lisa asked, her voice filled with a mix of curiosity and delight.

"Not just the park," Don said, his grin widening. "We're going boating."

Lisa laughed, her mood already lighter. "Boating? In this weather?"

"You'll be fine," Don assured her, pulling a scarf from his pocket and wrapping it gently around her neck. "I'll keep you warm."

Rowing Through Autumn

The boat rocked gently as Don rowed them out onto the still waters of the park's lake. The air was crisp, but the sunlight streaming through the golden leaves provided just enough warmth to make the chill bearable.

Lisa leaned back, letting herself relax for the first time in what felt like weeks. She watched Don struggle with the oars, his exaggerated grunts and mock frustration drawing laughter from her.

"Are you even trying?" she teased, her voice laced with amusement.

"I'll have you know," Don replied, pretending to wipe sweat from his brow, "this is hard work. You could offer to help, you know."

Lisa smirked, reaching for one of the oars. "Fine. Move over, Hercules. Let me show you how it's done."

They swapped places, and Lisa took the oars with determination. At first, her strokes were uneven, sending the boat spinning in circles.

"Oh, very impressive," Don said, laughing as he clutched the sides of the boat for balance.

"Hey!" Lisa shot back, laughing too. "I'm getting the hang of it!"

After a few more attempts, she found her rhythm, and Don clapped mockingly. "Well done, Captain. Shall we head for the open seas?"

They spent the next hour exploring the lake, their laughter echoing across the water. It was the kind of carefree joy Lisa hadn't felt in ages, and she savored every moment of it.

An Unexpected Moment

As they drifted near the edge of the lake, Lisa paused, her gaze drifting to the fiery leaves reflected in the water.

"This is beautiful," she said softly, her voice tinged with awe.

Don set the oars aside and leaned forward, his eyes fixed on her. "You're beautiful."

Lisa turned to him, her cheeks flushing again. "Don..."

He reached for her hand, his touch warm despite the chill in the air. "I know things have been hard lately. I know you've been carrying so much. But I want you to know...you don't have to carry it alone. I'm here, Lisa. For all of it. For you."

Her throat tightened at his words, emotion welling up inside her. "Thank you, Don," she whispered, her voice barely audible. "You don't know how much that means to me."

"I think I do," he replied, his gaze steady and sincere.

Without thinking, Lisa leaned forward, brushing her lips against his. The kiss was soft, unhurried, but filled with all the emotions they couldn't put into words. When they pulled apart, Don smiled, his boyish crease appearing at the corners of his mouth.

"I think I like this boating thing," he said, his voice teasing.

Lisa laughed, her heart lighter than it had been in weeks. "Me too."

A Night to Remember

Later that evening, they returned to Lisa's apartment, still buzzing from their day together. Don had picked up dinner from a small Italian restaurant, and they sat on the couch, sharing stories and laughter over plates of pasta and glasses of wine.

Lisa felt a warmth she hadn't known in a long time—a sense of contentment that came not from the absence of struggles, but from the presence of someone who made those struggles bearable.

As the night wore on, Don leaned back, his arm draped around her shoulders. "So, what's next on our adventure list?"

Lisa smiled, her head resting against his chest. "I don't know. But as long as you're there, I think I'll be okay."

Don kissed the top of her head, his voice soft. "You'll be more than okay, Lisa. You'll be amazing. Because that's who you are."

In that moment, surrounded by love and laughter, Lisa allowed herself to believe that brighter days were ahead. They still had battles to face, but together, she and Don could weather any storm.

And for the first time in a long time, she felt truly hopeful.

Chapter 20: Whispers of Tomorrow

The autumn chill swept through New York, a crispier crispness in the air hinting at the oncoming winter. Lisa wrapped her scarf tightly around her neck as she and Don strolled hand in hand through Central Park. The trees were painted in fiery shades of red, orange, and gold, their leaves crunching beneath their boots with every step.

Don had been in a particularly playful mood all morning, stopping at every food cart to sample pretzels, roasted chestnuts, and hot apple cider. His laughter was contagious, and Lisa found herself caught up in his infectious energy, savoring the way he brought warmth and light into her life.

"Come on," Don said, tugging her toward a carousel tucked away in the park. His boyish grin made her heart skip a beat. "Let's ride."

Lisa chuckled, shaking her head. "Don, that's for kids."

"So? Aren't we allowed to feel like kids sometimes?" He waggled his eyebrows. "Besides, I'm not taking no for an answer."

Before she could protest further, Don was already buying tickets. Moments later, they were climbing onto the carousel, surrounded by painted horses frozen in mid-gallop. Lisa chose a golden one with a silver mane, while Don insisted on riding a black stallion next to her.

The carousel began to turn, its lights twinkling as cheerful music played. Don reached for her hand, his eyes sparkling with mischief. "Hold on, or you might fall off."

Lisa laughed, gripping his hand tightly. "You're impossible."

"And you love it," he shot back, his grin widening.

As the ride spun faster, Lisa's laughter bubbled up, unrestrained and joyous.

For a little while, it felt like they were the only two people in the world, their laughter echoing through the park like music. Don mimed galloping on his horse, drawing giggles from a nearby child who declared him the "funniest grown-up ever." Lisa felt her heart swell—Don had a way of making her feel weightless, even in the heaviest moments.

When the ride slowed and finally stopped, Don helped her down from the horse, his hand lingering on hers. "See? You had fun."

She smiled, leaning into him. "Okay, you win this one."

"I always win," he teased, planting a quick kiss on her forehead.

Their playful banter carried them through the park, the warmth of their connection keeping the autumn chill at bay. They stopped by Bow Bridge, leaning against the railing as they watched rowboats glide across the lake. The city's skyline rose in the distance, a reminder of the world waiting beyond this moment of serenity.

"I love it here," Lisa said softly, her gaze fixed on the water. "It's so peaceful."

Don nodded, his hand brushing against hers. "It reminds me of us. Finding something beautiful in the middle of chaos."

Lisa turned to him, her heart swelling at his words. "You have a way of saying the most unexpected things."

Don shrugged, his eyes twinkling. "What can I say? You inspire me."

They stayed there for a while, the world fading away as they shared stories, laughter, and quiet moments of reflection. Don told Lisa about his childhood misadventures, painting vivid pictures of scraped knees and mischievous pranks. Lisa shared stories of her own—of climbing mango trees in Grenada, racing her brothers through the countryside, and sneaking bites of her mother's freshly baked coconut tarts before they cooled.

Their laughter drew the attention of an elderly couple passing by. The woman smiled knowingly, her eyes crinkling at the corners. "You two look like you're in your own little world," she said, her voice warm and kind.

Lisa blushed, but Don grinned unabashedly. "We are," he replied, squeezing Lisa's hand. "It's a nice place to be."

The couple walked on, leaving Lisa and Don to savor the moment. The afternoon sun dipped lower, casting a golden glow over the park. Lisa felt a sense of contentment she hadn't known in years—a sense that, for now, everything was exactly as it should be.

As they wandered through the bustling streets of Manhattan, Don pulled Lisa into a small boutique. "I have an idea," he said, his voice tinged with excitement.

"What kind of idea?" Lisa asked, her curiosity piqued.

"You'll see," he replied mysteriously, disappearing into the aisles. A few moments later, he returned with a wide-brimmed hat and oversized sunglasses. He placed them on her with a flourish, stepping back to admire his handiwork.

"Perfect," he declared, grinning. "Now you're ready for the paparazzi."

Lisa laughed, shaking her head. "You're ridiculous."

"Ridiculously in love with you," he corrected, earning a playful shove from Lisa.

They spent the rest of the day exploring the city, Don insisting on snapping photos of Lisa at every landmark. By the time they returned to her apartment, her cheeks ached from smiling. Don had a way of making even the most ordinary days feel extraordinary.

That evening, as they lay together on the couch, Don reached for Lisa's hand. His expression was thoughtful, almost hesitant.

"There's something I've been meaning to tell you," he began quietly.

Lisa turned to him, her heart skipping a beat. "What is it?"

Don hesitated, then smiled, his vulnerability shining through. "I've been thinking about our trip to Grenada. About how right it felt to be there with you. And I realized... I don't just want to visit. I want us to build something lasting."

Lisa's breath caught. "You mean...?"

"I mean I want to make you a part of my forever," he said softly. "Wherever that takes us—Grenada, New York, anywhere—we'll figure it out together."

Tears welled in Lisa's eyes as she leaned into him. "Don, you've already given me so much. I never thought I'd feel this way again, and it's because of you."

Don wrapped his arms around her, holding her close. "You're my home, Lisa. You always will be."

In that moment, Lisa felt a profound sense of peace. For the first time in years, she allowed herself to dream of a future filled with love, laughter, and endless possibilities.

They fell asleep that night entwined, their hearts beating in unison, ready to face whatever challenges lay ahead. Together.

Chapter 21: Snowflakes and Laughter

Lisa stared out of the window at the falling snow, her breath fogging the glass. The white, glittering powder blanketed the city, softening its sharp edges and painting the skyline in a way she found both enchanting and intimidating. Growing up in the Caribbean, she'd only ever seen snow in movies or on postcards. It was beautiful, yes, but entirely foreign.

When Don first mentioned ice skating, she'd laughed nervously, waving the idea away. "Don't be ridiculous," she'd said. "I can barely walk on a wet tile floor without slipping."

But Don, with his mischievous grin and unrelenting charm, wouldn't let her off the hook. "You've survived hurricanes and thunderstorms, Lisa. You can survive a little ice. Trust me."

Now, as they stood in Rockefeller Center amidst the towering Christmas tree and the gliding skaters, Lisa wondered if she might have overestimated her resilience.

"Don," she whispered, clutching his arm as they approached the rink. "I'm starting to think this was a mistake."

Don chuckled, wrapping an arm around her shoulders. "Come on, island girl. It's time you learned how to have some real winter fun."

Lisa shot him a look that was equal parts nervous and annoyed. "Fun? This looks like an accident waiting to happen."

Don leaned closer, his voice low and teasing. "Don't worry. If you fall, I'll be there to catch you—after I stop laughing."

Lisa smacked his arm playfully. "You're terrible."

Don laced up Lisa's skates with the precision of someone who had done this a hundred times before. "The trick," he explained, "is to keep your knees slightly bent. Stay balanced, don't lock your legs, and—"

"Don't fall?" Lisa interrupted, her wide eyes betraying her nerves.

"Exactly." Don grinned, standing and holding out his hand. "Now, let's get you out there."

With great reluctance, Lisa let Don guide her onto the ice. Her legs wobbled immediately, and she clung to his arm like a lifeline. "This is insane," she muttered, her grip tightening as her feet slid unsteadily beneath her.

"You're doing fine," Don said, biting back a laugh. "Just take it slow."

Slow was an understatement. Lisa shuffled forward, her movements awkward and jerky, while Don glided effortlessly beside her. The contrast was so stark that a nearby couple chuckled as they passed.

"Don't look at them," Lisa muttered, feeling her cheeks flush. "This is humiliating."

Don couldn't help but laugh. "Oh, come on, Lisa. You're not that bad. Look, you haven't fallen yet."

As if on cue, Lisa's foot slipped, and she stumbled. Don caught her just in time, his laughter bubbling over as he steadied her. "Okay, maybe I spoke too soon."

Lisa glared at him, though she couldn't suppress a small smile. "You're enjoying this way too much."

"Absolutely," Don admitted, his grin widening. "But I'm proud of you for trying."

As the evening went on, Lisa began to find her rhythm—or at least something resembling it. With Don's patient guidance and steady hand, she managed to skate a short distance without clinging to him for dear life. It wasn't graceful, but it was progress.

"There you go!" Don cheered as Lisa completed a wobbly loop around the rink. "See? You're a natural."

Lisa rolled her eyes but couldn't hide her smile. "If by 'natural,' you mean 'barely surviving,' then yes."

Don slid up beside her, his arm slipping around her waist. "I mean you're amazing," he said softly, his teasing replaced by a genuine warmth that made Lisa's heart flutter.

For a moment, they stood together in the middle of the rink, the world around them blurring into a swirl of lights and laughter. Lisa looked up at Don, her nerves forgotten as she leaned into his embrace.

"I never thought I'd enjoy something like this," she admitted.

Don smiled, pressing a soft kiss to her forehead. "There's a first time for everything."

Back at Lisa's apartment, the warmth of the fireplace was a welcome contrast to the biting cold outside. They sat together on the couch, wrapped in a shared blanket, sipping hot chocolate that Don had expertly spiked with a splash of Bailey's.

"So," Don said, his tone playful, "what's the verdict? Are you ready to become a professional ice skater?"

Lisa laughed, shaking her head. "I think I'll stick to sandy beaches and turquoise waters, thank you very much."

Don smirked. "Fair enough. But you have to admit, you were pretty impressive out there."

Lisa arched an eyebrow. "Impressive? Don, I looked like a baby giraffe on roller skates."

"An adorable baby giraffe," Don teased, earning a playful nudge from Lisa.

They fell into a comfortable silence, the crackling of the fire and the occasional sound of traffic outside filling the space. Lisa leaned her head on Don's shoulder, feeling a deep sense of contentment.

"Thank you," she said softly.

"For what?" Don asked, his voice equally gentle.

"For pushing me," Lisa replied. "For showing me that I can do things I never thought I could. And for making me laugh along the way."

Don turned to her, his eyes warm and full of affection. "That's what love's about, Lisa. Pushing each other, laughing together, and holding on tight—especially when the ice gets slippery."

Lisa smiled, her heart swelling with gratitude and love. "I'm lucky to have you."

Don kissed her then, slow and tender, and Lisa felt the world around her fade away. In his arms, she found a kind of magic that no winter wonderland could replicate—a warmth that melted the coldest fears and replaced them with a love that felt as vast and endless as the Caribbean Sea.

Chapter 22: Uncharted Roads

The winter evening sky shimmered with stars as Lisa and Don strolled along the bustling streets of New York. The festive lights from the nearby buildings added a warm glow to the icy sidewalks, casting reflections on the slushy streets. For the first time in weeks, Lisa felt a lightness in her steps, a sense of peace as if the world, with all its chaos, had pressed pause just for them.

"Tell me something, Don," Lisa said, wrapping her scarf tighter against the crisp air. "What was your first winter like? Was it as disastrous as mine?"

Don chuckled, slipping his gloved hand into hers. "Oh, you mean when I skated on ice like a newborn deer? Absolutely. I was terrible at everything—snowball fights, sledding, you name it."

Lisa tilted her head, her eyebrows raised in mock disbelief. "You? The great Don, stumbling on ice? Hard to imagine."

"Laugh all you want, but I was a disaster. My brother still teases me about it. Let's just say I've come a long way since then," he admitted with a sheepish grin. "But enough about me. You held your own out there, Lisa."

She rolled her eyes. "Barely. I think my dignity is still somewhere on that rink."

Don stopped walking and turned to her, his expression serious but playful. "Dignity is overrated. You were brave, and that's what matters. Plus," he added with a smirk, "you made it a lot more fun for me."

Lisa swatted his arm, laughing. "You're insufferable."

"And yet, you adore me," he teased, pulling her closer.

Lisa leaned into him, her laughter softening into a warm smile. She felt a sense of security in his arms, a steadiness that was becoming her anchor. But beneath her joy, there was a flicker of unease she couldn't ignore—the unresolved tension with Lyron, the looming shadow of Margaret. These thoughts were like unwelcome guests, lurking at the edges of her happiness.

Don seemed to sense her shift in mood. He stepped back slightly, cupping her face in his gloved hands. "What's going on in that beautiful mind of yours?"

Lisa hesitated, debating whether to voice her worries. But this was Don—her partner, her confidant. If she couldn't share her burdens with him, who could she turn to?

"It's Lyron," she admitted, her voice barely above a whisper. "I've been thinking about him a lot. I feel like I'm running out of ways to reach him."

Don's expression softened, his thumbs gently brushing her cheeks. "Lisa, you've done more than most people would even attempt. You've shown him love and patience. That's all you can do right now. The rest has to come from him."

"I know," she said, her voice heavy with resignation. "But it's hard not to feel helpless."

Don nodded, his gaze steady. "You're not helpless. You're strong, Lisa. And Lyron will see that in time. Trust me."

She sighed, leaning her forehead against his chest. "I just wish time didn't feel so endless."

Later that evening, they returned to Lisa's apartment, their cheeks rosy from the cold. Don had insisted on stopping by a bakery on their way back, and now the warm, sweet scent of fresh pastries filled the room.

Lisa set the table, lighting a few candles for ambiance, while Don unpacked the box of treats. "I may have gone overboard," he said, sheepishly revealing an array of éclairs, danishes, and tarts.

Lisa laughed, shaking her head. "Overboard? This is a feast."

"Well," Don said, placing a plate in front of her, "you deserve it. Consider it a celebration of surviving your first skating adventure."

They settled into the cozy setting, the flickering candlelight casting soft shadows on the walls. As they ate, their conversation drifted to lighter topics—

Don's childhood antics with his siblings, Lisa's favorite Caribbean dishes, and their shared dreams for the future.

"What do you miss most about Grenada?" Don asked, leaning back in his chair.

Lisa paused, her fork hovering over her plate. "The simplicity," she said after a moment. "Life there is slower, more connected. You don't have to fight to keep relationships alive—they just thrive naturally. And the garden... I miss growing my own crops, I miss picking fresh corn, watermelons and salad greens grown with my own hands."

Don smiled thoughtfully. "We'll go back soon. And next time, I'll plan for a longer trip. Maybe even learn to catch fishes with your brother again."

Lisa laughed. "You? Fishing? That's something I'd pay to see."

"Don't underestimate me," Don said, feigning offense. "I've got hidden talents you know."

They both laughed, the sound echoing in the warm, candlelit room. For a moment, the weight of the world lifted, leaving only the joy of their shared connection.

As the night wore on, Don suggested a movie, and they curled up on the couch together, a soft blanket draped over their legs. Lisa found herself stealing glances at him, marveling at how he seemed to fit so effortlessly into her life. He wasn't just her partner; he was her sanctuary, her safe harbor in the storm.

Don caught her looking and raised an eyebrow. "What?"

Lisa shook her head, smiling. "Nothing. Just thinking how lucky I am."

He leaned in, brushing a kiss against her temple. "If anyone's lucky, it's me."

As the movie played, Lisa rested her head on Don's shoulder, her hand entwined with his. For the first time in what felt like forever, she allowed herself to simply be. To exist in this moment of peace and love, without the shadows of the past or the worries of the future.

For now, that was enough.

Chapter 23: Unfamiliar Comforts

The following morning, Lisa awoke to the comforting aroma of freshly brewed coffee wafting through the small apartment. She stretched languidly, her muscles still pleasantly sore from their snow adventures the day before. A soft hum carried from the kitchen, and Lisa couldn't help but smile as she recognized Don's off-key rendition of an old Motown classic.

She padded into the kitchen, the warmth of the apartment a stark contrast to the frosty scene beyond the window. Don was standing at the counter, pouring coffee into two mugs, his hair tousled and his face bearing the unmistakable ease of someone at peace.

"Good morning, sleeping beauty," he teased without looking up.

Lisa chuckled, wrapping her arms around herself. "Good morning. And what tune was that? Sounds like something from your rebellious youth."

Don turned, a mock-offended expression on his face. "I'll have you know that song is a classic. You just don't have taste."

She raised an eyebrow as she accepted the mug he offered. "Says the man who thought pairing chocolate milk with rum was a good idea."

Don's laughter filled the kitchen. "That was a creative experiment, thank you very much."

Lisa took a sip of her coffee, savoring its warmth. She couldn't remember the last time she had felt so content, so lighthearted. The cold world outside was momentarily forgotten, replaced by the gentle glow of domesticity.

"You have a way of making mornings feel magical," she said softly, meeting his gaze.

Don's expression softened, a small smile playing on his lips. "I'm just try to keep up with you, Lisa."

Later that day, Don sprang a surprise on Lisa. "How about we hit the road?" he asked, leaning casually against the doorway.

Lisa eyed him suspiciously. "You're being cryptic again. Where are we going?"

His lips twitched into a mischievous grin. "It's a surprise. Trust me."

Lisa's curiosity piqued. She had learned by now that Don's surprises always led to memorable moments. Bundling up against the cold, they set off in his car, the city's skyline soon giving way to the sprawling countryside blanketed in snow.

"Are you kidnapping me?" Lisa asked teasingly, glancing at him from the passenger seat.

Don smirked, his hands steady on the wheel. "Only if it means I get to keep you forever."

Lisa laughed, shaking her head. "You're impossible."

After an hour of winding roads and playful banter, they arrived at their destination—a cozy, rustic lodge nestled in a grove of pine trees. Smoke curled from the chimney, and warm golden light spilled from the windows, promising comfort and charm.

"Don," Lisa gasped, her eyes wide. "This is beautiful."

"Wait until you see inside," he said, leading her up the stone path.

The lodge was even more enchanting than it appeared from the outside. A roaring fireplace dominated the center of the room, its warmth wrapping around them like a soft blanket. The air was filled with the scent of pine and cinnamon, and Lisa felt as though she had stepped into a postcard.

Don checked them in, his grin widening as he watched Lisa take it all in. "Figured you could use a little getaway. Plus, I hear their hot chocolate is life-changing."

Lisa's heart swelled at the thoughtfulness behind the gesture. "You're amazing, you know that?"

He shrugged, his expression playful. "I have my moments."

After settling into their cozy room, Lisa and Don ventured outside to explore the snow-covered grounds. The air was crisp, each breath forming little puffs of mist as they walked hand-in-hand through the woods. Don, ever the teaser, couldn't resist tossing a snowball at her when she wasn't looking.

"Don!" Lisa shrieked, spinning around as snow clung to her coat.

"What?" he said innocently, already scooping up another handful of snow. "It's a winter tradition."

Lisa bent to gather her own snowball, her Caribbean pride refusing to back down. She hurled it with surprising accuracy, catching Don square in the chest.

He staggered dramatically, clutching his chest. "Betrayed! By my own love."

Lisa smirked, brushing her hands together. "Don't underestimate me. I've had plenty of practice pelting stones at mango trees to pick ripe mangoes. Trust me, that makes me an expert at snow fights."

Don's eyes widened in mock alarm. "Oh no. I'm up against a professional. I'm doomed."

Lisa laughed, scooping up another snowball. "You better watch out, or this professional is going to make sure you regret underestimating her."

The playful war resumed, with Don trying—and failing—to outmaneuver Lisa's expert aim. Each time he tried to sneak around her, she managed to land another snowball with precision, leaving him laughing and breathless.

"You're ruthless," he declared, brushing snow from his coat.

"Just skilled," Lisa retorted with a grin. "I told you—mango season is serious business in Grenada."

That evening, they curled up by the lodge's fireplace, mugs of the famous hot chocolate in hand. Lisa took a sip, her eyes widening as the rich, velvety liquid coated her tongue.

"Okay, you weren't kidding. This is divine."

Don grinned, his own mug half-empty. "Told you."

They sat in comfortable silence, the crackle of the firewood providing a soothing soundtrack. Lisa found herself reflecting on how far they had come—how this man had brought so much light into her life, even during her darkest moments.

"I don't think I've ever been this happy," she admitted softly, her gaze fixed on the flames.

Don turned to her, his expression tender. "You deserve it, Lisa. Every bit of it."

She looked at him, her heart full. "So do you, Don."

He leaned in, brushing a soft kiss against her lips. It was a simple, quiet moment, but it carried the weight of everything they had shared—their struggles, their joys, their unwavering love.

The next morning, as they prepared to leave the lodge, Don turned to Lisa, his eyes twinkling with mischief. "You know, I've been thinking."

"Uh-oh," Lisa said, feigning dread. "What now?"

"I think we need to make this a tradition," he said, wrapping an arm around her waist. "Snowball fights, hot chocolate, romantic lodges—it's our thing now."

Lisa laughed, her heart brimming with joy. "I think I could get used to that."

As they drove back to the city, Lisa found herself daydreaming about their future—of more adventures, more laughter, more love. For the first time in a long while, she felt like everything was falling into place.

And she couldn't wait to see what came next.

Chapter 24: A Feast for the Heart

The cooking date turned into a delightful dance of laughter and learning as Lisa and Don navigated the art of Grenadian cuisine. While the kitchen had filled with the tantalizing aroma of simmering coconut milk and spices, Lisa decided it was time to introduce Don to a staple beverage that was as much a part of her childhood as oil down.

"Now that you've peeled bananas and survived the scotch bonnet, it's time for your next lesson," Lisa announced, pulling out a bag of fresh limes.

Don raised an eyebrow. "Lime juice? Is this going to be as dangerous as the scotch bonnet?"

Lisa laughed, shaking her head. "No danger this time. But if you want to really feel the Grenadian spirit with your oil down, you need a glass of ice-cold lime juice. No exceptions."

She grabbed a cutting board and knife, handing them to Don. "Start by slicing these in half. And make sure you don't waste any juice!"

Don picked up a lime, inspecting it with exaggerated seriousness. "You know, for a guy from the city, this is uncharted territory. We just buy bottled juice here. Squeezing limes is practically a foreign concept."

Lisa rolled her eyes, but she couldn't help smiling. "You're about to learn what real lime juice tastes like. Trust me, once you try this, you'll never look at bottled juice the same way again."

As Don began slicing the limes, Lisa prepared a bowl with a strainer to catch the seeds. She handed him a simple citrus reamer, demonstrating how to twist the lime halves to extract every drop of juice.

Don watched her closely, mimicking her movements. "This isn't so bad," he admitted, grinning as the juice began to collect in the bowl.

Lisa laughed. "See? You're a natural, but this is the city method, the island method is like this." Lisa took two halves of lime, one in each hand and squeeze then with her fingers. "This, is the island way, see, it's much quicker."

"Wow! You need masculine hands to squeeze these limes down to a pulp." Don said grinning. "Let me at 'em! Super Don to the rescue!"

Lisa chuckled. As Don worked, Lisa leaned against the counter, a nostalgic smile on her face. "You know, when I was a kid, we had lime trees growing all around. The trees have very sharp prickles on the branches, and getting to the limes, we had to be so careful not to get these prickles into our feet. We'd sweetened it with brown sugar—never white—and add water. That was the perfect drink after a hot day in the fields or playing in the yard."

Don paused, looking up at her. "That sounds... amazing. You must've had such a different childhood from mine. I can't imagine picking fresh limes right off a tree."

"It was special," Lisa said softly, her voice tinged with both fondness and longing. "The juice tasted fresher somehow, like it carried the sun with it. I miss those days sometimes."

Don squeezed the last lime, his hands sticky with juice, and looked at her with a teasing grin. "Well, I don't have a lime tree to pick from, but I think I've done a pretty good job here."

Lisa inspected his work, nodding approvingly. "Not bad for a city boy. Now for the most important part—the sweetening."

She poured the juice into a pitcher, adding water and a generous helping of brown sugar. Stirring it with a long spoon, she handed Don a spoonful of juice to taste. Two glasses filled with ice waited on the counter to pour the golden-green liquid into.

"Moment of truth," she said, watching him expectantly.

Don took a sip, his eyes widening. "Wow. This is... incredible. It's tart, but the brown sugar gives it this deep sweetness. You're right—this is nothing like bottled juice."

Lisa beamed. "I told you! It's like tasting a piece of Grenada. Even in this cold New York weather, it brings a little warmth, doesn't it? It's like a little taste of sunshine."

Don nodded, raising his glass in a mock toast. "To lime juice—and to the best teacher a guy could ask for."

They laughed, clinking their glasses together before settling at the table with their meal. The oil down was rich and flavorful, the lime juice refreshing, and the laughter they shared made the experience unforgettable.

Later, as they cleaned up, Don couldn't resist teasing Lisa about her "expert instructions."

"You really take this lime juice thing seriously," he joked, drying the pitcher.

Lisa smirked, tossing him a kitchen towel. "Of course I do. It's a matter of national pride. If you'd grown up competing with your brothers to see who could make the best juice, you'd take it seriously too."

Don laughed, pulling her into a hug. "Well, for the record, I think you win. Best lime juice—and best oil down—I've ever had."

Lisa rolled her eyes playfully but leaned into his embrace, her heart full. In moments like these, she felt the weight of her worries lift, replaced by a simple, profound joy.

As they stood there, the city lights flickering outside the window, Lisa couldn't help but feel grateful. For the food that connected her to her roots. For the man who made her laugh and lightened her load. And for the promise of more evenings like this—filled with love, laughter, and the taste of home.

That night, as they sat on the couch sipping the last of the lime juice, Don turned to Lisa with a mischievous grin.

"So, when's the next cooking lesson?" he asked.

Lisa laughed, shaking her head. "You're insatiable."

"Hey, if it means more time with you—and more lime juice—I'm all in," Don said, raising his glass.

Lisa smiled, clinking her glass against his. "Then you'd better be ready. Next time, we're making pigeon peas soup with Grenadian dumplings."

Don groaned dramatically, but his laughter filled the room, blending perfectly with Lisa's. In that moment, their world felt warm and complete, the taste of lime juice lingering like a sweet memory of home.

Chapter 25: Finding His Voice

Lisa woke to the sound of a rich baritone humming in the kitchen. She smiled as she sat up, recognizing the melody—it was one of Don's many impromptu "concerts," something she had grown to adore about him. The man could turn a mundane chore like washing dishes into a Broadway performance, complete with exaggerated vibrato and the occasional drumbeat on the countertop.

Wrapping herself in a cozy robe, she padded out to the kitchen. There he was, pouring coffee, singing a lively, offbeat rendition of an old blues song, his voice filling the small space. He noticed her and turned, holding the coffee pot like a microphone.

"Good morning, beautiful!" he crooned dramatically, bowing as if addressing an audience.

Lisa laughed, shaking her head. "You're impossible, you know that?"

"But you love it," Don said with a grin, setting the coffee pot down and pouring her a mug.

"I do," she admitted, taking the cup from him. "You have a way of making everything...brighter."

Don returned to his makeshift stage—the kitchen counter—singing a rock ballad this time. Lisa leaned against the doorway, her mug cradled in her hands, watching him. His wild, goofy energy was infectious, and though the genre wasn't her favorite, she couldn't help but enjoy the show.

"You know," she said when he paused for a sip of water, "you've got a really good voice."

Don raised an eyebrow, smirking. "You think so? I always figured I was just good at being loud."

Lisa shook her head. "No, I mean it. You've got real talent, Don. I think you should do something with it."

He chuckled, waving her off. "Oh, come on. I'm just messing around."

"I'm serious," Lisa insisted, setting her mug down. "You could write your own songs. Perform them. I think you'd be amazing."

Don shrugged, but there was a glimmer of intrigue in his eyes. "I don't know... I've never thought about it like that. Singing's just something I do for fun."

Lisa stepped closer, placing a hand on his arm. "Fun is where it starts, Don. But you've got a gift, and gifts are meant to be shared. I think you should try."

He looked at her, the usual teasing glint in his eyes replaced with something softer, more contemplative. "You really think so?"

"I do," she said firmly. "And I'd love to help you get started."

The day unfolded with a renewed sense of purpose. As they strolled through the winter market, Don hummed bits of melodies, experimenting with lyrics that came to mind. Lisa encouraged him, laughing at his wilder lines but always pointing out the moments of brilliance hidden in his playful verses.

"You know," she said as they stopped at a food stall, "your goofy songs always make me laugh, but when you really sing—when you put your heart into it—it's something special."

Don smiled, his cheeks reddening slightly. "You've got a way of making me feel like I could do anything, Lisa."

"Maybe because you can," she replied, her voice warm with conviction.

That evening, back at their apartment, Lisa sat at the dining table with her laptop, the memory of Don's impromptu performances swirling in her mind. Inspired, she began working on a new song for the album she'd been quietly crafting—a project close to her heart.

The lyrics flowed easily, a melody taking shape in her mind. She imagined Don singing it, his voice giving life to the words she was pouring onto the page. It wasn't her usual style, but it felt right for him—wild, raw, and full of emotion.

"What are you working on?" Don asked, leaning over her shoulder, his breath warm against her cheek.

Lisa tilted the screen toward him. "A song. For you."

"For me?" he asked, his eyes widening.

"I've been thinking," Lisa said, turning to face him. "You've got a voice that people need to hear. And I think this song could be the start of something amazing for you."

Don read the lyrics, his expression shifting from curiosity to something deeper. "This is...beautiful, Lisa. But you really think I can pull it off?"

"I know you can," she said, her voice steady. "And I'll be right here to help you every step of the way."

Don sat down beside her, the usual playfulness in his demeanor giving way to a quiet determination. "All right," he said after a moment. "Let's do it."

Lisa smiled, her heart swelling with pride. This was the beginning of something new, not just for Don, but for both of them.

The next few days were filled with music. Don experimented with melodies while Lisa fine-tuned the lyrics, their collaboration bringing them closer in ways they hadn't expected. Lisa found herself falling even more in love with Don's vibrant, unapologetic energy, and he, in turn, was inspired by her unwavering belief in him.

One afternoon, as Don worked on the song, Lisa prepared a fresh batch of lime juice in the kitchen. "You need to stay hydrated if you're going to be a rock star," she teased, handing him a glass.

Don took a sip, his eyes lighting up. "This is amazing. How do you always make everything taste so good?"

"Years of practice," Lisa said with a wink. "Back in Grenada, a glass of ice-cold lime juice or gospo juice at every meal made everything feel just right. It's a little taste of island warmth, even in the middle of a New York winter."

Don grinned, raising his glass. "To lime juice and big dreams."

"To lime juice and big dreams," Lisa echoed, clinking her glass against his.

As the usual blast of snowfall blanketed the city, Lisa and Don stood by the window, watching the world outside transform into a winter wonderland.

"Think we'll ever perform this song together?" Don asked, his arm around her shoulders.

Lisa looked up at him, her eyes shining. "I think we'll do a lot of things together, Don. And this is just the beginning."

They shared a quiet moment, the sound of their song lingering softly in the background, a reminder of the new journey they were embarking on—one filled with laughter, music, and the promise of love.

Chapter 26: The Song of Their Love

Lisa sat at her writing desk, a quiet determination etched on her face as she stared at the blank page before her. The memories of the early days of her relationship with Don swirled in her mind—days filled with uncertainty, where every smile and fleeting touch was a question left unanswered. She had struggled then, not knowing if Don truly cared for her or if she was just a fleeting thought passing thought in his life.

The sound of Don humming in the kitchen brought a soft smile to her lips. That same playful energy she had long for to be her constant throughout their journey. But now, she understood the complexities beneath it—the battles he had fought within himself, the cage he had felt trapped in, and the walls he had to tear down to be with her.

As if on cue, Don appeared in the doorway, his presence warm and familiar. "What are you working on?" he asked, leaning against the doorframe.

"A song," Lisa replied, tapping her pen against the notebook. "One that tells our story."

Don crossed the room, sitting on the edge of her desk. "Our story, huh? That's a lot to fit into one song."

Lisa laughed softly, looking up at him. "It is. But it's worth telling."

He reached out, brushing a strand of hair from her face. "You've been thinking about those early days, haven't you?"

She nodded. "I can't help it. I think about how much I doubted everything— how much I doubted you—and now I see how far we've come. But I also think about how hard it was for you, how trapped you must have felt."

Don's expression grew serious, a shadow crossing his features. "It wasn't easy," he admitted. "There were so many things pulling me in different directions—Myrna, the restrictions at work, my own fears. I wanted to be with you, Lisa. I just didn't know how to move forward without tearing everything apart."

Lisa reached for his hand, her touch grounding him. "You don't have to explain, Don. I understand now. But back then... I didn't know what to think. Every time you pulled away, I thought it was because you didn't care."

"I cared," Don said firmly, his voice filled with emotion. "I cared more than I knew how to handle. That's why I kept coming back, knowing that it wasn't fair to you, I couldn't stay away."

Lisa's heart swelled at his words, the raw honesty in his voice a testament to how far they had come. "That's what this song is about," she said softly. "About love that refuses to be caged, no matter how many walls are built around it."

Don tilted his head, a faint smile playing on his lips. "What do you have so far?"

Lisa flipped to the page where she had begun drafting the lyrics. "It's not finished, but here's the chorus:

You can't cage love, its wild and free,
It will break through chains, to fly to where its meant to be.
You can't stop hearts from finding their place,
Love will break free and win the race."

Don read the words, his smile widening. "Lisa, that's incredible. It's...us. It reflects everything we've been through... the love we've fought for..."

Lisa interrupted, "...the restrictions of the hotel, the way we had to hide to express our feelings every time – thank God for the elevator, it saved our butts so many times." Lisa laughed as she recalled those stolen moments.

Don chuckled. "That's right... nothing could stop love you know."

Lisa's eyes sparkled with emotion. "That's why I want this to be the lead song for my album. It's not just our story—it's Lyron's too. It's about the walls Margaret has built around him, and how love will break through them one day."

Don nodded, his expression thoughtful. "It's perfect. It's the message we need to share with the world; and your book, *Beauty Waiting in the Shadows*, it pairs perfectly with this song. Lisa you're a genius."

They spent the rest of the evening working on the song together. Don strummed a melody on his guitar while Lisa refined the lyrics, their collaboration a seamless blend of their strengths. The song took shape, each verse a reflection of their journey—the struggles, the doubts, the triumphs.

As the final note hung in the air, Don looked at Lisa with a mix of pride and admiration. "This is it," he said quietly. "This is the song that's going to lead your album."

Lisa smiled, her heart full. "I couldn't have done it without you, honey."

"You inspired it," Don replied. "This is as much yours as it is ours."

The next morning, Lisa woke to the sound of Don humming the melody they had created. She found him in the kitchen, flipping pancakes and singing softly to himself.

"You're practicing already?" she teased, leaning against the counter.

He turned, his grin playful. "Just getting ready for the big debut."

Lisa laughed, pouring herself a cup of coffee. "Well, you'd better be ready. This song is going to put you on the map."

Don's expression softened, a hint of vulnerability in his eyes. "I don't care about that, Lisa. As long as it makes you proud, that's all that matters to me."

Lisa stepped closer, wrapping her arms around him. "You've already made me proud, Don. Now let's show the world what we can do together."

As the days passed, Lisa and Don worked tirelessly to perfect the song. They recorded a demo, Lisa's heart swelling with pride every time she heard Don's voice bring the lyrics to life. The song was raw, powerful, and deeply personal—a testament to the love that had grown between them and the battles they had fought to keep it alive.

"You Can't Cage Love" became the centerpiece of Lisa's album, a beacon of hope and resilience. And as they prepared to share it with the world, Lisa knew that this was just the beginning of their journey—a journey that would continue to break through walls and defy all odds.

Bottom of Form

Chapter 27: Planning Paradise

The cold New York winter seemed to stretch endlessly, but for Lisa, thoughts of her sunny homeland kept her spirits high. She and Don had been deep into planning their next trip back to Grenada, and the anticipation brought a warmth to their hearts that the icy winds couldn't touch. Lisa could see it in the way Don's eyes lit up whenever they talked about the trip. She'd caught him more than once scrolling through photos of Caribbean beaches on his phone, a dreamy smile on his face.

One evening, Don walked into the kitchen, rubbing his hands together to warm them. "Lisa," he began, grinning mischievously, "you've introduced me to oil down, fried bakes, and lime juice. But I want to learn more. What's next on the Grenadian menu?"

Lisa turned from where she was organizing the pantry, her eyes gleaming with excitement. "How about pelau? It's one of my favorites. A hearty one-pot dish with rice, chicken, vegetables, and all the flavors of home. I will teach you. Next time we can make dumpling and peas."

Don leaned against the counter, crossing his arms. "Sounds amazing. And don't forget—I'm becoming quite an expert in the kitchen thanks to you."

Lisa smirked, playfully nudging him with her shoulder. "We'll see about that, Chef Don."

They spent the evening preparing the dish together, and the kitchen filled with the tantalizing aroma of marinated chicken, caramelized brown sugar, and freshly chopped herbs. Lisa guided Don through every step, her instructions peppered with stories of her childhood in Grenada.

"Back home," Lisa said, as she browned the chicken, "when I was growing up, pigeon peas soup or as we called it, 'dumpling and peas' used to be almost a national dish. Just as we cook the oil down today for Independence Day, dumpling and peas was the pot everyone was bubbling on Cambulae night, that was the night before carnival day. I remember helping my mom pick fresh pigeon peas from the garden. I'd get in trouble for eating them raw because I couldn't wait!"

Everything we celebrated back then was done with a feast of dumpling and peas. When it was harvesting time in the fields, we would make what was called a 'Maroon.' Where all the villagers would gather to help the farmer harvest his crop. And dumpling and peas would be bubbling on the outdoor fire to feed everyone.

But pelau? Well, that's for anytime, especially if you're going to the beach or having a family picnic.

Don chuckled as he carefully measured rice into the pot. "So, this is like a Grenadian comfort food?"

"You could say that," Lisa said with a smile. "It's the kind of meal that brings everyone together."

As they worked, Don's natural goofiness emerged. He hummed a tune, adding exaggerated flourishes to his movements as he stirred the pot. Lisa couldn't help but laugh, her heart swelling with affection.

"You're ridiculous," she teased, shaking her head.

"Ridiculously talented, you mean," Don shot back, winking at her.

When the pelau was finally ready, they sat down to eat, the warmth of the dish contrasting with the chill outside. Don took his first bite and let out a satisfied groan. "Lisa, this is incredible. I'm officially in love with Grenadian food—and you."

Lisa laughed, her cheeks warming. "Well, you've got good taste."

After dinner, they settled on the couch, sipping cups of hot cocoa. Lisa pulled out her laptop, scrolling through a list of places they wanted to visit in Grenada.

"I've been thinking," she said, her voice thoughtful. "We should spend some time in Carriacou this time. It's quieter, less touristy, and the beaches are stunning."

Don nodded. "I'm all for that. Maybe we could rent a small villa by the water. Just us, the ocean, and plenty of Grenadian food."

Lisa's heart fluttered at the thought. "That sounds perfect."

They talked late into the night, planning their itinerary and sharing stories. Lisa recounted memories of her childhood, from climbing mango trees to swimming in the river and catching crayfish under the river stones. Don, in turn, shared tales of his own adventures, painting a vivid picture of his city life before they met.

As the conversation slowed, Lisa leaned against Don, a contented sigh escaping her lips. "Thank you for this," she said softly.

"For what?" he asked, resting his chin on her head.

"For wanting to be part of my world," she replied. "For making this dream of ours a reality."

Don kissed her temple, his voice tender. "Lisa, it's my dream too. I've never felt more alive than when I'm with you."

As they drifted off to sleep that night, their plans for Grenada felt like more than just a vacation. It was a symbol of their shared future, a testament to how far they'd come together. And while the journey hadn't been easy, they knew that with love, patience, and a touch of humor, they could face anything that came their way.

Chapter 28: The Calm Before the Storm

The icy embrace of New York's winter had grown heavier as the days ticked closer to Lisa and Don's anticipated escape to Grenada. The chill outside was relentless, but inside their cozy home, a warmth had settled between them, one built on love, shared dreams, and the excitement of what lay ahead. Lisa had been tirelessly organizing the details of their trip, making sure everything would be perfect. Don, in his typical laid-back style, trusted her completely but couldn't resist teasing her about her meticulous nature.

"You know," Don quipped one morning as Lisa scribbled furiously in her planner, "I think you're planning every second of our trip. Should I schedule bathroom breaks too?"

Lisa shot him a playful glare. "If I don't plan, you'll probably try to wing it and forget something important—like booking the hotel."

He raised his hands in mock surrender. "Fair point. But trust me, the only thing I'll forget is how to stop having fun with you."

Lisa laughed, shaking her head. Don always knew how to lighten the mood, and for that, she was grateful. They were in the middle of one of their rare quiet weekends, the kind Lisa had come to cherish. No outside noise, no pressing deadlines—just the two of them.

"I think we should do something today," Don said, breaking the peaceful silence. "Something fun, something different."

Lisa raised an eyebrow. "Fun like what?"

"Bowling," he declared, his face lighting up.

"Bowling?" Lisa repeated, laughing. "Don, the last time I tried bowling, I nearly sprained my wrist."

"Perfect," Don teased, stepping closer. "That means I'll win. Come on, it'll be a blast. Unless, of course, you're scared to lose..."

Lisa narrowed her eyes, a playful smirk tugging at her lips. "You're on, Mr. Big Shot. But don't cry when I win."

A couple of hours later, they were at a lively bowling alley downtown. The neon lights cast a warm glow over the lanes, and the air buzzed with laughter, the clatter of pins, and the occasional groan of disappointment when a ball veered into the gutter. Don, ever the competitor, was in his element, showing off with exaggerated warm-up stretches.

"Pay attention, Lisa," he said, grabbing his bowling ball with dramatic flair. "You're about to witness greatness."

Lisa rolled her eyes but couldn't suppress a laugh. She watched as Don took his stance, lined up his shot, and released the ball with what he clearly thought was expert precision. The ball veered slightly to the left, knocking down seven pins.

"Not bad," Lisa admitted as Don turned to her, grinning like a kid.

"Not bad?" he repeated, feigning offense. "That was practically perfect."

When it was Lisa's turn, she approached the lane with exaggerated seriousness, her face a mask of mock concentration. She gripped the ball tightly, muttering under her breath, "Let's see what you've got."

Her first roll wobbled down the lane, narrowly avoiding the gutter before knocking over four pins. Don clapped enthusiastically, his teasing grin back in place. "Impressive start, rookie. Want me to give you some tips?"

Lisa smirked. "I don't need tips. I just need practice—and don't forget, I'm a Caribbean girl. I've got years of practice pelting stones to pick mangoes++. You're lucky this isn't a snowball fight."

Don laughed, shaking his head. "Alright, mango pelting queen. Let's see if you can handle the pressure."

The game continued, filled with playful banter, exaggerated celebrations, and more than a few gutter balls on Lisa's part. But by the end, she had managed to score a respectable spare, much to Don's mock chagrin.

"I let you have that one," he said as they returned their shoes.

"Sure you did," Lisa replied, nudging him. "Just admit it—I'm a natural."

After bowling, the day unfolded like an adventure. They explored the city, stopping at a small café for hot chocolate and wandering through a nearby park blanketed in snow. The crisp air bit at their cheeks, but the warmth between them made it feel like spring.

As they strolled hand in hand, Lisa found herself marveling at how far they had come. The man beside her, goofy and kind, had become her anchor, her safe space in a world that often felt chaotic. She glanced up at him, her heart swelling with gratitude.

"What?" Don asked, catching her gaze.

"Nothing," Lisa said, smiling. "Just thinking about how lucky I am."

Don stopped walking, turning to face her. "Lisa, I'm the lucky one. You've brought so much light into my life. I don't say it enough, but I hope you know how much you mean to me."

Lisa felt her cheeks flush, not from the cold but from the sincerity in his voice. "I know, Don. And I feel the same way."

That evening, as they relaxed at home, their conversation turned to Grenada. Lisa brought out her travel plans, showing Don pictures of places they would visit.

"I can't wait to take you to Grand Anse Beach again," she said, her voice brimming with excitement. "The water is so clear, and the sand feels like silk this time of year."

"And I can't wait to eat more of your food," Don added. "Do you think your son will cook for us while we're there?"

"David's cooking puts mine to shame," Lisa admitted with a laugh. "You'll love it."

They spent hours talking about the trip, their laughter filling the room as they imagined all the adventures they would have. Don suggested they try scuba diving, while Lisa insisted on taking him to the local market to experience Grenadian spices firsthand.

As the night wore on, Don leaned back, a contented smile on his face. "Lisa, this trip isn't just a vacation for me. It's a chance to know you even better. To understand your world, your roots."

Lisa rested her head on his shoulder, her heart full. "And it's a chance for me to share my world with you. Grenada is more than a place to me—it's home. And now, you're part of that."

Don kissed the top of her head, his voice soft. "I can't wait, Lisa. I really can't."

As they drifted off to sleep that night, their thoughts were filled with dreams of the Caribbean—the sun, the sea, and the promise of new memories waiting to be made. For Lisa and Don, this trip was more than just an escape; it was a step toward a future built on love, laughter, and the shared hope of what was to come.

Chapter 29: Anticipating Paradise

The days before their trip to Grenada were filled with a mix of excitement and nostalgia. Lisa and Don spent hours talking, laughing, and planning the adventures they would share, but as they packed their suitcases and shopped for tropical wear, old memories resurfaced.

One evening, Lisa sat cross-legged on the couch, folding a lightweight dress and carefully tucking it into her suitcase. Don was seated nearby, flipping through a travel guide she had picked up, his excitement barely contained.

"We're definitely going to Grand Anse beach again," he said, circling a picture of the iconic beach with a pen. "But I also want to see the waterfalls this time. Annandale Falls, right?"

Lisa nodded, her smile warm. "Annandale is beautiful. And maybe this time we can visit Seven Sisters Falls too. It's a hike, but it's worth it."

Don grinned. "I'm game. I'll even carry the picnic basket if you promise not to laugh when I slip on the rocks."

Lisa chuckled, but her laughter faded into a thoughtful silence. She reached for her cup of tea, her gaze lingering on Don. "You know," she began, "I've been thinking a lot about how far we've come. From where we started to now...it feels like a dream."

Don set the travel guide aside, sensing the shift in her mood. "What's on your mind?"

Lisa hesitated, then met his gaze. "Back then, when we first started noticing each other, I didn't even know why I liked you so much. I knew absolutely nothing about you, Don—not your background, your likes, or even if you were single. And yet, there was this...this pull, like my heart recognized something before my mind could figure it out."

Don leaned forward, his expression softening. "I felt it too," he admitted. "It scared me at first. I wasn't sure what it meant or if I was even ready for it."

Lisa smiled faintly, remembering the early days when she had tossed and turned at night, wondering if she was imagining the connection. "What did you see in me?" she asked, her voice tinged with curiosity. "What made you notice me?"

Don's face lit up with a tender smile. "It was everything," he said. "The way you carried yourself—calm, kind, but with this quiet confidence. And your smile...Lisa, your smile could light up a room. I'd watch you interact with people, and it was like you had this aura, this natural beauty and grace that couldn't be ignored. I couldn't stop thinking about you."

Lisa blushed, her heart swelling at his words. "I had no idea you were watching me like that," she said softly.

Don's expression grew more serious. "I need to say something, though. Back then, when I was avoiding you...I know it hurt you, and I'm sorry for that. I was confused, trying to figure out my own feelings and what to do about them. I never wanted to cause you pain."

Lisa reached for his hand, her touch gentle. "It did hurt," she admitted. "There were nights I couldn't sleep, wondering what I did wrong or why you weren't talking to me. But I see now that you needed that time to figure things out. And in a way, it made us stronger."

Don squeezed her hand, his eyes filled with gratitude. "You never gave up on me, even when I gave you every reason to. That's what made me fall for you, Lisa. Your patience, your faith in us, even when I didn't deserve it."

Lisa smiled, her heart lightened by his honesty. "I'm glad I didn't give up. Look at us now—planning a trip to Grenada, ready to make new memories. I couldn't have imagined this back then."

Don leaned back, his gaze thoughtful. "It's funny," he said. "There were times I thought I'd blown it, that I'd let you slip away because I was too scared to act. But here we are. And I wouldn't trade this for anything."

Lisa chuckled, a playful glint in her eyes. "Well, you almost blew it. But you've redeemed yourself."

Don laughed, holding up his hands in mock surrender. "Noted. I'll spend the rest of my life making it up to you."

They both fell into a comfortable silence, the only sound the rhythmic hum of the heater as it battled the lingering chill of March. Lisa glanced at her suitcase, already envisioning the vibrant colors of Grenada—the lush greenery, the turquoise waters, the golden sands.

"What are you looking forward to the most when we get there?" Lisa asked, breaking the silence.

Don tilted his head, considering the question. "Honestly? Just seeing the world through your eyes. You light up whenever you talk about Grenada, and I can't wait to experience it with you again. Oh, and the lime juice," he added with a grin. "But only if I can help make it this time."

Lisa laughed, nudging his shoulder. "You're getting too good at this, Don. Fine, you can help—but no complaining about squeezing the limes."

"Deal," Don said, leaning in to kiss her forehead.

As the night wore on, they continued reminiscing about their journey—how far they had come, the challenges they had faced, and the love that had grown stronger with each passing day.

Lisa closed her laptop, her heart full as she leaned against Don. "I'm so glad we found each other," she whispered.

"So am I," Don replied, wrapping an arm around her. "Grenada is going to be incredible, Lisa. And it's just the beginning of all the adventures we'll share."

Lisa rested her head on his shoulder, her thoughts drifting to the island she loved and the man beside her. Together, they were creating a life filled with hope, love, and endless possibilities.

Tomorrow, the journey would begin. But tonight, they cherished the quiet anticipation, knowing that the best was yet to come.

Chapter 30: A Return to the Warmth of Grenada

The Grenadian air wrapped around them like a familiar embrace the moment Lisa and Don stepped off the plane. The scent of saltwater mingled with the faint aroma of nutmeg and spices, a sensory signature of the island that immediately brought a smile to Lisa's face. Don closed his eyes, taking a deep breath as if trying to inhale the very soul of Grenada.

"I missed this," Don said, grinning as he opened his eyes.

Bain's hearty laughter rang out as he approached them in the arrivals area. "Lisa! Don! Welcome back!"

Lisa rushed into her brother's arms, hugging him tightly. "It's so good to be home, Bain. I've missed this place—and you!"

Don shook Bain's hand firmly, his grin widening. "Bain, good to see you again. I've been counting the days to get back here. And dreaming of the lime juice."

Bain laughed, clapping Don on the shoulder. "Well, we've got plenty of limes waiting for you. Let's get you both settled first, and then we'll talk about juice."

The drive to Lisa's home was a cheerful mix of chatter and sightseeing. Don leaned against the van window, marveling at the vibrant bursts of bougainvillea lining the roads and the rolling hills that seemed to stretch endlessly toward the horizon.

"It's even more beautiful than I remembered," Don said, his voice tinged with awe.

Lisa smiled, taking his hand in hers. "Wait until you see what I have planned for us this time. There's so much more of Grenada to explore."

As they pulled into the yard, Bain gestured proudly toward the house. "Welcome home, Lisa. It's been waiting for you."

David stood on the veranda, waving enthusiastically. "Mom! Don! It's about time you two got here!"

Lisa climbed out of the van, rushing to hug her eldest son. "David! You're as handsome as ever."

David chuckled, his deep voice resonating warmly. "And you're as flattering as ever, Mom."

He turned to Don, shaking his hand with a firm grip. "Welcome back, Don. Ready to dive into some real Grenadian food?"

"You know it," Don replied with a grin. "But only if you're cooking."

David laughed. "You're in luck. I've got a feast waiting for you inside."

Exploring Bain's Garden

A few days into their stay, Bain suggested a visit to his garden. "Don, if you want to see the magic behind the lime juice you keep raving about, I've got something to show you," he said, his eyes twinkling.

Intrigued, Don eagerly followed Bain and Lisa to the back of the property. They wove through rows of fruit trees and vibrant crops until they reached a sprawling lime tree, its branches heavy with green and yellow limes.

"This is it," Bain declared, pointing at the tree proudly. "The tree is one of my most productive lime trees, you can pick as many as you need."

Don's face lit up as he stared at the tree in awe. "This is where the magic happens? I feel like I've met a celebrity."

Lisa laughed, grabbing a small basket. "Come on, let's pick some limes. But watch out for the prickles on the branches—they're sharp. And be careful where you step, you don't want to get prickles in your feet."

She demonstrated how to pick the fruit safely, carefully avoiding the small but fierce thorns. Don watched her with amusement.

"You make it look so easy," Don said, reaching for a ripe lime. "Ow!" He yanked his hand back, inspecting a small scratch on his finger.

Lisa laughed, gently taking his hand. "I warned you about the prickles, city boy." She kissed his finger teasingly giggling at the look on his face.

Bain chuckled as he watched them. "Don, you're getting a proper Grenadian initiation today. You'll appreciate that juice even more now."

Don grinned, undeterred. "This is worth every scratch."

They filled the basket with a mix of ripe and green limes, Lisa occasionally teasing Don about his overly cautious picking technique. When Bain handed him a second basket, Don threw Lisa a mock-serious look.

"Don't laugh. I'm practically a pro now," he said, plucking a lime with exaggerated care.

Lisa and Bain burst into laughter, and Don joined in, savoring the light-hearted moment.

Lime Juice and Laughter

That evening, Lisa brought out the freshly picked limes and set them on the kitchen counter. "Alright, Don," she said, placing a knife and a pitcher in front of him. "You're in charge of making the lime juice."

Don rolled up his sleeves, ready to take on the challenge. "This is my moment to shine," he declared.

As Lisa guided him through the process, they joked and teased each other. Don insisted on tasting the juice after every few stirs, claiming he was "perfecting the art."

When the juice was finally ready, Lisa added a splash of vanilla essence, stirring it with care. Don poured himself a glass, taking a sip with an exaggeratedly critical expression.

"Well?" Lisa asked, raising an eyebrow.

Don's face broke into a grin. "Best lime juice I've ever had. Even better than last time."

"Because you helped," Lisa teased, handing him another glass. "Fresh squeezed limes directly from the tree, nothing could beat that!"

David walked in just then, taking a sip from the pitcher. "Not bad, Don. You might just have a future as a Grenadian lime juice maker."

Bain nodded in agreement, his eyes sparkling with amusement. "You've earned your stripes today, Don."

Don raised his glass in a toast. "To good limes and better company."

They clinked glasses, their laughter filling the kitchen as the sun dipped below the horizon, casting a warm glow over the house.

A Moment of Reflection

Later that night, Lisa and Don sat on the veranda, the cool evening breeze brushing against their skin. The stars were scattered across the sky like diamonds, and the sound of crickets provided a soothing backdrop.

Lisa leaned against Don, her voice soft. "I love seeing you here, Don. You fit right in."

Don smiled, wrapping an arm around her. "That's because I have the best guide. Grenada feels like home because of you."

Lisa sighed contentedly, her heart full. "There's so much more to show you. Tomorrow, we'll hike to Seven Sisters Falls. You're going to love it."

"I already do," Don said, pressing a kiss to her temple. "And I love you, Lisa. Thank you for sharing this world with me."

As they sat together under the Grenadian sky, Lisa couldn't help but feel that this was exactly where they were meant to be—surrounded by family, laughter, and the simple joys of life. For the first time in years, everything felt right.

Chapter 31: Waterfalls and Nature's Wonder

The morning sun broke through the dense greenery surrounding Bain's home, painting the garden in golden hues. Lisa and Don stood near the van, ready for their adventure to one of Grenada's hidden treasures: the Seven Sisters Waterfalls. Lisa's excitement was infectious, and Don couldn't help but grin as she rattled off stories about the island's natural beauty.

"Trust me," Lisa said, adjusting the straps of her hiking boots, "you're going to fall in love with this place."

"I already love it here," Don replied, pulling her into a quick embrace. "But I'm ready to see what all the fuss is about."

Bain handed Don a walking stick. "You'll need this. The trail can get tricky, especially if it's muddy. And don't forget to keep an eye out for tree branches that could get in the way"

Don raised an eyebrow. "Ah cha! A few branches can't slow me down, eh Lisa."

Lisa chuckled, giving him a playful nudge. "You'll see. Just watch your step."

The Journey to Seven Sisters

The drive to the start of the trail was picturesque, with winding roads that climbed into the lush hills of Grand Etang. Along the way, Don marveled at the vibrant foliage—giant ferns, towering bamboo groves, and flowering trees that seemed to stretch endlessly toward the sky.

When they arrived, a local guide greeted them with a warm smile. "Welcome to Seven Sisters. My name's Marlon, and I'll be showing you the way today."

As they set off, Marlon shared tidbits about the area. "The Seven Sisters Waterfalls are part of the Grand Etang Forest Reserve," he explained. "The hike isn't too long, but it can be a bit steep in places. Just take your time and enjoy the scenery."

The trail wound through dense jungle, the air thick with the earthy scent of damp soil and leaves. Lisa pointed out the various plants she remembered from her childhood—wild ginger, heliconia, and towering breadfruit trees.

"Smell this," she said, crushing a leaf between her fingers and holding it up to Don's nose.

"Wow," Don said, inhaling the sharp, citrusy scent. "What is that?"

"Bay leaf," Lisa replied. "Grenadians use it in everything—soups, stews, even cocoa tea."

Marlon chimed in. "It's also good for keeping mosquitoes away. Just rub it on your skin."

Don filed the information away, making a mental note to take a few leaves back with him.

The Seven Sisters Waterfalls

After about an hour of hiking, the sound of rushing water grew louder, signaling their approach. When they finally reached the first of the waterfalls, Don stopped in his tracks, his eyes widening in awe.

The cascade of water tumbled over the rocks, pooling into a crystal-clear basin below. The sunlight filtered through the trees, casting dappled patterns on the water's surface.

"This is...breathtaking," Don said, his voice filled with wonder.

Lisa smiled, slipping off her shoes. "Wait until you feel the water. It's cold, but it's worth it."

She waded into the pool, gasping as the cool water lapped at her skin. Don followed, laughing as the chill hit him. They swam toward the base of the falls, letting the cascading water splash over them.

Marlon stood nearby, watching with amusement. "You two look like you're enjoying yourselves."

"We are!" Lisa called back, her laughter echoing against the rock walls.

After a while, they sat on the smooth rocks near the edge of the pool, letting the sun dry their skin. Lisa leaned her head on Don's shoulder, her heart full. "This," she said softly, "is one of my favorite places in the world. And now I get to share it with you."

Don kissed her forehead. "Thank you for bringing me here, Lisa. I'll never forget this."

A Stop at Grand Etang Lake

On their way back, Marlon suggested a detour to Grand Etang Lake. "It's not far from here," he said. "And if you're lucky, you'll see the monkeys."

Don's curiosity was piqued, and Lisa agreed eagerly. "The lake is beautiful," she said. "You'll love it."

The drive to Grand Etang was short, and soon they were standing at the edge of the serene crater lake, its surface shimmering like glass under the afternoon sun. Marlon explained its origins as they walked along the path.

"Grand Etang Lake is a volcanic crater lake," he said. "It's over 1,700 feet above sea level and fed by underground springs. Some people say it's bottomless."

"Bottomless?" Don echoed, raising an eyebrow.

"It's a legend," Marlon said with a grin. "But it adds to the mystery of the place."

As they continued, they noticed movement in the trees above. Moments later, a small group of Mona monkeys appeared, their curious faces peeking through the foliage.

Lisa gasped in delight. "There they are!"

Marlon handed Don a banana. "Hold this out. They'll come to you."

Don hesitated for a moment before extending the fruit. One of the monkeys cautiously approached, snatching the banana with nimble fingers before retreating to a nearby branch.

"This is amazing," Don said, watching the monkeys as they chattered and played among the trees.

Lisa laughed as one particularly bold monkey jumped onto a low branch near her, tilting its head as if examining her. "I think this one likes me," she said.

"It has good taste," Don replied, grinning.

They spent the rest of the afternoon exploring the area, learning about the flora and fauna from Marlon. When it was time to leave, Don turned to Lisa, his expression thoughtful.

"This place," he said, gesturing to the lake and the surrounding forest, "it feels magical. Like it's alive."

Lisa smiled, taking his hand. "That's Grenada. It's not just a place—it's a feeling."

As they drove back to Bain's house, the sun dipped lower in the sky, casting a warm, golden glow over the island. Lisa and Don sat close together, their hands intertwined, their hearts full. They were rediscovering Grenada, but more importantly, they were rediscovering each other.

Chapter 32: A Feast at Grand Anse

The sun hung high in the Grenadian sky as Lisa and Don arrived at her home in Grand Anse. Lisa breathed in the familiar scent of her favorite dish cooking, mingled with the aroma of freshly picked local seasonings wafting from the kitchen.

Inside, David was busy at the stove, the unmistakable sound of bubbling goodness filling the air. He glanced up as his mother and Don entered, a broad smile lighting up his face.

"Mom! Don! You're just in time," he said, covering the pot of Grenada's national dish, oil down. "This is going to be the best you've ever had."

Lisa approached the stove, peeking into the pot filled with layers of breadfruit, callaloo, dumplings, salted meat, and aromatic herbs. The golden turmeric-infused coconut milk simmered, coating everything in a fragrant sauce.

"It smells amazing," Lisa said, reaching over to give David a light pat on the back. "You've outdone yourself."

David grinned. "I learned from the best."

Lisa chuckled, shaking her head. "Don't forget to save some for your father. Have you called him yet?"

David paused, his expression sheepish. "I was going to after I finished cooking."

Lisa raised an eyebrow, crossing her arms. "David, you know he's not the best cook. Make sure he gets enough. And call him now. I don't want him waiting too late to eat."

David sighed but nodded, grabbing his phone from the counter. "Alright,

alright, I'll call him now."

Don, who had been leaning against the doorway, watched the exchange with quiet admiration. He was struck once again by Lisa's unyielding kindness and her commitment to family. Despite everything she had been through with Ronald, she still made sure he was cared for.

As David dialed, Don approached Lisa, placing a hand on her shoulder. "You're incredible, you know that?"

Lisa turned to him, her brow furrowing slightly. "What do you mean?"

"The way you look after everyone," Don said softly. "Even Ronald. You don't have to, but you do it anyway. It says a lot about who you are."

Lisa smiled, her eyes softening. "Ronald is still their father. Whatever happened between us doesn't change that. And as long as he's in their lives, I'll do my part to make sure they stay connected. It's important."

Don pulled her into a brief hug, his voice filled with warmth. "You have such a big heart, Lisa. I'm lucky to be a part of it."

The Feast

As the oil down reached its final stage of cooking, Lisa set the table.

David carried the steaming pot of oil down to the table, setting it in the center like a crown jewel. "Alright, everyone," he announced, "time to dig in!"

The family gathered around, their laughter and conversation blending with the sound of waves in the distance. Don took his first bite of oil down and closed his eyes, savoring the explosion of flavors.

"This," he declared, "is the best meal I've ever had. David, you're a genius."

David laughed, holding up his hands in mock surrender. "Hey, credit goes to Mom for teaching me. I just perfected it."

Lisa rolled her eyes, playfully swatting his arm. "Don't let it go to your head."

A Visit from Ronald

Later that afternoon, Ronald arrived to collect his portion of the meal. Lisa greeted him warmly, handing him a neatly packed container of food.

"Thanks, Lisa," Ronald said, his tone sincere. "You didn't have to do this."

Lisa waved him off. "Nonsense. It's oil down, Ronald. You can't miss out on this."

Don observed the interaction from a distance, impressed by the ease between them. Despite their history, there was no tension—only a quiet understanding and a shared commitment to their family.

As Ronald turned to leave, he paused, looking back at Lisa. "I appreciate it, Lisa. And... thanks for reminding the kids to check in on me. It means a lot."

Lisa smiled gently. "They're your children, Ronald. It's what families do."

When he was gone, Don came up beside her, slipping his arm around her waist. "You never cease to amaze me, Lisa."

She leaned into him, her expression thoughtful. "It's not always easy, Don. But it's worth it. For the kids, for the family—it's worth it."

A Perfect Evening

As the sun dipped below the horizon, Lisa and Don sat on the veranda, sipping glasses of freshly made lime juice. Don held up his glass, swirling the contents.

"Lisa," he said with a mock-serious tone, "this lime juice...it's life-changing."

Lisa laughed, shaking her head. "You're obsessed."

"Can you blame me?" Don teased, taking another sip. "It's perfect. Sweet, tangy, refreshing—just like you."

Lisa rolled her eyes but couldn't hide her smile. "You're impossible."

"And you love it," Don shot back, grinning.

As the stars began to twinkle in the night sky, Lisa rested her head on Don's shoulder, her heart full. She had her family, her home, and the love of a good man. For now, life was as perfect as the adventures they have embarked on under the Grenadian sky.

Top of Form

Bottom of Form

Chapter 33: Sailing to Carriacou and Petit Martinique

The morning sun bathed Grenada in its warm glow, casting a golden shimmer over the water as Lisa and Don stood at the ferry terminal. The harbor buzzed with life—vendors selling fresh fruits, the scent of spices wafting through the air, and travelers chatting excitedly. Today, they are boarding the ferry to Carriacou, the largest of Grenada's sister islands, with a plan to visit Petit Martinique.

Don adjusted his sunglasses, grinning as he took in the lively scene. "I've been looking forward to this all week," he said.

Lisa chuckled, her excitement mirroring his. "You're going to love Carriacou. It's quieter, more laid-back, but it's full of charm. And Petit Martinique? It's like stepping into another world."

As the ferry's horn blared, signaling departure, Lisa and Don climbed aboard, finding seats at the upper deck. The ferry swayed gently as it pulled away from the dock, and the expanse of the open sea stretched out before them like an endless canvas.

Don leaned back in his seat, the ocean breeze tousling his hair. "This is the life," he said, turning to Lisa. "Blue skies, clear water, and you by my side. What more could I ask for?"

Lisa smiled, resting her hand on his. "Maybe some grilled fish and callaloo when we get there?"

Don laughed, nodding. "Now you're talking."

Arrival in Carriacou

The ferry docked at Hillsborough, Carriacou's main town, its colorful buildings standing out against the lush green hills. Lisa led Don down the plank, her pride growing as she introduced him to this quieter slice of Grenada.

"This is Hillsborough," Lisa said, gesturing to the quaint streets lined with shops and eateries. "It's small, but it has a lot of heart."

They strolled through the town, stopping at a seaside café for a taste of local flavors. Plates of fried jackfish with rice and a side of callaloo arrived, the aroma making Don's mouth water.

"Okay," Don said after his first bite, "this might be the best fish I've ever had. The seasoning is incredible."

Lisa laughed. "Told you, there's nothing like the taste of fish from the waters of Grenada. The flavor of everything you taste from Grenada is always more robust and inviting to the palette."

After lunch, they visited Belair National Park, where the ruins of old plantations told stories of the island's history. Don was captivated, taking photos and asking Lisa endless questions about the island's past.

"It's amazing how much history is packed into such a small place," he said. "Every corner has a story."

Sandy Island Paradise

Later that afternoon, they hired a boat to take them to Sandy Island, a tiny strip of sand surrounded by crystal-clear waters. The moment they set foot on the island, Don's eyes lit up.

"This is paradise," he said, his voice filled with wonder.

They spent the next hour snorkeling, discovering vibrant coral reefs teeming with life. Lisa pointed out schools of fish darting between the rocks, their scales catching the sunlight.

Don surfaced, laughing. "I could stay here forever. Why didn't we come here sooner?"

Lisa smiled, treading water beside him. "Because some things are worth the wait."

As the sun began its descent, their boat returned to take them back to

Carriacou.

Petit Martinique

The ferry ride to Petit Martinique was brief, but the smaller island felt like a world apart. Known for its rich fishing traditions, the island exuded tranquility.

"Welcome to Petit Martinique," Lisa said as they stepped onto the sandy beach. "This is as authentic as it gets."

They wandered through the quiet village, where fishermen mended their nets and children played in the sand. Don marveled at the simplicity of life here, his usual city intensity melting away.

They ended the day with freshly grilled lobster at a small beachfront shack. The salty breeze and the sound of waves created the perfect backdrop for their meal.

"Lisa," Don said, watching the stars overhead, "I don't think I've ever felt this relaxed. This place...it feels like a dream."

Lisa leaned her head on his shoulder. "That's the magic of the islands. They remind you of what really matters."

Reflections on the Ride Back

The ferry ride back to Grenada was serene, the evening's sunset stretching out on the horizon like a painting draped in orange, red and grey hues, as the boat cut smoothly through the rough waters. Lisa and Don sat close together, wrapped in a light blanket to ward off the evening's coolness.

"Thank you for bringing me here," Don said, his voice soft. "I feel like I'm seeing a piece of your heart."

Lisa smiled, her hand resting over his. "And thank you for sharing it with me. There's still so much to see, so much to do. This is just the beginning."

As the ferry approached Grenada's harbor, the lights of St. George's twinkling in the distance, Lisa felt a wave of contentment. The journey, the islands, and the love she shared with Don were all part of a story she knew she would cherish forever.

Bottom of Form

Chapter 34: All of Me for All of You

The rhythm of life in Grenada had settled into a comfortable flow for Lisa and Don. Each day brought new adventures, but there was something different about this trip compared to their first. On their previous visit, they had explored some well-known spots and pristine beaches, but this time, they couldn't miss the charm of Carriacou and Petit Martinique. Lisa wanted to take Don deeper into her world, to places rich with her memories and stories.

One morning, as the sun filtered through the mango trees outside their window, Lisa was struck by a wave of inspiration. She had spent the night thinking back on the early days of her relationship with Don—the yearning, the uncertainty with Myrna, and the dreams that kept her going when things seemed impossible. She remembered a romantic note that she had written him back then where she told him how much she was thinking of him and how much she was longing to be with him.

Lisa rose quietly, not wanting to wake Don, and opened her laptop. The house was silent except for the gentle rustle of leaves outside, and Lisa began to write, her fingers moving swiftly across the keyboard.

All of Me for All of You

Verse 1
Every moment of every day,
I keep thinking about you baby.
Thinking of a place where we could be,
With non one in between, Just you and me.

Chorus
I want to give you all of me, in exchange for all of you,
I want to melt in your arms like ice cream on a sunny day.
Oh baby my lips are tingling for your kiss,
And every part of me is craving for your touch.
Verse 2
But the uncertainty of baby leaves me with much longing
To know if me or her you admire
Should I let you or should I stay
Let me know clearly your desire
Please don't leave me waiting in vain
My heart could not take the pain of losing you forever

Lisa smiled as the words poured out, each lyric carrying a piece of her heart. She thought back to those days in her hotel room, lying awake at night, longing for Don. His silence had been unbearable—emails unanswered, no phone calls, no sign that he was thinking of her the way she thought of him. But despite the ache, she had held onto the hope that one day, she could give all of herself to him, and that he would do the same.

By the time Don woke, Lisa had the foundation of her song written. He shuffled into the kitchen, still groggy but smiling when he saw her. "Morning, beautiful," he said, his voice warm.

"Good morning," Lisa replied, pouring him a cup of freshly brewed cocoa tea. "I was up early. Couldn't sleep."

Don raised an eyebrow. "Thinking about me, I hope?"

Lisa laughed, handing him the mug. "Actually, yes. You've been inspiring me more than you know."

He leaned against the counter, sipping his tea. "What were you working on?"

Lisa hesitated for a moment, then turned her laptop to face him. "It's a song. I was thinking back to...before we got together. When everything felt so uncertain."

Don read the lyrics, his expression softening. "Lisa, this is beautiful. It's...

us."

She nodded. "It's all the things I couldn't say back then. All the things I felt but didn't know if you'd ever feel the same."

Don set down his mug and reached for her hand. "You don't have to wonder anymore, honey. I'm here. I've always been here. Just couldn't bring myself to telling you, I'm sorry."

Later that day, Lisa and Don set out to explore other parts of Grenada, some of which they had visited before. Their first stop was the Belmont Estate, a historic cocoa plantation nestled in the lush countryside. They had been there on their first visit, but Lisa loved watching Don's face light up as he learned about the traditional methods of chocolate making. They were able to see the actual cocoa trees, touched the cocoa pods, and sampled the cocoa beans drying in the sun. They also learnt of the fermenting process before the beans were ready for processing into chocolate. They sampled rich, velvety chocolate, and Don couldn't resist teasing Lisa about her enthusiasm for the sweet treat.

"You have a chocolate addiction," he said, grinning as she reached for another sample.

Lisa playfully nudged him. "And you have a teasing addiction."

Don was fascinated as they walked through the estate, learning about the process of cocoa farming and chocolate-making. Lisa watched him with amusement, his curiosity reminding her of a child discovering something new.

"Did you know chocolate could be this complicated?" he asked, examining a cocoa pod.

Lisa laughed. "You should see the finished product. They make the best dark chocolate here. With so many different local flavors to choose from."

"Only if you promise to share it with me," he said, winking.

They spent hours exploring, tasting, and laughing. Don even tried his hand at grinding cocoa beans, his attempts earning cheers and playful jabs from the staff.

"You're a natural," one of the guides said with a grin.

"Or a disaster waiting to happen," Lisa teased, snapping a photo of him.

Their laughter echoed through the estate as they wandered the grounds, marveling at the beauty of the island.

From there, they visited Levera National Park, where they stood on the windswept shore and watched the waves crash against the rocks. The rugged beauty of the coastline left them both in awe.

"This place feels like the edge of the world," Don said, his voice tinged with wonder.

Lisa slipped her hand into his. "It's one of my favorite spots. It reminds me that even in the wildest storms, there's beauty."

That evening, back at the house, Lisa shared more of her song with Don. They sat together on the veranda, the stars twinkling above them, and she hummed the melody she had in mind. Don listened intently, his arm around her shoulders, as she poured her heart into the song.

"Lisa," he said when she finished, "this is going to be something special. I can feel it."

She smiled, leaning into him. "I was thinking...maybe this should be part of the album. What do you think?"

Don nodded. "It has to be. It's our story. And I think the world needs to hear it."

As they sat under the Grenadian sky, Lisa felt a profound sense of peace. The journey they had taken—the struggles, the heartbreak, and now the joy—had all led them here. And with Don by her side, she knew they were just beginning to write the next chapter of their story.

Chapter 35: The Story of Us

The soft hum of the evening enveloped the house as Lisa settled into her favorite spot on the veranda, her laptop resting on her lap. The day's adventures had stirred something deep within her—a longing not just to remember the moments but to preserve them. She wasn't writing a song this time. This was different. She was chronicling the love story that had taken her by surprise, swept her off her feet, and brought her to this place of contentment and renewal.

Their story had been anything but ordinary, and Lisa felt compelled to put it into words, not just for herself but for others who might one day find hope in it. She glanced up as Don walked out with two steaming mugs of cocoa tea, setting one beside her.

"You've been quiet," he said, sitting next to her. "What's going on in that beautiful mind of yours?"

Lisa smiled, tilting her head to rest on his shoulder for a moment. "I'm writing our story," she said softly. "From the first moment we met to all the chaos and beauty that's followed. I want to capture it—every twist and turn."

Don chuckled, taking a sip of his tea. "You mean the story of a goofy hotel manager and a stunning Caribbean queen who turned his life upside down?"

Lisa laughed, her eyes sparkling in the dim light. "Something like that. But more...epic. You know, the kind of story that makes people laugh, cry, and believe in love again."

Don smirked. "No pressure or anything."

Lisa nudged him playfully. "Oh, hush. You know you're the hero in this story."

"Hero, huh?" he teased, leaning back in his chair. "Then I better start practicing my dashing poses."

Lisa rolled her eyes, but her smile remained. His humor was part of what she loved most about him. No matter how heavy life got, Don had a way of lightening the load, of bringing joy even in the midst of uncertainty.

"Seriously, though," she said, turning back to her laptop. "I've been thinking a lot about where we started. About the days I spent in that hotel room, wondering if you'd ever start noticing me again. About the times when Myrna was doing everything in her power to put distance between us."

Don raised an eyebrow. "Notice you? Lisa, I noticed you the second you walked through those doors. I just didn't know what to do about it."

Lisa looked at him, surprised. "Really?"

He nodded, his expression softening. "I was stuck in a mess I didn't know how to get out of. Myrna...the job...everything felt so tangled. And then there you were—this bright, beautiful light—and I was afraid of ruining it. I didn't think I deserved you."

Lisa's chest tightened at his words. She reached for his hand, intertwining their fingers. "You didn't have to deserve me, Don. You just had to be you."

He smiled, bringing her hand to his lips. "And look where we are now."

Lisa's thoughts drifted back to those early days—the longing, the uncertainty, the moments she lay awake at night, dreaming of the life they could have together. She had doubted herself, doubted him, but something always kept her holding on, even when she decided she had to break things off with him.

"I want to include everything," she said after a moment. "The times we struggled, the times we almost gave up, and the moments that made it all worth it."

Don nodded, his gaze steady. "Then tell it all, Lisa. The good, the bad, the crazy. That's what makes it real."

That evening, back at the house, Lisa returned to her laptop. The day had given her so much to reflect on—the simplicity of their joy, the beauty of rediscovering her roots with Don by her side.

Don joined her again, this time with a plate of fresh fruit. "Writing more?" he asked, offering her a slice of mango.

Lisa nodded, chewing thoughtfully. "Today reminded me of why I started this. It's not just our story. It's a reminder that love isn't perfect, but it's worth it."

Don leaned back, a satisfied smile on his face. "I like that. 'Not perfect, but worth it.' Sounds like a good title for your next book."

Lisa laughed. "Maybe. But first, I have to finish writing this one."

"And when you do," Don said, his tone serious, "I'll be the first in line to read it."

Lisa smiled, her heart full. With Don beside her and the pages of their story unfolding, she felt more certain than ever that their best chapters were still ahead.

Chapter 36: An Unexpected Reunion

The sun rose gently over Grenada, casting a golden glow on the island as Lisa and Don prepared for another day of exploration. Today's plan was to visit the Annandale Waterfall, a lush, serene spot nestled in the hills. Lisa loved the idea of showing Don more of the island's natural beauty, and Don was eager for another adventure.

As they packed a small bag with snacks and towels, Don hummed a tune under his breath, his voice filling the room. Lisa paused, smiling at him. His natural habit of singing while doing mundane tasks had become one of her favorite things about him.

"Is that a new song?" she asked, tilting her head.

Don grinned. "Just something I'm making up as I go. You like it?"

Lisa nodded, her heart swelling. "I love it. You really should take your singing more seriously, Don. You've got something special."

He shrugged, a little bashfully. "Maybe. But I don't know if I'm ready for all that yet."

Lisa smiled, deciding not to press him. For now, she was content to enjoy his impromptu serenades.

The drive to Annandale Waterfall was short but scenic. The road wound through lush green hills, with glimpses of the Caribbean Sea peeking through the trees. Lisa pointed out local landmarks as they went, her voice animated with nostalgia.

When they arrived, the sound of rushing water filled the air, mingling with the chirping of birds and the rustle of leaves. The waterfall was breathtaking, its cascading streams tumbling into a clear, inviting pool surrounded by vibrant tropical plants.

Don's eyes widened as he took it in. "This is incredible," he said, his voice filled with awe.

Lisa beamed. "I knew you'd love it. This is one of my favorite places too."

They spent the morning exploring the area, dipping their feet in the cool water and taking photos. Don, always playful, splashed Lisa unexpectedly, earning a mock glare and a retaliatory splash. Their laughter echoed through the clearing, blending with the sounds of nature.

As they sat on a nearby rock to rest, munching on fresh mangoes they'd packed, a familiar voice called out.

"Lisa? Is that you?"

Lisa turned, her heart skipping a beat as she recognized the voice. It was her childhood friend, Marva, whom she hadn't seen in years.

"Marva!" Lisa exclaimed, standing to embrace her friend.

Marva laughed, her arms wrapping tightly around Lisa. "I can't believe it! What are the chances of running into you here?"

Don watched the reunion with a warm smile, standing to introduce himself when Lisa gestured to him.

"This is Don," Lisa said, her voice brimming with pride. "My...boyfriend."

Don extended a hand, grinning. "Nice to meet you, Marva."

Marva shook his hand, her eyes twinkling. "You've got good taste, Lisa. He's a keeper."

Lisa laughed, her cheeks flushing slightly. "I know, right?"

The three of them spent the next hour catching up, with Marva sharing stories about the island and her family. Lisa listened intently, her heart full as she reconnected with someone from her past.

Later, as they drove back to the house, Lisa felt a sense of gratitude. The trip had already been filled with so many wonderful moments—adventures, reconnections, and the quiet, steady presence of Don by her side.

"I think today was one of my favorites," Don said, breaking the comfortable silence.

Lisa glanced at him, her heart swelling. "Why is that?"

"Because I got to see another piece of your world," he replied simply. "And it just keeps getting better."

Lisa reached for his hand, intertwining their fingers. "I feel the same way, Don. Thank you for being here with me—for loving this place as much as I do."

Don smiled, his eyes warm. "I don't just love this place, Lisa. I love you."

Her breath caught at his words, the sincerity in his voice making her heart ache in the best way.

"I love you too," she whispered.

The sun dipped lower in the sky as they drove, its golden light casting a glow over the island. For Lisa, it felt like the perfect end to another chapter in their story—a story that was only just beginning.

Chapter 37: A Feast of Love

The warm Grenadian sun kissed the earth as Lisa and Don made their way through the familiar roads of her childhood home, the scenery lush and alive with vibrant greenery. This trip wasn't just about revisiting of cherished places or connecting with her brother Bain and her son David—it was also about confronting a piece of her past. Today, they would visit Ronald, Lisa's ex-husband. Though the idea had initially made Lisa uneasy, she knew it was important. Their shared history couldn't be erased, and she hoped introducing Don would help solidify the family's unity.

A Warm Welcome

When they arrived at Ronald's house, Lisa's heart was pounding. She glanced at Don, whose calm presence helped to ease her nerves. "He's a good man," Lisa said softly, as if convincing herself as much as Don.

Ronald opened the door with a broad smile, his demeanor warm and inviting. His eyes softened when he saw Lisa, and he extended his hand to Don with genuine friendliness.

"You must be Don," Ronald said, shaking his hand firmly. "Lisa's told me a lot about you."

"All good, I hope," Don said, smiling.

"All good," Ronald confirmed with a chuckle. He turned to Lisa, his voice tinged with emotion. "It's really good to see you, Lisa. You look happy."

"I am," Lisa replied, smiling warmly. "And thank you, Ronald, for making this easy."

Ronald nodded, his gaze briefly flicking to Don. "Well, anyone who makes

Lisa happy is good in my books."

They spent the next few minutes talking, the conversation light and amicable. Ronald shared updates about his life and reminisced about the family memories they'd shared before things had fallen apart. Lisa was relieved by his openness and grateful that he welcomed Don without any hesitation.

When it was time to leave, Ronald hugged Lisa, his embrace a gesture of closure and understanding. "You deserve happiness, Lisa," he said softly.

"Thank you, Ronald," she replied, her voice thick with gratitude.

Mango Picking Excitment

After the emotional visit with Ronald, they travelled back to her brother's home. Lisa decided it was time for something lighter.

Lisa laughed excitedly, unable to hide what she was thinking. Are you ready to meet my childhood celebrity?" Don looked puzzled.

They walked to a nearby mango tree, its branches laden with ripe, golden fruits way up in the tree. Lisa picked up an average size stone from the ground and handed it to Don.

"In Grenada, we don't wait for mangoes to fall—we make them fall," she said with a mischievous grin.

Don raised an eyebrow, looking at the stone in his hand. "And how do we do that?"

"Watch and learn," Lisa replied, aiming her stone at a mango high in the tree. She threw it with precision, but the mango stubbornly remained on the branch.

Don smirked. "Impressive... if the goal was to scare the mango into falling."

"Quiet, you," Lisa said, laughing as she picked up another stone. She tried again, but the mango remained untouched.

Don hefted the stone in his hand, taking aim, his expression serious. With a swift flick of his arm, the stone soared through the air and hit a mango squarely, knocking it to the ground.

"Beginner's luck!" Lisa exclaimed, clapping her hands as Don retrieved the fruit.

Don smirked, tossing the mango in the air. "I'll take it. Want to see if I can do it again?"

To Lisa's astonishment, Don repeated his feat, bringing down a grap of three mangoes. He handed the fruits to her with a triumphant grin.

"Well, aren't you the expert now," Lisa said, feigning annoyance but unable to hide her amusement.

"Maybe you should stick to pelting breadfruit," Don teased. "Or was it stones for fun as a kid?"

Lisa burst out laughing. "Hey, I've had plenty of practice pelting stones to pick mangoes, thank you very much. But clearly, this tree has it out for me. Perhaps it's been holding a grudge against me all these years."

They spent the next hour laughing and teasing each other, Don playfully dodging Lisa's mock threats to "teach him a lesson" for showing her up.

A Breakfast Feast

The next morning, David surprised them with a breakfast of freshly sliced roast breadfruit and fried fish, a mixture of snapper and butterfish, perfect for a feast. David, already in the kitchen, was busy preparing the meal.

The breadfruit slices were deeped in salted water and fried to golden perfection, while the fish, deeply seasoned with a blend of grated garlic and fresh herbs, fried in another pan. The aroma filled the house, mingling with the rich, chocolatey scent of Grenadian cocoa tea simmering on the stove.

When the meal was served, Don couldn't hide his excitement. "This is amazing," he said, digging into the fried breadfruit. "I've never had anything like this."

Lisa grinned, savoring the warm, nutty flavor of the breadfruit. "This is a Grenadian breakfast at its finest."

"And the cocoa tea," Don added, taking a sip, it was infused with bay leaves and cinnamon, with a touch of grated tanka bean. "I could drink this every day."

David beamed with pride. "You'll have to come back often for the real deal."

As they ate, the morning was filled with laughter and stories, the warmth of family creating a memory Lisa knew she would treasure forever.

When Don raised his mug of cocoa tea, a playful smile on his face, Lisa couldn't help but laugh. "To mango-pelting champions everywhere," he said, earning a round of laughter from the table.

"To mango-pelting champions," Lisa echoed, her heart full as their cups clanked together.

Chapter 38: Sweet Fruits of Home

The days of Lisa and Don's vacation in Grenada were winding down, but Lisa wasn't ready to let Don leave without experiencing one more cherished piece of her childhood. Behind Bain's house, where Lisa had spent countless days playing as a child, stood two fruit trees she had adored—the sugar apple and sapodilla trees. These trees were more than just sources of fruit; they were symbols of her childhood freedom, adventure, and the sweet simplicity of life on the island.

Early that morning, as the first rays of sunlight crept over the horizon, Lisa decided it was time to introduce Don to her favorite fruit trees. She woke him with a soft nudge, her excitement barely contained.

"Come on," she whispered, her eyes sparkling. "I have something special to show you."

Don groaned, pulling a pillow over his face. "Is this payback for the snow-skating lesson?"

Lisa laughed, tugging at the pillow. "No, this is about the heart of Grenada. Trust me, you'll love it."

Reluctantly, Don rolled out of bed, quickly pulling on a shirt and jeans. As they walked through the cool morning air toward Bain's backyard, the scent of dew and fresh earth greeted them, along with the cheerful chirping of birds in the trees.

"This," Lisa said, stopping in front of a large, gnarled tree, "is the sugar apple tree. My favorite."

Don tilted his head, examining the tree with curiosity. Its branches were dotted with pale green fruit, their skin rough and segmented. "Those are the sugar apples you've been talking about?"

Lisa nodded with a grin. "The very ones. They're sweet and creamy, like dessert straight from nature. But you can't just pick them any way you want— they're delicate. You have to twist them off gently when they're ripe."

Don stepped closer, reaching for a fruit. "Like this?"

Lisa quickly grabbed his hand, laughing. "Not so fast! These are not ready yet. See how firm they are? That means they need more time. When they're ripe, they'll be soft, and they'll practically fall off the branch with a little twist."

Don smirked, folding his arms. "So no stones? No tree shaking?"

Lisa gasped in mock indignation. "Stones? This isn't mango picking, Don! This tree demands respect."

Tales of the Fruit Bandit

Lisa led Don around to show him the sapodilla tree, its dusty, rough, almost rounded fruits nestled among shiny leaves. She reached up, stretching to a lowered branch to touch one of the fruits, almost with reverence.

"These," she said, her voice tinged with nostalgia, "are sapodillas. They taste like brown sugar with a hint of caramel. But they're not in season right now, they're still young. When they're ripe, they're soft and brown, and you pick them by hand just like the sugar apples; but like the sugar apples, you can also pick then when they're full and put them to ripe."

Don ran his fingers over the rough bark of the tree. "So no stones for these either?"

Lisa shook her head, smiling. "No stones, but you have to climb to get them way up in the branches - Just patience and a good eye for ripeness."

As they stood beneath the sapodilla tree, Lisa's gaze grew distant, her mind wandering back to her childhood. "I used to climb this very tree to get the ripe fruits before the birds did. Sometimes, I'd sit up there for hours, just watching the world go by – the tree was much shorter then."

Don looked up at the tree, imagining a younger Lisa perched among its branches. "You were a regular fruit ninja, weren't you?"

Lisa laughed, her eyes sparkling with mischief. "It was serious business! If you waited too long, the birds would peck at every last fruit. It was a game of wits—me against them."

Don chuckled, his admiration for her growing. "I can just picture you up there, swinging from branch to branch like a regular Tarzan."

"I wasn't swinging," Lisa corrected with a grin. "But I was pretty good at spotting the ripe ones. And let me tell you, there's nothing like splitting open and biting into a ripe sapodilla you've just picked."

Breakfast and Banter

As they walked back toward the house, Bain met them near the kitchen door, carrying a tray of sliced roasted breadfruit and fried fish. The aroma wafted through the air, making Don's stomach growl audibly.

"Breakfast is ready," Bain announced, setting the tray on the table.

Lisa grinned, reaching for a slice of the golden-ripe, roasted breadfruit. It was sweet and starchy and tasted divine. "This is why you have to come back, Don. Grenada spoils you with food."

As they sat down to eat, Bain shared stories about his farm, his fishing expeditions, and life on the island. Don listened intently, soaking in every detail. Lisa couldn't help but feel a sense of pride as she watched Don bond with her brother over their shared love of the simple, fulfilling life Grenada offered.

The Sugar Apple Tree, Revisited

Later that afternoon, Lisa brought Don back to the sugar apple tree. The sun was warm on their backs, and the birds chirped overhead, darting between the branches.

"So," Don said, rubbing his hands together, "what's the plan? How do I win this sugar apple battle against the birds?"

Lisa rolled her eyes, laughing. "The plan is patience. But let's see if we can find one ripe enough to pick."

They examined the tree carefully, Lisa showing Don how to spot the ripening fruit. After a few minutes, she reached up and gently twisted a ripe sugar apple from the branch, holding it up triumphantly.

"This is what the birds were after. Got one!" she declared.

Don grinned, reaching for the fruit. "Let me try."

He spotted another on hiding within the branch that looked promising and carefully repeated Lisa's technique. With a little effort, the fruit came loose, and he held it up like a trophy.

"Beginner's luck," Lisa teased.

"Beginner's skill," Don shot back, his eyes twinkling.

They sat beneath the tree, sharing the sugar apples as Lisa told more stories of her childhood adventures. Don listened, captivated by her tales of climbing trees, competing with birds, and savoring the sweet fruits of her homeland.

"Lisa," he said after a while, his voice soft, "I can see why you love this place so much. It's not just the beauty or the food—it's the life here. It's you."

Lisa smiled, her heart full. "And now it's part of you too."

As they sat together beneath the tree, the world seemed to fade away, leaving only the two of them, the warm Caribbean breeze, and the sweet taste of sugar apples on their lips.

Chapter 39: Moonlight Whispers

The beach was their sanctuary that evening, a stretch of sand and sea that seemed to exist just for Lisa and Don. With every step they took along Grand Anse Beach, the fading sunlight wrapped them in a golden glow. Lisa felt as though the island itself were saying goodbye in the only way it knew—through its beauty, warmth, and the symphony of waves lapping against the shore.

Don paused to admire the scenery, his face serene. "This place is something else," he murmured, his voice barely above the sound of the water.

Lisa smiled, brushing her hand against his. "It's the kind of place that stays with you. No matter where you go, a piece of it comes along with you."

The sun dipped lower, its fiery hues melting into the horizon. They found themselves a secluded spot where the beach curved inward like an embrace. A lone fisherman's boat rocked gently in the distance, silhouetted against the glowing sky.

Lisa took Don's hand, leading him closer to the water. "Let's make this our last memory here," she said softly, her voice tinged with the bittersweetness of their approaching departure.

Don chuckled, slipping his arm around her waist. "As long as it involves you, it's a memory I'll never forget."

They sat down on the cool sand, watching as the last rays of sunlight disappeared and the stars began to prick the sky. Lisa tilted her head back, marveling at how vast and endless it all seemed.

"I used to dream about moments like this," she confessed, her voice tender. "Sitting here with someone I love, feeling the world fall away."

Don turned to her, his gaze warm and steady. "Did those dreams feel the same way as this does?"

Lisa looked at him, her heart swelling. "This is way better. Because they have you in it."

Don's lips curved into a smile, and he leaned in, pressing a kiss to her temple.

The Splendor of Moonlight

By the time they returned to her house, the moon had risen, its silvery glow illuminating the yard in a soft, ethereal light. Don stopped in his tracks, looking around with wide-eyed wonder.

"I've never noticed moonlight like this before," he said, his voice hushed. "Not in New York. There's always too much light from the city. But here..."

He gestured to the trees, their leaves glistening as though dipped in liquid silver. The shadows cast by the branches danced gently across the ground, creating a scene that felt almost otherworldly.

Lisa watched him with a smile, her heart full at seeing him so captivated. "This is the Grenadian moonlight," she said with a playful lilt. "It's special, just like everything else here."

Don turned to her, his face glowing with a boyish excitement. "I feel like I've stepped into a painting. This is... breathtaking."

Lisa took his hand, leading him toward the house. "Come on in, let's see how it looks through the window."

Inside, the moonlight spilled through the open window of their room, casting a soft glow across the walls and bed. Don stood by the window, the curtains drawn, staring out at the trees swaying gently in the night breeze.

"You know," he said quietly, "I didn't think I'd find a place that could feel like this. Peaceful. Magical."

Lisa joined him by the window, leaning her head on his shoulder. "It's not just the place, Don. It's us. Being here together makes it what it is."

Don turned to her, his expression tender. "You're right. And I'm not feeling ready to leave it just yet."

Sweet Stories Beneath the Stars

Lisa smiled and pulled him toward the bed, where they sat side by side, the moonlight wrapping them in its embrace. "Before we leave," she began, her tone light, "there's something else you should know about this place."

Don arched an eyebrow. "Another fruit tree story?"

Lisa laughed, shaking her head. "Not quite. But when I was little, I used to believe the moonlight here could grant wishes. My friends and I would sit outside and whisper our dreams to it, thinking it could hear us."

Don's eyes twinkled. "And did it ever work?"

She shrugged with a grin. "Sometimes. But I think the magic wasn't in the moonlight—it was in the hope we felt when we believed in something."

Don nodded thoughtfully, reaching out to take her hand. "So, what would you wish for now, if you still believed in moonlight magic?"

Lisa paused, her gaze drifting to the glowing trees outside. "I'd wish for this feeling to last forever. For us to always have moments like this, no matter where we are."

Don's grip on her hand tightened slightly, and he leaned closer. "I'd wish for the same."

They sat there for a long time, sharing whispered stories and laughter, their voices blending with the soft hum of the night. The moonlight poured over them, a silent witness to their love.

As Lisa drifted to sleep later that night, wrapped in Don's arms, she felt a deep sense of peace. Their vacation might be ending, but the memories they had created would remain, lighting their path forward like the moonlight that had illuminated their final night in paradise.

Chapter 40: Homeward Bound

The airplane hummed steadily as it cut through the clouds, leaving behind the warmth of Grenada's sun and carrying Lisa and Don back to New York's cooler embrace. Lisa gazed out of the window, watching as the turquoise waters of the Caribbean Sea grew smaller and smaller, fading into the vast blue of the sky.

Don sat beside her, quietly flipping through the in-flight magazine, though Lisa could sense his mind wasn't entirely on the glossy pages. Every now and then, his hand would find hers, his thumb brushing lightly over her fingers—a small gesture, but one that grounded her amidst the mix of emotions swirling inside.

Lisa sighed, leaning back against her seat. She had tried to keep her thoughts on the beautiful memories they had made—the laughter, the moonlit whispers, the joy of seeing Don bond with her family—but as the miles between them and Grenada grew, another thought kept pushing its way to the forefront: Lyron.

It had been years since she last saw her son. The ache of his absence had never dulled, no matter how much time passed. Margaret's interference had created a barrier so impenetrable that Lisa had nearly lost hope. Nearly.

As the clouds drifted past the window, her mind wandered to the little boy Lyron used to be—the one who would crawl into her lap with a book, who would burst into fits of laughter at her silly voices. She thought about his bright smile, his boundless energy, and the way he used to hold her hand so tightly as if he was afraid to let go.

Lisa swallowed hard, blinking back the sting of tears. That little boy felt so far away now, replaced by a man she didn't know anymore—a man she longed to reconnect with but couldn't seem to reach.

Don's Quiet Comfort

"You okay?" Don's voice broke through her thoughts, gentle and filled with concern.

Lisa turned to him, her lips curving into a faint smile. "I'm fine," she said, though her voice betrayed her weariness.

Don set the magazine aside, giving her his full attention. "You're thinking about Lyron, aren't you?"

She nodded, her gaze falling to her lap. "I can't help it, Don. I don't even know where to start. Every time I think I might have a way to reach him, it feels like Margaret is one step ahead, blocking me. It's like she's made it her life's mission to keep us apart."

Don reached for her hand, his grip firm and reassuring. "You'll find a way, Lisa. I know you will. You've already overcome so much—this is just one more challenge. And I'm here to help you, whatever it takes."

Lisa looked at him, her heart swelling with gratitude. Don's unwavering support was a balm to her weary soul. "Thank you," she said softly. "I don't know what I'd do without you."

He smiled, his eyes warm. "You won't ever have to find out."

The Weight of Uncertainty

As the plane began its descent, Lisa couldn't shake the sense of urgency growing inside her. She wanted to believe Don's words, to hold on to the hope that she would one day reconnect with her son. But the road ahead felt impossibly long, and the uncertainty was suffocating.

After they landed and made their way through the airport, the crisp New York air hit her like a jolt—a stark contrast to Grenada's tropical warmth. Lisa tightened her scarf around her neck, the chill biting at her skin.

Don hailed a cab, and as they slid into the backseat, Lisa stared out at the cityscape flashing by. The bustling streets, the towering buildings, the relentless pace of life—it was all so different from the serene beauty they had just left behind.

"Home sweet home," Don said with a wry smile, sensing her mood.

Lisa chuckled softly. "It's...different, that's for sure."

A Quiet Resolve

Back at her apartment, Lisa unpacked her bags with a sense of quiet determination. Each item she pulled out—a seashell from the beach, the cocoa balls and spices from her brother Bain, a photo of her and Don with David—all felt like a piece of Grenada she was carrying forward.

As she tucked the photo into the frame on her nightstand, she paused, running her fingers over the edges. Her family. It wasn't whole without Lyron.

Sitting on the edge of the bed, Lisa let out a slow breath. She didn't have the answers yet. She didn't know how to break through Margaret's walls or how to find her way back to her son. But she knew one thing: she wouldn't give up.

Don appeared in the doorway, leaning against the frame with a soft smile. "You look deep in thought again."

Lisa glanced at him, a spark of determination in her eyes. "I'm just...thinking about what comes next."

He walked over, sitting beside her and wrapping an arm around her shoulders. "Whatever it is, we'll face it together. You're not alone anymore."

She leaned into him, finding comfort in his presence. "I know," she said softly. "And that makes all the difference."

As the city buzzed outside their window, Lisa allowed herself a moment of hope. The journey ahead might be uncertain, but with Don by her side, she felt stronger, more capable. And though she didn't know how or when, she believed that one day, she would find her way back to Lyron.

Chapter 41: A Question of Forever

The flight back to New York was a quiet one for Lisa and Don. The glow of their Grenadian escape still lingered in their smiles, but as the plane touched down and the bustling energy of the city greeted them, the realities of life began to seep back in. Lisa couldn't help but feel the familiar pang of longing for her son, Lyron, and the weight of uncertainty surrounding him. Don, however, was quietly brimming with determination. He had spent the last days of their vacation reflecting on their love and now carried a secret he couldn't keep much longer.

Settling Back In

The chill of New York was a stark contrast to Grenada's warmth, but Don's apartment welcomed them with its familiar coziness. They set down their bags, exchanging tired smiles as they shed their travel coats.

"Home sweet home," Lisa said softly, though her voice carried a note of wistfulness. She wandered to the window, gazing at the skyline illuminated by city lights.

Don came up behind her, wrapping his arms around her waist. "What's on your mind?" he asked, his voice gentle.

Lisa leaned back into him, taking comfort in his steady presence. "Lyron," she admitted. "I can't help but wonder if he's okay, if he's thinking of me."

Don kissed the top of her head. "We'll figure it out, Lisa. I know it feels impossible right now, but we'll find a way."

She turned in his arms, offering a small smile. "Thank you. You always know how to make me feel like I'm not alone in this."

"You're not," Don said, his eyes locking with hers. "And you never will be."

Dinner and Determination

Don had insisted on preparing dinner, claiming it was his way of easing them back into their routine. Lisa sat at the kitchen counter, sipping a glass of wine and watching him work. His casual ease, the way he hummed quietly to himself as he chopped vegetables, filled her heart with warmth.

"You're quite the chef these days," Lisa teased, resting her chin in her hand.

Don shot her a grin. "Well, I've had a pretty great teacher."

They ate together, the meal simple but satisfying. Conversation flowed easily, filled with stories from their trip and lighthearted teasing. But Don's mind was elsewhere, turning over the words he'd been rehearsing for days.

After dinner, they moved to the couch, the city lights casting a soft glow in the room. Lisa curled up beside Don, her head resting on his shoulder. She felt a rare contentment despite the worries lingering at the edges of her mind.

"Lisa," Don said suddenly, his voice breaking the comfortable silence.

She looked up at him, her brow lifting slightly. "Yes?"

Don shifted, his hand dipping into his pocket. "There's something I've been meaning to say. Something I've been thinking about for a long time."

Lisa sat up, her heart quickening as she watched him pull out a small velvet box. Her breath caught as he opened it, revealing a stunning ring that sparkled in the dim light.

"Lisa," Don began, his voice steady but filled with emotion, "meeting you changed everything for me. You've shown me what love really looks like—patient, kind, unwavering. You've been my strength, my joy, and my reason to keep moving forward."

Lisa's eyes filled with tears, her hand covering her mouth as he continued.

"I never thought I'd find someone like you, someone who sees all of me and still chooses to stay. I want to spend the rest of my life proving that I'll always choose you, too. So, Lisa, will you marry me?"

For a moment, Lisa couldn't speak, her heart overwhelmed with love and disbelief. Then, slowly, she nodded, her voice trembling as she said, "Yes, Don. A thousand times, yes."

Don's face lit up with relief and joy as he slid the ring onto her finger. They both stared at it for a moment, the reality of their promise settling over them like a warm embrace. Then, Don pulled her into his arms, their kiss deep and filled with the certainty of their love.

Celebrating the Moment

The rest of the evening was a blur of laughter, kisses, and shared dreams. Don brought out a bottle of champagne he'd been saving, and they toasted to their future, their glasses clinking softly in the quiet of the apartment.

Lisa couldn't stop glancing at the ring, her heart swelling with each look. "It's perfect," she said softly, meeting Don's gaze.

"You're perfect," he replied, brushing a strand of hair from her face. "And I can't wait to spend forever with you."

They fell asleep that night tangled in each other's arms, their hearts full and their minds spinning with the possibilities of the life they were building together.

The Morning After

Lisa woke to the soft light filtering through the blinds and the warmth of Don's arms around her. For a moment, she simply lay there, letting the reality of their engagement sink in. She turned to Don, her smile breaking wide as she saw him watching her.

"Good morning, fiancée," he said, his voice thick with affection.

"Good morning, fiancé," Lisa replied, her laughter soft and melodic.

They spent the morning wrapped in a bubble of bliss, savoring the first day of their engagement. Don cooked breakfast—pancakes this time, much to Lisa's amusement—and they talked about everything and nothing, their love weaving through each word and gesture.

Planning the Future

Later, as they walked through the city, hand in hand, they began to dream out loud about their wedding. Lisa wanted something intimate yet special, surrounded by the people they loved most. Don wanted whatever would make her happiest.

"We'll make it perfect," Don promised as they stopped by a park bench. "Whatever you want, we'll make it happen."

Lisa rested her head on his shoulder, her heart full. "All I want is you, Don."

"And you'll have me," he said, pressing a kiss to her hair. "Always."

As they sat there, surrounded by the hum of the city, Lisa felt a deep sense of peace. Despite the challenges that still lay ahead, she knew they were stronger together. With Don by her side, she could face anything—and for the first time in a long while, she allowed herself to believe in the beauty of the future they were creating.

Chapter 42: Family Ties and Wedding Plans

The days following Don's proposal were a blend of excitement and a flurry of preparations. Lisa found herself caught up in a whirlwind of wedding planning, but every detail, every decision brought her a sense of joy she hadn't experienced in years. This wasn't just about a wedding—it was about merging two lives, two families, and two hearts into one.

Lisa and Don decided on an intimate ceremony with only their closest friends and family, focusing on the love that had carried them through so many challenges. Lisa wanted the event to reflect her vibrant Caribbean roots and Don's grounded, New York sensibility—a perfect fusion of their worlds.

Bringing in the Experts

One evening, as Lisa sat surrounded by bridal magazines and Pinterest boards, Don came over with two cups of tea and a playful grin. "I think it's time we called in the cavalry," he said, placing a steaming cup in front of her.

Lisa raised an eyebrow. "The cavalry?"

"My sisters," Don replied. "Karen and Evelyn are pros at this kind of thing. They'll be thrilled to help."

Lisa hesitated. She wasn't used to relying on others, but the prospect of sharing the load—and the fun—was tempting. "Do you think they'd want to?" she asked.

Don chuckled. "Want to? They'll fight over who gets to do what. Trust me, Lisa, they already adore you."

An Afternoon with Karen and Evelyn

True to Don's words, his sisters, Karen and Evelyn, arrived the next afternoon, arms full of notebooks, fabric swatches, and infectious enthusiasm. Karen, the artistic one, had a natural eye for beauty and balance, while Evelyn, the organizer, brought a precision and energy that could rival a professional planner.

"So," Karen began, sketchpad in hand, "tell us your vision, Lisa."

Lisa glanced at Don for reassurance before speaking. "I'd like something elegant but warm. Soft blush tones, whites, and greenery—maybe touches of gold for a little shimmer. I want it to feel intimate and romantic, like a garden in full bloom."

Karen's eyes lit up. "Blush and greenery—classic and beautiful. We could use candles for that soft glow you're talking about."

Evelyn was already taking notes. "And the venue is St. Luke's, right? The stone walls there will be stunning with this palette."

Lisa nodded, smiling. "Yes, and David is working on the menu in Grenada. He's planning a fusion of Caribbean and American flavors."

Karen grinned. "Perfect. I can already picture it—guests enjoying his amazing food in a setting that feels like a dream."

Details and Laughter

The afternoon flew by as the four of them brainstormed, laughed, and shared ideas. Karen sketched out floral arrangements—cascading bouquets with eucalyptus and peonies, soft and romantic. Evelyn mapped out a timeline for the day, ensuring everything would run smoothly.

At one point, Karen turned to Lisa with a mischievous smile. "Do you have your dress yet? Or is that next on the list?"

Lisa blushed. "Not yet. I have a few ideas, but I haven't made a decision."

Evelyn clapped her hands. "Then we'll go shopping together. It'll be a girls' day out!"

Lisa laughed, feeling a warmth she hadn't known she was missing. Don's sisters had embraced her so fully, making her feel like part of the family long before the wedding day.

A Quiet Moment

After Karen and Evelyn left, Lisa and Don sat together on the couch, the apartment now quiet after the lively energy of the afternoon. Lisa leaned her head on Don's shoulder, a contented sigh escaping her lips.

"Your sisters are amazing," she said. "I don't know how I ever thought I could plan this wedding without them."

Don chuckled, pressing a kiss to her hair. "They love you. They've been waiting for someone like you to come into my life."

Lisa smiled, her heart full. "And I've been waiting for you."

Don tilted her chin up, meeting her gaze. "This is just the beginning, Lisa. Our life together—it's going to be incredible."

Dreaming of the Future

The days passed in a flurry of excitement. Lisa and Don chose invitations, coordinated with the florist, and finalized their guest list. Don's sisters were ever-present, their enthusiasm turning every task into a celebration.

One evening, as Lisa sat flipping through photos of wedding venues, Don came up behind her, wrapping his arms around her shoulders. "What's next on the list?" he asked, his voice warm and playful.

Lisa smiled. "Finalizing the decorations. I want everything to feel perfect."

Don kissed her cheek. "It already is. As long as we're together, Lisa, it's perfect."

A Toast to Love

One week before the wedding, Karen and Evelyn hosted a small gathering at their home to celebrate the upcoming nuptials. It was an evening filled with laughter, heartfelt toasts, and shared memories.

Karen raised her glass, her eyes sparkling. "To Don and Lisa—a love that's brought out the best in both of you. We couldn't be happier for you."

Lisa glanced at Don, her heart swelling as she clinked glasses with him. "To us," she whispered.

"To us," he replied, his voice filled with love.

As the evening wound down, Lisa felt a deep sense of gratitude. She had found not only a partner in Don but also a family that embraced her fully. With each passing day, the life they were building felt more real, more beautiful, and more complete.

And as they left Karen and Evelyn's home that night, hand in hand under the glow of the city lights, Lisa knew that their future together would be everything she had ever dreamed of—and more.

Chapter 43: Shadows of the Past

The days leading up to Lisa and Don's wedding brimmed with excitement and anticipation, but underneath the surface, tension simmered. Myrna had begun to stir trouble again. Her sudden reappearance, cloaked in concern for their son Jonathan, had placed a cloud over what should have been a joyous time.

Lisa was at home, carefully packing boxes for the wedding, when her phone buzzed on the coffee table. The notification glowed: *Myrna*. Her chest tightened. She had hoped the hotel confrontation was the end of the drama, but clearly, Myrna had more to say.

She hesitated before unlocking her phone and opening the message.

"Lisa, you don't know the full story about Don. I think it's time we talk. For your sake, I hope you'll hear me out."

Lisa stared at the words, her stomach twisting. What was Myrna playing at now? She took a deep breath, trying to steady herself, but the unease crept in like a shadow. The tone of the message was deliberately ambiguous, calculated to unsettle.

When Don walked in a few minutes later, Lisa handed him the phone without a word. He read the message, his jaw tightening.

"This is ridiculous," he muttered. "She's just trying to stir up trouble. You know that, right?"

Lisa nodded, her voice trembled slightly as she replied. "I know. But what does she mean by 'the full story'? What could she possibly think I don't already know?"

Don rubbed his temples, frustration flickering across his face. "Lisa, I don't want her dragging you into this. Myrna has always had a knack for creating chaos—making herself the victim and twisting everything to suit her narrative."

"But she's not backing down, Don," Lisa said, her voice firm despite the worry in her eyes. "If I ignore her, she'll just escalate. I think we need to confront this together."

Don hesitated, visibly torn. "I don't want you to get hurt. Myrna knows how to push buttons. She's manipulative, and I won't let her ruin this for us."

Lisa reached for his hand, squeezing it gently. "We'll face her together, Don. She can't break what we've built."

Reluctantly, Don agreed, and they arranged to meet Myrna the next day.

The Confrontation

The café was quiet when Lisa and Don arrived, the late afternoon sun casting long shadows across the room. Myrna was already seated at a corner table, her posture poised but tense. She watched them approach with an unreadable expression, her lips pressed into a thin line.

"Myrna," Don said tersely as they sat down. "What do you want?"

Myrna's eyes flicked to Lisa, her gaze sharp. "I'm here for Lisa's sake, not yours. She deserves to know who she's really marrying."

Lisa's heart raced, but she kept her voice calm. "If you have something to say, Myrna, say it."

Myrna leaned forward, her tone low and deliberate. "Don didn't tell you everything about our relationship. Did he ever mention the times he walked out on me? Or the way he ignored Jonathan for weeks at a time? He made promises he didn't keep, Lisa. And if he did it to me, he'll do it to you."

Lisa's breath caught, the words landing like sharp blows. She turned to Don, searching his face for answers.

"That's not true," Don said firmly, his voice steady but tinged with anger. "I stayed in that relationship longer than I should have—for Jonathan. You know that, Myrna. And when it ended, it was because we both knew it wasn't working. Don't twist the truth."

Myrna's expression darkened. "You can justify it all you want, Don, but the fact remains: you have a pattern of walking away. Lisa deserves better than that."

Lisa felt a wave of frustration and pain rise within her. She met Myrna's gaze, her voice firm. "Don has been nothing but honest with me about his past. I know it wasn't perfect, but none of us are. What matters is who he is now, and I trust him."

Myrna's eyes narrowed. "Trust him all you want, Lisa. Just don't say I didn't warn you when he lets you down."

Don stood abruptly, his fists clenched at his sides. "That's enough, Myrna. You don't get to come here and try to ruin what we have. I won't let you poison this relationship the way you tried to poison everything else."

Lisa rose slowly, her composure steady despite the turmoil inside her. She looked at Myrna with a mixture of compassion and resolve. "I'm sorry for whatever pain you're holding onto, Myrna. But Don and I are moving forward, and nothing you say will change that."

Myrna's expression faltered, a flicker of vulnerability crossing her face before she masked it with cold indifference. "Fine," she said, standing. "But don't expect me to support this. Jonathan deserves better than being caught in the middle of your fantasy."

She walked away, leaving Lisa and Don standing in the café, the tension hanging heavy in the air.

Rebuilding Strength

As they drove home, Lisa was quiet, her thoughts tangled. Don reached over, placing a hand on her knee.

"Lisa," he said softly, his voice breaking the silence. "You know she's just trying to get under your skin, right? None of what she said was true."

Lisa nodded, her voice hesitant. "I know, Don. But it's hard not to let it affect me. She's so... persistent."

Don pulled the car into the driveway and turned to face her. "Listen to me. Myrna thrives on control. This is her way of trying to hold onto something she lost. But she can't touch what we have, Lisa. I love you, and nothing will change that."

Lisa took a deep breath, his words steadying her. She reached for his hand, squeezing it tightly. "I love you too, Don. And I won't let her win. We've come too far to let anyone tear us apart."

A Love Unshaken

That night, as they lay in bed, Lisa rested her head on Don's chest, listening to the steady rhythm of his heartbeat. Despite Myrna's attempt to sow doubt, she felt a renewed sense of certainty in their love.

"We'll get through this," Don murmured, stroking her hair. "Together."

Lisa smiled, the tension of the day melting away. "Together."

And as they drifted off to sleep, wrapped in each other's arms, they knew that no shadow from the past could extinguish the light of their future.

Chapter 44: A New Challenge

The days before the wedding were a flurry of final preparations, filled with excitement and a touch of nervous energy. But amidst the joyful anticipation, another challenge emerged—this time, from a quieter, more hesitant voice from Don's past.

Don had a daughter named Emma from a previous relationship, a bright and curious 12-year-old who adored her father but had grown up without much consistency in their relationship. Her mother, Angela, had always been respectful of Don's choices but now, as his wedding approached, she found herself compelled to reach out.

A Letter from the Past

One evening, as Lisa and Don were sorting through RSVP cards, Don's phone buzzed with a message. He glanced at it, his brow furrowing slightly as he read.

"It's from Angela," he said, holding up the screen. "She wants to talk. She says it's about Emma."

Lisa set down the stack of envelopes in her hands, her gaze steady. "What does she want to talk about?"

Don sighed, rubbing the back of his neck. "She's worried about the wedding, I think. She didn't say much, but it sounds like Emma has questions—concerns."

Lisa nodded thoughtfully. "It's natural for her to feel a little uncertain, Don. This is a big change for her, and she probably just needs reassurance."

Don gave her a small smile, his admiration for her patience shining through.

"You're right. I'll call Angela tomorrow and see if we can set up a time to talk."

A Conversation of Concerns

The next afternoon, Don sat in the living room, his phone pressed to his ear as Lisa listened quietly from the kitchen.

"Angela, I get it," Don said, his tone calm but firm. "Emma's my daughter, and her feelings matter to me. What's going on?"

Angela's voice was soft on the other end of the line, tinged with worry. "Don, she's just... she's confused. She doesn't know Lisa, and she's scared. She feels like you're moving into a new life without her."

Don's heart ached at the thought. "I'm not moving into a new life without her. Lisa and I both want Emma to be part of this."

"I believe you," Angela said gently. "But Emma doesn't know that yet. She needs to see it, to feel it. And honestly, Don, I'm just wondering... are you sure about all of this? Marrying someone from another country, someone Emma barely knows—it's a lot."

Don glanced toward Lisa, who was now pretending to focus on rearranging the centerpiece on the dining table. "Angela, I've never been more sure about anything in my life. Lisa is incredible, and she's already making an effort to understand and include Emma. We're in this for the long haul, and I want Emma to see that."

Angela hesitated, then sighed. "Okay, Don. But promise me you'll be patient with her. This is new for all of us."

"I promise," Don said, his voice steady. "I'll do whatever it takes."

Meeting Emma

A few days later, Don arranged for Emma to come over for dinner. Lisa was nervous but determined to make Emma feel welcome. She spent the afternoon preparing a meal that she hoped would appeal to the young girl—spaghetti and meatballs, Emma's favorite according to Don.

When Emma arrived with Angela, her posture was guarded, her eyes taking in the apartment and then settling on Lisa with a mix of curiosity and skepticism. Lisa greeted her warmly, keeping her tone light and friendly.

"Hi, Emma," Lisa said with a smile. "I've heard so much about you. It's so nice to finally meet you."

Emma nodded politely but didn't say much, clinging to her small backpack as though it were a shield.

As they sat down for dinner, the atmosphere was a little tense at first, but Don worked to ease the mood, cracking jokes and sharing lighthearted stories. Lisa followed his lead, asking Emma about her favorite subjects in school and the books she liked to read.

It was a slow process, but by the time dessert was served—a homemade chocolate cake that Lisa had baked—Emma's demeanor had softened slightly.

"This is really good," Emma said quietly, glancing at Lisa as she took another bite.

"Thank you, Emma," Lisa said warmly. "I'm glad you like it. If you ever want, we could bake something together next time."

Emma looked up, a flicker of interest in her eyes, but she quickly masked it with a shrug. "Maybe."

A Small Breakthrough

After dinner, Don and Lisa invited Emma to help pick out a few decorations for the wedding. Lisa brought out a box of ribbon samples, asking Emma for her opinion on colors. The young girl hesitated but eventually joined them, her natural creativity shining through as she offered suggestions.

"I like this one," Emma said, holding up a pale lavender ribbon. "It's pretty but not too flashy."

Lisa smiled, her heart lifting at the small connection. "That's a great choice. I think it'll look beautiful."

As the evening wore on, Emma seemed to relax more, even laughing at one of Don's corny jokes. Angela, who had been quietly observing, gave Lisa a small nod of approval before leaving to let Emma spend the night with her father.

When it was just the three of them, Don suggested watching a movie. Emma picked out one of her favorites, and they all settled onto the couch. Lisa noticed how Emma leaned against Don, her trust in him evident despite her earlier hesitations.

A Step Forward

The next morning, as Emma was getting ready to leave, she hesitated by the door, looking up at Lisa. "Thank you for dinner," she said softly. "And for... you know, trying."

Lisa crouched down slightly to meet her eyes, her expression sincere. "Emma, I'm not trying to take anyone's place. I just want to be here for you and your dad. I hope we can get to know each other better."

Emma nodded, a small smile tugging at her lips. "Okay."

As Don walked Emma out, Lisa felt a swell of hope. It wasn't a complete breakthrough, but it was a step in the right direction—a foundation for something deeper.

When Don returned, he pulled Lisa into a hug, his gratitude evident. "Thank you," he murmured. "For being so patient, so understanding. You're amazing."

Lisa smiled, resting her head against his chest. "We're in this together, Don. Always."

Planning for the Future

As the days passed, Emma continued to warm up to Lisa, and Angela's initial concerns began to ease. Don and Lisa focused on preparing for their wedding, but now with a renewed sense of unity. They knew the journey wouldn't be without its challenges, but their love and commitment gave them the strength to face whatever came their way.

And as they moved forward, hand in hand, they carried with them the knowledge that their family, however imperfect, was growing stronger with each step.

Chapter 45: A Test of Love and Strength

The countdown to Lisa and Don's wedding was in full swing. Excitement and anticipation filled the air as they finalized the seating chart, tasted cakes, and reviewed vows late into the evenings. But life has a way of testing even the most steadfast of hearts, and their joy was about to face a devastating blow.

One evening, Lisa was sorting through her jewelry box, contemplating which piece to wear on her wedding day, when Don's phone rang. He glanced at the screen and frowned. *Myrna.*

Don hesitated before answering. "Hello?"

The voice on the other end was frantic, trembling. "Don, it's Jonathan... He's in the hospital. He was badly beaten. They don't know if he'll make it."

The room seemed to freeze. Lisa stopped what she was doing, her eyes locking onto Don's pale face.

"What?" Don's voice cracked as he stood abruptly, gripping the phone. "Where is he? What happened?"

"They don't know much," Myrna sobbed. "Someone found him unconscious and called for help. He's in critical condition."

"I'll be right there," Don said, his voice shaking.

Lisa was already grabbing her coat. "I'm coming with you."

A Long, Uncertain Night

The drive to the hospital was tense and silent, the air thick with unspoken fears. Don's hands gripped the steering wheel tightly, his jaw set. Lisa reached over, placing her hand on his arm in silent reassurance.

When they arrived, Myrna was in the waiting area, pacing with her arms folded. Her face was blotchy from crying, and she looked up as they approached. "Don..." Her voice broke as she rushed toward him.

"What happened?" Don asked, his voice strained.

"They don't know yet," Myrna said, wiping her face. "They found him in an alley, barely alive. He's in surgery now."

Lisa's chest tightened. She could see the devastation in Don's eyes, and it reminded her of the helplessness she'd felt when she lost Lyron. She resolved to do whatever it took to help Don through this.

The Waiting Game

Hours passed in the dimly lit waiting room. Don sat with his head in his hands, Lisa's hand resting gently on his back. Myrna paced nearby, muttering under her breath, her grief palpable but her demeanor sharp.

A doctor finally emerged, his expression calm but serious. "Mr. Parker?"

Don stood, Lisa rising beside him.

"Jonathan is out of surgery," the doctor said. "He sustained significant injuries, including a fractured skull and internal bleeding. We were able to stabilize him, but he's still in critical condition. The next 24 to 48 hours will be crucial."

"Can I see him?" Don asked.

The doctor hesitated. "He's unconscious, but you can sit with him for a while."

Don nodded and glanced at Lisa. "Will you come with me?"

Lisa smiled softly. "Of course."

Myrna accompanied them into the room sobbing under her breath as she saw her son.

A Father's Pain

Jonathan lay motionless in the hospital bed, his face bruised and swollen, his body hooked up to monitors and IV lines. The beeping of the machines was the only sound in the room.

Don sat beside him, taking his son's hand gently. "Hey, buddy," he whispered, his voice thick with emotion. "It's me. I'm here."

Lisa stood quietly by the door, giving Myrna and Don the space they needed. Her heart ached for Don, for the pain she could see etched into his every movement. Myrna looked uneasy, starring at Jonathan, pain and worry etched on her face.

As Don spoke to Jonathan, Lisa's mind drifted to Lyron. She thought of the nights she'd cried herself to sleep, praying for her son, imagining him out there, lost and unreachable. She understood Don's agony in a way she wished she didn't.

Lisa Steps In

Later, as Don sat with Jonathan, Lisa approached the nurses' station. She introduced herself and offered her assistance, drawing on her years of nursing experience. She knew hospital protocols and boundaries but wanted to ensure Jonathan was receiving the best care.

When she returned to the waiting room, Myrna was sitting alone, her face buried in her hands. Lisa hesitated before sitting beside her.

"Myrna," she said gently. "I know this is hard, but Jonathan is strong. He'll fight through this."

Myrna looked up, her eyes red and tired. "Do you really believe that?"

"Yes," Lisa said firmly. "And he needs us—all of us—to be strong for him."

Myrna nodded, her expression softening slightly. For the first time, there was no hostility, only shared pain.

A Difficult Decision

As the hours turned into days, Jonathan's condition improved slightly. Don spent every waking moment at the hospital, and Lisa was right there beside him, offering support and handling logistics so he could focus on his son.

One evening, as they sat in the waiting room, Don turned to Lisa, his eyes filled with guilt and sorrow. "Lisa, I need to talk to you about the wedding."

Lisa's heart sank, but she kept her expression calm. "What is it?"

Don sighed deeply, running a hand through his hair. "I can't do this right now. Jonathan needs me, and I can't focus on anything else until he's okay. I think we need to postpone."

Lisa reached for his hand, her gaze steady and full of love. "Don, your son comes first. Always. We'll have our day when the time is right."

Tears filled Don's eyes as he pulled her into an embrace. "Thank you, Lisa. For understanding. For being here."

A New Perspective

In the days that followed, Lisa threw herself into supporting Don and Jonathan. She coordinated with hospital staff, kept Don's family updated, and made sure he ate and rested. Her quiet strength didn't go unnoticed.

Don's sisters visited often, bringing food and offering comfort. One evening, Karen pulled Lisa aside. "You've been incredible through all of this," she said. "I don't know how Don would've managed without you."

Lisa smiled, her eyes misty. "I just want to be there for him, the way he's been there for me."

As Jonathan slowly recovered, Lisa began to see glimmers of hope in Don's eyes again. They were far from out of the woods, but the love and resilience they shared gave them the strength to face whatever came next.

And as they sat together in the hospital, holding hands and watching over Jonathan, Lisa knew that their love was unshakable—a beacon of light even in the darkest of times.

Chapter 46: Strength Amid the Storm

The days following Jonathan's ordeal passed in a haze of tension and exhaustion. Though his physical recovery was progressing, the psychological toll of his involvement with dangerous individuals was far from resolved. The hospital maintained tight security around Jonathan's room, but the undercurrent of danger lingered, leaving Don and Lisa constantly on edge.

Lisa emerged as the rock of the family during this turbulent time. Her natural strength and deep faith guided her every action as she coordinated hospital visits, comforted Don, and provided quiet but firm support to everyone around her.

A Father's Guilt

One morning, Lisa stood in the kitchen preparing tea when Don entered, his shoulders heavy with worry and his phone clutched tightly in his hand. His face was drawn, his eyes betraying the burden he carried.

"What is it?" Lisa asked, setting down the kettle and meeting his gaze.

Don sighed deeply, running a hand through his hair. "I just got off the phone with the detective handling Jonathan's case. It's confirmed—he got caught up with a gang."

Though Lisa had suspected as much, hearing it out loud sent a pang through her heart. "Did they say how it started?"

Don sat heavily at the kitchen table, shaking his head. "Not much detail, but they think it's been going on for months. Myrna didn't mention anything to me. Maybe she didn't know... or thought she could handle it alone."

Lisa moved closer, her hand resting gently on his shoulder. "Don, you can't blame yourself for this. Jonathan made his own decisions, but he's still young. What matters now is how we move forward—how we help him get out of this mess."

Don reached up to cover her hand with his, his grip firm but trembling slightly. "I feel like I failed him, Lisa. Like I wasn't there when he needed me most."

"You didn't fail him," Lisa said firmly, her voice steady with conviction. "You're here now, and that's what matters. Jonathan needs you to be strong, and he needs to know he can lean on you. This would be very crucial for his recovery going forward."

Don's eyes glistened as he looked up at her. "You always seem to know the right thing to say. How do you do it?"

Lisa offered him a small, tender smile. "Because I've been there. I know what it feels like to be terrified of losing someone you love. But fear doesn't help—you have to act, even when it's hard."

At Jonathan's Side

Later that day, Lisa accompanied Don to the hospital. The sterile air of the room contrasted sharply with the warmth Lisa exuded as she entered, her presence instantly filling the space with comfort. Jonathan lay in bed, his face pale but alert. His eyes opened slowly, landing first on Don and then on Lisa, his expression wavering between vulnerability and hesitation.

"Dad..." Jonathan's voice was hoarse, barely audible.

Don leaned closer, his own voice steady despite the emotion coursing through him. "I'm here, son."

Jonathan's gaze shifted to Lisa, curiosity flickering in his tired eyes. She smiled warmly, her tone soft but resolute. "You've been through a lot, Jonathan. But you're going to get through this. We're here to help."

Jonathan nodded faintly, his eyes closing again as exhaustion pulled him under. Lisa exchanged a glance with Don, her determination etched into every line of her face. She silently vowed to see this through—to ensure that Jonathan had a chance at redemption.

A Family United

Returning home that evening, Lisa and Don were greeted by the sight of Don's family gathered in the living room. His sisters, Karen and Evelyn, had come to lend their support, along with Emma, Jonathan's younger sister. The room was filled with a quiet strength, an unspoken agreement that they would face this crisis together.

As they settled into their seats, Lisa took the lead. Her voice was calm but carried an undeniable authority. "We need to show Jonathan that he has a strong support system. He needs to know he's not alone, but we also have to be firm. He has to understand the consequences of his choices."

Don nodded, his expression resolute. "Lisa's right. This isn't just about helping him recover—it's about keeping him on the right path moving forward."

Karen reached out to squeeze Lisa's hand. "Thank you for being here for us. I don't know how you stay so composed through all of this."

Lisa smiled faintly, her gaze warm. "Because I've been through my own storms. And I know that the only way to get through them is to stay focused on what matters most—faith, love, and family."

Evelyn leaned forward, her voice thick with emotion. "Don's lucky to have you, Lisa. We all are."

Don's eyes softened as he looked at Lisa, his admiration clear. "I don't know how we'd get through this without you."

A Test of Faith

As the days passed, Lisa leaned heavily on her faith, spending quiet moments in prayer and reflection. She believed that God's grace would see them through, even when the challenges seemed insurmountable.

One evening, after a particularly difficult meeting with the police, Don sat beside Lisa in their dimly lit living room. His exhaustion was evident, but there was also a glimmer of hope in his eyes.

"You've been my anchor, Lisa," he said, his voice raw with emotion. "I don't know how you keep going, but you've kept me from falling apart."

Lisa took his hand, her touch gentle but firm. "Because we're in this together,

Don. Love isn't just about the good times—it's about standing by each other when things get tough."

Don pulled her into a tight embrace, his gratitude spilling over. "You've shown me what love really means. I'll never stop being thankful for you."

Quiet Resolve

That night, as they lay in bed, Lisa stared at the ceiling, her thoughts a jumble of fear, hope, and determination. She whispered a silent prayer, asking for strength, guidance, and healing for their family. Beside her, Don held her hand tightly, their connection unbreakable.

The road ahead was still uncertain, but together, they felt ready to face whatever challenges lay in wait. Their faith, love, and resilience would be their guiding lights, leading them through the storm to the promise of brighter days.

Chapter 47: The Leap of Faith

Lisa sat at Jonathan's bedside, her hand resting lightly on his arm as she studied his face. His bruises were healing, but his eyes still carried the weight of the fear and danger that had followed him for months. She could see his mind working, the restless energy of someone desperate to reclaim control of his life.

Jonathan glanced toward the door, lowering his voice as he spoke. "Lisa... I've been thinking. These people won't stop unless someone makes them. They'll keep pushing, keep coming, until they think they've won."

Lisa tilted her head, her calm expression hiding the churn of emotions in her chest. "You're right," she said softly. "But they're also not as invincible as they want you to believe. They have weaknesses, Jonathan. We just have to find the right way to expose them."

Jonathan looked at her, hesitant but determined. "I think I can lead them into a trap," he whispered. "I know how they operate. I know what they want. If we play this right, they'll walk straight into the hands of the police."

Lisa sat back, her mind racing. She thought of Lyron, her own son, and the years of anguish she'd endured because of Margaret's manipulations. She wasn't going to let Jonathan face the same kind of torment. Not if she could help it.

"You're not doing this alone," Lisa said firmly. "But we're going to do it carefully, Jonathan. No risks, no shortcuts. And we're going to pray through every step."

The Plan

Lisa stayed with Jonathan as they pieced together the details of the plan. She would be the one to set it in motion, assuming all the risk while keeping Jonathan safely in the hospital. The adversaries wanted access to a physical package they believed Jonathan could deliver, so Lisa decided to give them exactly what they wanted—but on her terms.

The next day, Lisa quietly reached out to Don's brother, a retired police officer. Without revealing the full scope of her plan, she explained enough to get his cooperation. She asked for a discreet team of officers who could intervene at a critical moment. Her confidence and resolve left no room for doubt, and Don's brother agreed to help.

Lisa prayed silently as she prepared, her faith lifting to God, her guiding light. She thought of Lyron, of the countless nights she had cried out to God for his safety, and felt a renewed determination. She wouldn't let another young man be destroyed by fear and manipulation.

The Execution

That evening, Lisa slipped out of the hospital with a simple bag in hand. Inside was a decoy package—a mix of innocuous papers and harmless electronics designed to look convincing. She knew the adversaries wouldn't be able to tell the difference until it was too late.

Lisa walked to the rendezvous point, a secluded area near a busy plaza where plainclothes officers were already stationed. Her heart pounded, but her steps were steady, her face calm. She recited a quiet prayer under her breath, asking for strength and protection.

As she approached the meeting spot, two men emerged from the shadows. Their eyes were sharp and suspicious, their movements deliberate as they scanned her and the surroundings.

"You have what we want?" one of them asked, his voice cold.

Lisa met his gaze without flinching. "It's all here," she said, holding up the bag. "But I want to make sure this is the last time you bother Jonathan. He's done."

The man sneered, reaching for the bag. "That's not your call to make."

Lisa held her ground, her voice firm. "It is now. You want this? Take it. But after this, you leave him alone. No more threats, no more messages."

The second man stepped closer, his eyes narrowing. "You're awfully brave, lady. You don't know who you're dealing with."

Lisa felt her heart race, but she stood tall. "And you don't know who's watching," she replied, her tone unwavering. She handed over the bag, her hand steady.

The men exchanged a glance, then turned to leave. But before they could take more than a few steps, officers emerged from every direction, their movements swift and precise. The men froze, realizing too late that they'd been caught.

"Police! Drop the bag and put your hands up!" one officer commanded.

The men hesitated for a moment before complying, the weight of their mistake sinking in as they were cuffed and led away. Lisa exhaled slowly, relief washing over her as the officers secured the area.

One of the officers approached her, nodding with respect. "You handled that perfectly, ma'am. They didn't see it coming."

Lisa gave a small, grateful smile. "Thank you. I just wanted to make sure no one else got hurt."

The Aftermath

Back at the hospital, Lisa returned to Jonathan's room, her face calm but her heart still racing from the adrenaline of the evening. Jonathan looked up as she entered, his expression a mix of concern and curiosity.

"What happened?" he asked.

Lisa sat beside him, taking his hand. "It's done. They're in custody. You're safe now."

Jonathan's shoulders sagged with relief, his eyes welling with gratitude. "You... you did this for me?"

Lisa smiled, her voice soft but full of conviction. "I would do it for anyone I love. And Jonathan, you're part of this family now. I wasn't going to let them take that away."

The news spread quickly among the hospital staff, who celebrated Jonathan's newfound safety with quiet relief. Don arrived soon after, and when he learned what had happened, he pulled Lisa into a fierce embrace.

"You're incredible," he whispered, his voice thick with emotion. "I don't know how you do it."

Lisa rested her head against his chest, her voice steady. "I just prayed, Don. I prayed and trusted that God would guide me. And He did."

Don's siblings gathered around them, their expressions a mix of awe and gratitude. For the first time in weeks, the tension that had hung over them seemed to lift, replaced by a sense of peace and hope.

As the night wore on, Lisa found herself reflecting on Lyron once more. She knew that her journey with him wasn't over, that her heart would always carry the ache of their separation. But in helping Jonathan, she had found a measure of healing—a chance to channel her love and faith into something that made a difference.

And as she sat beside Don, their hands intertwined, she knew that no matter what challenges lay ahead, they would face them together, strengthened by the love and courage that had brought them this far.

Chapter 48: A Beacon of Love

The days following the daring plan's success brought a sense of cautious relief to Don's family. Jonathan's recovery was steady, both physically and emotionally. The shadow that had loomed over him was finally lifting, and for the first time in weeks, Don and Lisa felt the possibility of returning to their normal lives.

It was a quiet evening at Don's apartment. The faint hum of the city outside created a soft backdrop as Lisa sat on the couch, a mug of chamomile tea cradled in her hands. Don was across from her, leaning back in his chair, his face a mixture of exhaustion and gratitude.

"You've been quiet tonight," Lisa said, her tone gentle but curious.

Don smiled faintly, running a hand through his hair. "Just... thinking. About everything. About you." His gaze softened as he looked at her. "I still can't believe what you did, Lisa. I didn't even know about the plan until it was over. And yet... you saved him. You saved all of us."

Lisa set her mug down, meeting his gaze. "Don, I wasn't going to let anything happen to Jonathan. Every time I thought about him, I saw Lyron. I saw the pain I've carried all these years, and I knew I had to act. I couldn't lose him too—not when I could do something to help."

Her words brought a silence that was both heavy and tender. Don leaned forward, his elbows resting on his knees as he clasped his hands together. "You've changed everything for me, Lisa. My family, my life—it all feels different now. Better. Because of you."

Lisa reached for his hand, her touch warm and steady. "Don, we've been through so much together already. But everything we've faced has only made us stronger. And I know that as long as we trust each other and trust God, there's nothing we can't overcome."

A Family Gathering

The following weekend, Don's siblings organized a small family dinner to celebrate Jonathan's recovery and thank Lisa for her unwavering courage. The apartment was filled with laughter and the comforting aroma of home-cooked food. Don's sisters, Karen and Evelyn, took charge of the kitchen, their dynamic energy bringing a sense of life to the room.

"You've got to teach us your secrets, Lisa," Evelyn said, nudging Lisa playfully as they worked side by side to prepare the table. "How do you stay so calm under pressure? I'd have been a wreck if I were in your shoes."

Lisa laughed softly, her hands deftly arranging a bouquet of fresh flowers for the centerpiece. "It's not about being fearless," she said. "It's about trusting that you're doing the right thing, even when it's hard. And praying—a lot of praying."

Karen paused from her task of slicing bread, her expression thoughtful. "You're incredible, you know that? Don couldn't have found anyone better for him. We all see it."

Lisa's cheeks warmed at the compliment. "Thank you. That means more than I can say."

As the evening unfolded, the family gathered around the dining table, their voices mingling in lively conversation. Jonathan sat beside Lisa, his demeanor lighter than it had been in weeks. He looked over at her, a smile tugging at the corners of his mouth.

"I owe you a lot, Lisa," he said quietly, his tone sincere. "You didn't have to do any of this, but you did. You went out of your way for me, and... I'll never forget it."

Lisa placed a hand on his shoulder, her eyes warm. "You don't owe me anything, Jonathan. You're family. That's what we do for each other."

Don watched the exchange with a full heart, his love for Lisa growing with every passing moment. As the evening wound down and the family began to disperse, he pulled Lisa aside, his expression serious yet tender.

A Promise Renewed

"Lisa," he began, his voice low. "I've been thinking about everything we've been through—the ups, the downs, the moments when I didn't know if we'd make it. And through it all, you've been my constant. My light."

Lisa tilted her head, a soft smile on her lips. "Don..."

"No, let me say this," he interrupted gently. "You've shown me what love really means. It's not just about the good times. It's about standing together when everything feels like it's falling apart. You've been my strength, Lisa. And I want you to know that I'll spend the rest of my life being that for you, too."

Tears shimmered in Lisa's eyes as she listened to his heartfelt words. She stepped closer, wrapping her arms around him as she rested her head against his chest. "You already are, Don. You're my anchor, my safe place. And I love you more than words can say."

As they stood together in the quiet of the evening, the promise of their future felt more certain than ever. They had weathered the storm, and though challenges would inevitably come, their love had proven unshakable.

Looking Ahead

In the days that followed, Lisa and Don returned to planning their wedding with renewed focus. The experience with Jonathan had brought them even closer, solidifying their bond and reminding them of what truly mattered.

Lisa found herself dreaming again—not just about the wedding, but about the life they would build together. She thought of the family they were creating, the love that had grown between them, and the faith that had carried them through their darkest moments.

As she sat at her desk one evening, penning the final details of their guest list, she felt a profound sense of gratitude. For Don, for his family, for the journey that had brought them to this place.

And as she looked toward the future, she knew that whatever lay ahead, they would face it hand in hand, their love a beacon of hope and strength that would guide them through all the days to come.

Chapter 49: Outdoor Reunions and Wedding Dreams

The weeks of tension and uncertainty had left their mark on Don's family, but with Jonathan's recovery progressing well and the shadow of danger lifting, they felt it was time to breathe again. To celebrate the newfound peace, Don's sister Karen suggested a family picnic—a way to blend fun with a bit of wedding planning. Lisa loved the idea, seeing it as an opportunity to bond further with Don's children and his siblings, Karen, Evelyn, and Robert.

On a bright Saturday morning, the family gathered at a sprawling park just outside the city. The air was crisp with the scent of freshly cut grass and blooming flowers, the promise of spring warming everyone's spirits. Lisa, dressed in a flowy floral blouse and jeans, carried a basket filled with homemade snacks as Don held a foldable chair in one hand and a cooler in the other.

The Family Comes Together

Emma and Jonathan arrived together, their energy cautious yet hopeful. Jonathan, still slightly reserved from his recent ordeal, gave Lisa a warm smile as he approached her. "Need any help with that?" he asked, motioning toward the basket.

"I think I've got it," Lisa replied with a grin. "But you can help set up the blankets."

Emma stood nearby, her gaze flitting between her father and Lisa. She seemed unsure of how to navigate her growing admiration for Lisa and her lingering skepticism. Yet, when Lisa approached her with a tray of fresh fruit, Emma softened.

"Thought you might like a snack," Lisa said warmly.

Emma hesitated, then smiled as she took a slice of mango. "Thanks," she said softly. "You always seem to have the good stuff."

"It's a Caribbean thing," Lisa replied with a wink, making Emma chuckle. The moment felt like a small breakthrough, a crack in the wall of uncertainty that had separated them.

Karen and Evelyn were already bustling about, setting up folding tables and arranging decorations. "We wanted to add a touch of wedding flair," Evelyn explained, motioning to the blush-pink tablecloths and small vases of wildflowers. "We figured this could double as a mini planning session."

Robert arrived last, lugging a portable grill and a cooler of marinated meats. "I'm in charge of the feast," he declared, his booming voice carrying across the field. "And I don't want any complaints."

Lisa laughed. "I wouldn't dream of it. I've heard your cooking is legendary."

Robert grinned, clearly pleased by the compliment. "You're smart, Lisa. No wonder Don fell for you."

Planning Amidst the Laughter

As the day unfolded, the family divided their time between playful activities and wedding planning. Lisa and Evelyn sat under a tree, flipping through fabric samples for bridesmaids' dresses while Karen sketched floral arrangement ideas in a notebook. Emma hovered nearby, quietly chiming in with her thoughts.

"I like the blush and greenery idea," Emma said, her voice tentative but sincere. "It's simple but elegant."

Lisa smiled warmly at her. "I couldn't agree more. And I'd love to hear any other ideas you have, Emma. You've got a great eye for this."

Emma's cheeks flushed with pride, and she nodded. "Thanks, Lisa. I'll think about it."

Meanwhile, Jonathan and Don joined Robert at the grill, their laughter carrying across the field. Jonathan seemed more at ease than Lisa had seen him in weeks, and it warmed her heart to see him enjoying the day. Don's siblings doted on him, their protective instincts still strong, but they also shared sly jokes that lightened the mood.

Playful Rivalries and Growing Bonds

After lunch, the family organized a friendly game of frisbee. Don and Robert captained opposing teams, with Lisa and Karen joining Don's side, while Evelyn and Emma teamed up with Robert. Jonathan served as the referee, his laughter bubbling up as he tried to keep the competitive spirit in check.

"You're going down, Robert," Don called, tossing the frisbee to Lisa with surprising accuracy.

Lisa caught it, her movements graceful. "Don't count your wins too soon!" she teased, aiming a perfect throw toward Karen, who sprinted to catch it.

Emma surprised everyone with her athleticism, intercepting Karen's throw and tossing it to Evelyn. "Guess we've got the dream team over here!" she called, her confidence growing.

The game ended in a tie, much to Robert's chagrin. "A tie?" he groaned, throwing up his hands. "I demand a rematch."

Lisa laughed, brushing a strand of hair from her face. "Next time, Robert. We'll settle the score."

Acknowledging Lisa's Place in the Family

As the sun dipped lower in the sky, the family gathered on blankets to relax. Karen and Evelyn passed around slices of cake, while Robert poured cups of sparkling cider. Don sat close to Lisa, his arm draped around her shoulders, his contentment evident in his relaxed posture.

Karen raised her glass. "I just want to say, Lisa, you've shown us all what love and strength really look like. Watching how you've supported Don, how you've stood by Jonathan and brought us all together... it's been incredible. You're not just part of Don's life—you're part of ours now, too."

Evelyn nodded, her eyes shining with emotion. "You've been a blessing to this family, Lisa. We couldn't have asked for a better match for Don."

Robert, usually the joker, added his own heartfelt words. "Lisa, you've got guts, and you've got heart. We're lucky to have you."

Lisa felt tears prick her eyes as she looked around at the family that had come to mean so much to her. "Thank you," she said, her voice thick with emotion. "You've all welcomed me with open arms, and I couldn't be more grateful. This family has become my home."

A Quiet Moment

Later, as the family packed up and the evening settled into a golden glow, Don and Lisa lingered behind. They walked hand in hand through the park, the quiet hum of nature surrounding them.

"Today was perfect," Lisa said softly, glancing up at him. "Your family... they're amazing."

"They think the same about you," Don replied, his gaze filled with warmth. "And they're right. You've brought something into my life I didn't even know I was missing."

Lisa smiled, leaning into him. "We've brought something to each other, Don. And I can't wait to see where this journey takes us."

As they stood beneath the fading light, their love felt stronger than ever, a beacon of hope and joy for the days to come.

Chapter 50: Final Preparations and a Family United

The following weeks buzzed with activity as the wedding day drew closer. The family's outdoor gathering had rejuvenated everyone, and now they were fully focused on finalizing the details. Lisa felt the momentum building, the joy and anticipation of the celebration ahead blending with the love that surrounded her and Don. Emma and Jonathan had settled into their roles within the family, and Don's siblings—Karen, Evelyn, and Robert—had become Lisa's staunch allies.

A Day of Decisions

One Saturday morning, Don and Lisa hosted a small planning meeting at their apartment. Lisa had spread out a variety of samples across the dining table—swatches of fabric, floral arrangement sketches, and a list of cake flavors. Evelyn arrived first, carrying a box of fresh pastries, followed by Karen with a bottle of sparkling juice. Robert walked in last, balancing a tray of coffee cups.

"You're lucky I like you, Lisa," Robert joked, setting the cups down with exaggerated care. "Otherwise, I wouldn't be hauling this much caffeine for anyone."

Lisa laughed, shaking her head. "I think you just wanted an excuse to avoid the florist meeting Karen dragged you into for last week."

"Guilty as charged," Robert admitted with a grin.

Emma and Jonathan joined shortly after, sliding into seats with an air of excitement. The siblings had been surprisingly enthusiastic about helping, and Lisa was touched by their growing engagement in the process.

Karen clapped her hands together. "Alright, team. We've got a lot to cover today. Lisa, what's at the top of the list?"

Lisa glanced at her notes. "Catering, for one. David has already sent over some menu ideas from Grenada, and I'd love your thoughts on incorporating them with more familiar options."

Jonathan perked up. "Can we have those macaroni pie he makes? I think it would be amazing."

Evelyn nodded in agreement. "And don't forget his fried plantains. They're a must."

Lisa jotted down their suggestions, smiling. "Perfect. I'll ask David to finalize the menu with these ideas in mind."

A Lighthearted Interlude

As the meeting continued, Emma's curiosity about the wedding traditions Lisa grew up with in Grenada prompted a lively conversation.

"Did you have big weddings back home?" Emma asked.

Lisa smiled, leaning back in her chair. "Oh, yes. Weddings were community events—lots of food, music, and dancing. And always a table filled with roti, cakes and other goodies made by the family."

"Roti?" Robert interrupted, feigning shock. "Why haven't you mentioned this tradition before? I feel cheated."

Karen rolled her eyes. "You'll survive, Robert. I'll ask David to add roti to the menu."

The group erupted into laughter, the warmth of their shared humor easing any lingering tensions from the past weeks.

A Surprise Gesture

As the day unfolded, Lisa noticed Emma lingering near the sample table, her expression contemplative. Lisa approached her gently. "What's on your mind, Emma?"

Emma hesitated before replying. "I was thinking... about something small I could do for the wedding. Like, maybe a speech or a reading. I just... I want it to be meaningful."

Lisa's heart swelled at the gesture. "Emma, that's a beautiful idea. Whatever you decide, it'll mean so much to us. Take your time and choose something that feels right."

Emma nodded, a shy smile spreading across her face. "Thanks, Lisa."

Meanwhile, Jonathan was in deep conversation with Don about his role as best man. "You sure you want me?" Jonathan asked, his tone tinged with disbelief.

"Absolutely," Don replied firmly. "You've come so far, and I can't imagine standing up there without you by my side."

Jonathan's expression softened, and he nodded. "Alright, Dad. I'll do it."

An Afternoon of Fun

After the planning session, Karen suggested a round of mini-golf at a nearby course. "We've earned a little fun," she said, nudging Robert playfully. "And I'm pretty sure I can beat you this time."

"You wish," Robert retorted, grabbing his keys. "Let's go."

The group piled into two cars and made their way to the course, where the lighthearted competition brought out everyone's playful sides. Emma surprised everyone with her precision, sinking several tricky shots in a row. "I learned from the best," she said with a grin, motioning to Lisa.

"Wait, what?" Lisa laughed. "I haven't even played this before!"

Emma smirked. "Natural talent, then."

Jonathan, meanwhile, kept up a steady stream of commentary, his dry humor making everyone laugh. Even Don, usually the steady and composed one, joined in the playful banter.

Acknowledging the Journey

As the sun began to set, the family gathered at a nearby café for a quick dinner. Over plates of steaming pasta and fresh bread, the conversation turned to the journey they had all been on.

"I have to say," Karen began, raising her glass, "we've all been through a lot lately. But seeing us here together, laughing, planning, and just being a family—it's a reminder of how far we've come."

Evelyn nodded. "And it's thanks to Lisa. You've brought us together in a way I didn't think was possible."

Robert raised his glass with a grin. "To Lisa. The real hero of this family."

Lisa blushed, feeling the warmth of their words settle in her heart. "Thank you," she said softly. "But this family was already strong. I'm just grateful to be part of it."

Don, seated beside her, took her hand in his, his gaze filled with love. "You've done more than just become part of it, Lisa. You've made it better. And I can't wait to officially call you my wife."

The group clinked their glasses together, the sound a joyful punctuation to the love and unity that had grown among them.

A Quiet Reflection

That night, as Lisa and Don returned home, they stood by the window, gazing at the city lights. Don wrapped his arms around her from behind, resting his chin on her shoulder.

"Today felt good," he said quietly. "Like everything is finally falling into place."

Lisa leaned into him, her heart full. "It did. And I can't wait to see what the future holds, Don."

As they stood there, wrapped in each other's embrace, the promise of their life together felt more certain than ever. They had faced challenges, overcome obstacles, and grown stronger through it all. Now, with their wedding day on the horizon, they were ready to step into the next chapter of their journey— together.

Chapter 51: A Bridal Shower and a Few Surprises

The final stretch toward Lisa and Don's wedding day brought a whirlwind of preparations and joyous anticipation. Karen, Evelyn, and Emma had conspired to host a surprise bridal shower for Lisa, ensuring that this moment would be unforgettable. For Lisa, the day was a blend of laughter, unexpected revelations, and a deeper connection to the family she was about to officially join.

The Surprise

On a breezy Saturday afternoon, Lisa thought she was heading to a quiet lunch with Karen and Evelyn. Instead, they brought her to a cozy garden venue decorated with twinkling fairy lights, elegant floral arrangements, and soft blush linens that mirrored the wedding's theme.

"Surprise!" came a chorus of voices as Lisa stepped into the garden. Don's siblings, friends, and even a few neighbors were gathered, their smiles wide and welcoming.

Lisa gasped, her hands flying to her mouth. "Oh my goodness, what is all this?"

"It's your bridal shower, Lisa," Karen said with a grin, looping an arm around her. "You didn't think we'd let you get married without a proper celebration, did you?"

Lisa laughed, her eyes shimmering with emotion. "You're all amazing. I don't even know what to say."

Evelyn stepped forward, handing her a delicate flower crown. "Start with 'thank you,' then let us spoil you for the afternoon."

Games and Laughter

The gathering was filled with warmth and camaraderie. The group played lighthearted games, including a trivia round titled *How Well Do You Know Don?* Evelyn read out questions ranging from Don's favorite childhood snack to his quirkiest habits, and Lisa answered with a mix of confidence and playful guesses.

"Favorite karaoke song?" Evelyn asked, her eyebrow raised.

Lisa paused, then smirked. "Anything from *The Greatest Showman*. Don thinks he's Hugh Jackman."

The room burst into laughter, and Karen nodded. "That is disturbingly accurate."

Later, the group divided into teams for a creative contest: designing wedding dresses out of toilet paper. Emma's team won by a landslide, their makeshift gown complete with a dramatic train and veil. Lisa couldn't stop laughing as Emma strutted across the garden, pretending to toss a bouquet.

Heartfelt Moments

As the games wound down, Karen called for everyone's attention. "Before we move on to presents, we thought it'd be nice to share some advice or kind words for Lisa as she gets ready to marry Don."

The atmosphere shifted, becoming softer and more intimate. One by one, guests shared their thoughts, blending humor with heartfelt sentiments.

Robert stood first, clearing his throat dramatically. "Lisa, marrying Don means you're marrying into this crazy bunch," he began, gesturing to the group. "But let me tell you, you're the glue that's been holding us together. You're marrying a good man, and I know he's marrying an even better woman."

Karen and Evelyn followed, their words brimming with love and gratitude. "Lisa," Karen said, "you've shown us what grace and strength look like. Don's lucky to have found you, and so are we."

Emma stepped forward next, her voice quieter but filled with sincerity. "Lisa, I wasn't sure about you at first," she admitted, glancing down shyly. "But you've shown me that you love my dad and all of us. You've made our family stronger, and I'm so glad you're here."

Lisa's eyes filled with tears as she listened, her heart swelling with gratitude. "Thank you," she said, her voice thick with emotion. "All of you. I've never felt so welcomed and loved. This family... you've given me more than I could have ever imagined."

A Special Gift

As the shower drew to a close, Evelyn stepped forward with a carefully wrapped box. "This is from all of us," she said, her eyes twinkling. "Something to remind you of how much you mean to us."

Lisa unwrapped the box to reveal a beautifully bound scrapbook. Inside were photos, notes, and memories from the past months—pictures from their outdoor gathering, handwritten messages from Don's children and siblings, and even a few keepsakes from Grenada.

Lisa turned the pages slowly, her fingers brushing over the heartfelt words and images. "This is... incredible," she whispered, her voice breaking. "Thank you so much. I'll treasure this forever."

Don's Evening Surprise

That evening, Lisa returned home, her heart full from the day's events. She walked into the apartment to find Don waiting for her with a bouquet of white roses.

"Hey, beautiful," he greeted, his smile warm and loving. "How was your day?"

Lisa smiled, stepping into his arms. "It was perfect. Your sisters and Emma outdid themselves."

Don pulled her close, resting his forehead against hers. "You deserve it. Every bit of joy and love this family gives you, Lisa, you've earned it a hundred times over."

Lisa gazed up at him, her heart swelling with love. "Don, I've never been this happy. And it's all because of you."

He kissed her softly, his touch lingering as he held her. "You make everything better, Lisa. I can't wait to call you my wife."

A Moment of Gratitude

Later that night, as Lisa sat by the window, gazing at the city lights, she reflected on the incredible journey that had brought her here. From the challenges they had faced together to the love they had built, every moment had been worth it.

Don joined her, sitting close and wrapping an arm around her. "Penny for your thoughts?"

Lisa smiled, leaning into him. "Just thinking about how blessed I am. This family, this love... it's more than I ever dreamed."

Don kissed the top of her head. "We're the blessed ones, Lisa. You've brought us together in ways we didn't think were possible."

As they sat together, the city quieting around them, Lisa felt a profound sense of peace. The wedding was near, and with each passing day, their love and unity grew stronger. Whatever the future held, Lisa knew they would face it together—side by side, as a family united in love.

Bottom of Form

Chapter 52: Final Preparations and a Father's Blessing

The week leading up to the wedding was a flurry of activity. The apartment buzzed with energy as Don's siblings—Karen, Evelyn, and Robert—took turns coordinating last-minute details. Emma and Jonathan pitched in where they could, their newfound comfort with Lisa shining through in their eagerness to help. Through it all, Lisa found herself at the center of a whirlwind of love and support, her heart swelling with gratitude.

A Morning of Reflection

On the morning of their final planning meeting, Lisa woke early, the faint light of dawn filtering through the curtains. She slipped out of bed quietly, letting Don sleep as she made her way to the kitchen. With a cup of tea in hand, she sat by the window, her thoughts drifting to Grenada.

She thought of her father, a man of quiet wisdom who had always believed in her strength. His voice echoed in her mind: *"Lisa, life isn't about waiting for the storm to pass. It's about learning to dance in the rain."*

Lisa smiled softly, imagining what he would say if he were here. *You've found someone who loves you as deeply as you deserve. Don't let anything hold you back.*

The Family Meeting

By mid-morning, the entire family had gathered at Karen's home for a final review of the wedding plans. The backyard, sprawling and serene, was the perfect setting for their meeting. Karen had laid out a table with coffee, pastries, and a stack of wedding itineraries.

"So," Karen began, clapping her hands together, "we're officially in the home stretch! Let's go over the timeline one more time."

As Karen ran through the schedule, Evelyn chimed in with updates on the floral arrangements, while Robert shared news about the DJ. Jonathan and Emma, seated together, listened intently, occasionally exchanging amused glances at their aunts' intensity.

Lisa couldn't help but laugh as the siblings debated over seating arrangements. "I'm just glad you all are handling this," she said, smiling. "You've made this process so much easier."

Evelyn waved her off with a grin. "It's what family does. Besides, this is fun for us."

A Special Moment with Emma

After the meeting, Emma approached Lisa as the others began tidying up. She hesitated for a moment before speaking, her voice soft.

"Lisa, can I talk to you?" Emma asked, glancing around nervously.

"Of course," Lisa replied, setting down her cup. She gestured to a nearby bench under a tree. "Let's sit."

As they settled onto the bench, Emma fidgeted with her hands. "I just... I wanted to say thank you. For everything. For how you've been there for my dad, for Jonathan, for all of us."

Lisa reached over, placing a gentle hand on Emma's. "You don't have to thank me, Emma. This family means everything to me. That includes you and Jonathan."

Emma nodded, her eyes misting slightly. "It wasn't easy at first. I wasn't sure what to think, but... you've shown me how much you care. You've made my dad so happy. And... I guess I just wanted you to know that I'm happy too."

Lisa's heart swelled with emotion as she pulled Emma into a warm hug. "That means the world to me, Emma. Thank you for trusting me."

Don's Visit with His Father

While Lisa bonded with Emma, Don drove across town to visit his father,

James. It was a quiet, reflective trip—one he had been meaning to make for weeks. James, a retired teacher with a sharp wit and a gentle demeanor, had always been a guiding force in Don's life.

As Don entered the cozy living room, his father greeted him with a warm smile. "There's my boy," James said, standing to embrace him. "You look good, son. Nervous?"

Don chuckled, sitting across from him. "A little. But mostly excited."

James nodded, his gaze thoughtful. "She's a remarkable woman, your Lisa. I see the way she looks at you—the way you look at her. That kind of love is rare, Don."

Don leaned forward, his voice earnest. "I know, Dad. She's everything I never thought I'd find. And she's brought so much light into my life."

James smiled, his eyes twinkling. "Then hold on to her. Love her fiercely, Don. And when life gets tough—and it will—remember why you chose each other."

Don felt a wave of gratitude for his father's wisdom. "Thanks, Dad. That means a lot."

Before he left, James handed him a small, wrapped box. "Something for the wedding day," he said with a wink. "Don't open it until then."

An Afternoon of Fun

Back at Karen's house, the family had decided to spend the afternoon enjoying the outdoors. They set up a makeshift volleyball net in the backyard, dividing into teams that mixed siblings, children, and Lisa.

Jonathan, still recovering but eager to participate, acted as the referee, his humor keeping everyone laughing. "Foul! Aunt Evelyn totally spiked that!" he called out, grinning.

"It was a *perfectly legal* spike!" Evelyn retorted, tossing the ball back into play.

Lisa found herself on a team with Don and Emma, their playful banter making her laugh until her sides ached. Don's competitive streak emerged, prompting Emma to tease him mercilessly.

"Dad, you're supposed to hit the ball, not the air," Emma quipped after Don missed a serve.

Lisa doubled over with laughter, her cheeks hurting from smiling so much. For the first time in weeks, the family felt truly at ease, their laughter echoing across the yard like a balm for the soul.

A Growing Bond

As the sun dipped lower in the sky, the group gathered around a fire pit, roasting marshmallows and sharing stories. Don's siblings took turns recounting embarrassing childhood memories of Don, much to Lisa's delight.

"Did you know," Karen began, her eyes sparkling with mischief, "that Don once got stuck in a tree because he was trying to impress a girl?"

Don groaned, burying his face in his hands as Lisa laughed. "Oh, I *need* to hear this," she said, leaning forward eagerly.

Emma chimed in. "And he still hasn't figured out how to properly serve in volleyball. Some things never change."

Lisa beamed at the ease and warmth around her. It wasn't just laughter—it was love, acceptance, and a growing sense of belonging that filled every corner of her heart.

A Quiet Moment

As the evening wound down, Don and Lisa found themselves sitting together by the fire, the rest of the family chatting in the background. Don took Lisa's hand, his thumb brushing over her knuckles.

"You know," he said softly, "seeing you with my family today... it feels like everything's falling into place. Like this is exactly where we're meant to be."

Lisa leaned into him, her voice equally quiet. "I feel it too, Don. Your family... they've made me feel so loved. And you... you've made all of this possible."

He pressed a kiss to her temple, his voice filled with emotion. "I can't wait to marry you, Lisa. To start this new chapter together."

As they sat by the fire, surrounded by the warmth of family and the love they had built, Lisa felt a deep sense of peace. Whatever challenges lay ahead, she knew they would face them together—with love, laughter, and faith guiding their way.

Chapter 53: An Unexpected Surprise

The wedding day was only days away, and excitement buzzed in the air. Lisa and Don had spent the morning reviewing the final details with Karen, Evelyn, and Robert. Emma and Jonathan, now fully immersed in the family dynamic, contributed ideas and playful quips that lightened the mood.

As the afternoon rolled in, the family decided to visit a quaint countryside estate just outside the city. It was a beautiful place—rolling green fields, a serene lake, and gardens in full bloom. They'd planned to take a break from the hustle of wedding preparations to simply enjoy each other's company.

Arriving at the Estate

The estate was picture-perfect, with its stone pathways winding through clusters of colorful flowers. Don drove the group in two cars, with Lisa sitting beside him. She gazed out at the landscape, her heart swelling with gratitude.

"This place is beautiful," she said softly, glancing at Don. "Thank you for this."

He reached over, taking her hand briefly as he kept his eyes on the road. "You deserve it, Lisa. We all do."

When they arrived, Karen and Evelyn were already setting up a picnic area by the lake. Emma and Jonathan raced ahead, laughing and teasing each other. Robert trailed behind, carrying a cooler and muttering something about being the family pack mule.

"Lisa, over here!" Karen called, waving enthusiastically.

Lisa smiled as she joined them, helping to spread out blankets and arrange the food. The estate's peaceful atmosphere was a balm for the family, a moment to breathe before the big day.

A Family Walk

After lunch, the group decided to explore the estate together. They strolled along a trail that wound through a grove of ancient oak trees, the sunlight filtering through the leaves in golden beams. Don walked beside Lisa, their hands intertwined, while Emma and Jonathan walked ahead, their playful banter filling the air.

"This feels like a dream," Lisa said, her voice filled with wonder. "I never imagined life could be this beautiful."

Don looked at her, his expression tender. "It's beautiful because you're here, Lisa. You've brought so much light into my life."

Lisa blushed, her heart fluttering at his words. She leaned into him slightly, savoring the warmth of his presence.

Ahead of them, Karen and Evelyn had paused to admire a small waterfall cascading into a crystal-clear stream. Robert and Jonathan took turns skipping stones across the water, their laughter echoing through the grove.

A Quiet Conversation

Later, as the family regrouped at the picnic area, Emma approached Lisa with a thoughtful expression.

"Lisa, can we talk?" Emma asked, her tone tentative.

Lisa nodded, motioning toward a bench beneath a shady tree. They sat side by side, the breeze rustling the leaves above them.

"I just wanted to say..." Emma began, her cheeks flushing slightly. "I'm sorry if I ever seemed... distant when we first met. I wasn't sure about everything, and I guess I let that get in the way, I told my mom that I didn't like you, but I take that back. I think you're cool."

Lisa smiled warmly, placing a reassuring hand on Emma's. "It's okay, Emma. I understand. Change is never easy, especially when it involves the people we love."

Emma nodded, her eyes shining with sincerity. "I can see now how much you love my dad—and how happy you make him. And Jonathan... he looks up to you so much. I just wanted to say thank you. For being there for him, for all of us."

Lisa felt a lump form in her throat as she squeezed Emma's hand. "Thank you for saying that, Emma. It means the world to me. I love your father, and I love this family. I'm so grateful to be part of it."

A Playful Afternoon

As the sun dipped lower in the sky, the family gathered for a game of tug-of-war by the lake. Karen and Evelyn were self-appointed captains, dividing the group into two teams. Lisa found herself on Don's team, along with Jonathan and Robert, while Emma joined Karen and Evelyn.

"This isn't fair," Emma teased, pointing at Don's team. "You've got Dad *and* Lisa. That's like having two powerhouses!"

Lisa laughed, shaking her head. "I wouldn't call myself a powerhouse, Emma."

Don grinned, giving her a playful nudge. "You underestimate yourself, Lisa. We've got this."

The game was filled with laughter and good-natured taunts. Don's team managed to win the first round, but Emma's team staged a comeback in the second. By the end, everyone was breathless and grinning, their competitive spirits replaced by shared joy.

A Toast to the Future

As the evening settled in, the family gathered by the lake to watch the sunset. The sky was ablaze with hues of orange and gold, the reflection shimmering on the water. Karen produced a bottle of sparkling cider and plastic flutes, passing them around for a toast.

"To family," Karen began, her voice filled with emotion. "To love, to laughter, and to this amazing new chapter for Don and Lisa."

The group raised their glasses, their voices overlapping as they echoed the sentiment. Lisa felt a wave of warmth wash over her, the love and acceptance of this family filling her heart.

Don turned to her, his gaze steady and full of affection. "And to you, Lisa. For bringing us all together and making my life complete."

Lisa's cheeks flushed as the family cheered, their voices blending with the sound of the breeze and the gentle lapping of the water.

As they stood together, watching the sun dip below the horizon, Lisa felt an overwhelming sense of peace. Despite the challenges they had faced, they had arrived at this moment stronger and more united than ever. And with Don's hand in hers, she knew their future was bright.

Chapter 54: Final Preparations

With just days remaining until the wedding, the energy in Don and Lisa's home buzzed with excitement. The family had grown closer than ever, each member taking on tasks to ensure the big day would be perfect. The previous day's outdoor adventure had left everyone with renewed spirits, and the tension of the past weeks seemed to dissipate, replaced by love and laughter.

Emma and Lisa Bond Over Dresses

In the morning, Lisa and Emma found themselves in the spare bedroom, where rows of bridesmaid dresses hung on a portable rack. Emma was helping Lisa finalize the selections for the wedding party, her enthusiasm infectious.

"This one," Emma said, holding up a blush-colored dress with delicate lace sleeves. "It's elegant but still fun. Aunty Karen will love it."

Lisa studied the dress, nodding with a smile. "You have a great eye, Emma. I think it's perfect too."

Emma beamed, clearly pleased. She hesitated for a moment before speaking again. "Lisa... can I tell you something?"

Lisa turned to her, sensing the shift in Emma's tone. "Of course, sweetheart. What's on your mind?"

Emma fiddled with the hem of the dress she was holding. "I know I told you that already, but I've always been close to Dad, you know? And when he told me about you, I wasn't sure how I felt about it. But... watching you these past few weeks, how you've been there for him and Jonathan... I get it now. You're exactly what he needed."

Lisa felt her heart swell with emotion. She reached out, pulling Emma into a warm hug. "Thank you, Emma. That means more to me than you know."

Emma hugged her back tightly. "I'm glad he found you. And I'm glad I get to call you family."

Don and Jonathan's Quiet Moment

Meanwhile, Don and Jonathan were in the backyard, setting up chairs and decorations for the rehearsal dinner. Don watched his son carefully position each chair, his movements deliberate. It had been a long road to get to this point, but seeing Jonathan here, engaged and focused, filled Don with pride.

"You're quiet today," Don said, breaking the silence.

Jonathan glanced at him, a small smile tugging at his lips. "Just thinking."

"About anything in particular?" Don asked, curious.

Jonathan paused, leaning on the back of a chair. "About how lucky I am. I've made so many mistakes, Dad. But you and Lisa... you never gave up on me."

Don stepped closer, placing a hand on Jonathan's shoulder. "We're family, son. That's what we do. And you've come a long way, Jonathan. I'm so proud of you."

Jonathan's smile widened. "Thanks, Dad. I'm proud of you too. Lisa's amazing, and I'm glad she's going to be part of our family."

The Family Reunites

By the afternoon, the entire family had gathered at Don and Lisa's home for a planning session. Karen arrived with a clipboard and an air of authority, ready to direct the group. Evelyn followed, carrying a box of centerpieces she had designed herself, each adorned with Lisa's chosen colors of blush, gold, and greenery. Robert came in last, balancing two trays of hors d'oeuvres he had picked up on the way.

"Alright, team," Karen said, clapping her hands. "Let's go over the final details."

The living room became a lively hub of activity as they reviewed the schedule, finalized the seating chart, and double-checked every element of the ceremony and reception. Laughter erupted as Robert tried to convince everyone that he should officiate the wedding, his over-the-top impressions of a pastor sending the room into fits of giggles.

"Robert, you'd have us all in tears from laughing too hard," Lisa said, wiping her eyes. "Let's stick to the original plan."

"Fine," Robert replied, feigning disappointment. "But don't blame me if the ceremony feels too serious!"

A Sweet Surprise

As the planning session wound down, Emma disappeared into the kitchen, returning with a small cake she had made herself. It was simple but beautifully decorated, with "To Love and Family" written in delicate icing on the top.

"I thought we could do a little pre-celebration," Emma said, setting the cake down on the coffee table. "You know, to remind ourselves what this is all about."

The gesture touched everyone, and as they gathered around to share the cake, the room was filled with warmth and gratitude. Lisa looked around at the faces of the people she had grown to love so deeply, her heart brimming with emotion.

Don's Late-Night Reflection

That night, after everyone had gone home, Don and Lisa sat together on the couch, the house quiet for the first time all day. Don drew Lisa close, resting his chin on the top of her head.

"You've brought so much into my life, Lisa," he murmured. "Love, hope, family... I don't know how I got so lucky."

Lisa tilted her head to look at him, her eyes soft and full of love. "We both got lucky, Don. And I think God knew exactly what He was doing when He brought us together."

He kissed her gently, his heart full. "I can't wait to marry you."

Lisa smiled against his lips, her voice barely a whisper. "And I can't wait to be your wife."

As they sat there, wrapped in each other's arms, they knew that no matter what challenges came their way, their love and faith would see them through.

Together, they had built something unshakable—a bond that would only grow stronger in the days and years to come.

Chapter 55: Rehearsal Day

The day before the wedding dawned bright and clear, a crisp breeze carrying the promise of a beautiful ceremony. The house buzzed with energy as everyone finalized their roles, outfits, and last-minute details for the rehearsal and dinner later that evening. Lisa woke early, her heart racing with anticipation. She stood by the window, watching the sunlight filter through the trees, reflecting on how far they had come.

The Morning Calm

Don found Lisa in the kitchen, brewing coffee and gazing out the window. He approached quietly, wrapping his arms around her waist and kissing her cheek.

"Good morning, almost Mrs. Parker," he teased, his voice warm.

Lisa turned to face him, her smile lighting up the room. "Good morning, almost husband."

They stood together in comfortable silence for a moment before Don spoke again. "Today's going to be hectic. Are you ready?"

Lisa nodded, her eyes twinkling. "As ready as I'll ever be. I just need a moment to take it all in."

Don cupped her face, his gaze tender. "Take all the moments you need. You've made all of this possible, Lisa. I don't think I could have done any of this without you."

Her smile softened, and she leaned into him. "We've done this together, Don. That's what makes it so special."

The Rehearsal

The church was alive with activity by mid-morning. Lisa's family had flown in, adding their own Caribbean flair to the festivities, and Don's siblings were already bustling around, ensuring everything was in place. Karen stood at the front, clipboard in hand, directing traffic like a seasoned wedding coordinator.

"Alright, everyone, let's get this started," she called out. "Groomsmen, line up here. Bridesmaids, you're on this side. Let's run through the processional."

Lisa's heart swelled as she watched Emma guide Jonathan into position. Despite their initial hesitation about the wedding, both had embraced their roles wholeheartedly. Jonathan, dressed sharply and standing tall, looked like a young man ready to take on the world. Emma, radiant and poised, glanced at Lisa and flashed a supportive smile.

The rehearsal unfolded smoothly, with only a few minor hiccups that brought laughter rather than stress. Don, ever the charmer, kept cracking jokes that had the entire wedding party in stitches.

As the pastor walked them through the vows, Lisa felt her chest tighten with emotion. She glanced at Don, who met her gaze with a look so full of love it nearly brought her to tears. In that moment, all the challenges they had faced faded away, leaving only the promise of their future together.

The Dinner

The rehearsal dinner was held at a charming outdoor venue adorned with twinkling lights and lush greenery. The tables were set with blush and gold accents, and the atmosphere was one of relaxed celebration. As guests arrived, they were greeted with laughter, hugs, and the warm embrace of a family coming together.

David, true to form, had prepared a Caribbean-inspired menu that delighted everyone. Stewed chicken, stewed pork, fried rice, fried plantains, and callaloo soup were just a few of the dishes that drew rave reviews. Lisa felt a pang of homesickness as she tasted the flavors of her childhood, but the presence of her family and Don's made it feel like home.

Halfway through the meal, Robert stood and tapped his glass, signaling for quiet. "I'd like to propose a toast," he announced, his voice carrying a mixture of humor and sincerity. "To my brother Don, who finally got it right." Laughter rippled through the crowd as Don rolled his eyes playfully. "And to Lisa, the woman who saw through his nonsense and chose to love him anyway."

The room erupted in applause and laughter as Robert raised his glass. "Here's to a lifetime of love, laughter, and no more drama. Cheers!"

A Quiet Moment

As the evening wound down, Don and Lisa slipped away from the crowd for a quiet moment under the stars. The night was cool, the sky clear and dotted with countless stars that seemed to stretch on forever. Don wrapped his jacket around Lisa's shoulders, pulling her close.

"This is it," he murmured, his voice tinged with awe. "Tomorrow, you'll be my wife."

Lisa smiled, resting her head against his chest. "It feels like we've waited a lifetime for this moment."

Don tilted her face up to his, his eyes reflecting the depth of his love. "And I'd wait a thousand more lifetimes for you."

They kissed softly, the world around them fading away as they focused solely on each other. In that moment, nothing else mattered—not the challenges they had faced, not the obstacles they had overcome. All that remained was their love, steady and unshakable.

The Night Before

Back at the house, Lisa's family gathered in the living room for a quiet evening of reminiscing and laughter. Her mother who had flown in from another country, sat beside her, holding her hand tightly.

"I'm so proud of you, Lisa," her mother said, her voice thick with emotion. "You've found a love that's strong and true. And I know your father is looking down, smiling at you."

Lisa felt tears prick her eyes as she leaned into her mother's embrace. "Thank you, Mom. I feel so blessed."

Upstairs, Don sat with Jonathan and Emma, sharing stories of his youth and offering them advice about life and love. The room was filled with laughter and warmth, a reflection of the family they had become.

As the clock struck midnight, Lisa stood at the window, gazing out at the moonlit sky. Tomorrow, she thought, everything changes. And yet, everything stays the same. With Don by her side, she knew they could face anything.

The Final Thought

Lisa knelt by her bed, hands clasped in prayer. "Thank you, Lord, for bringing us here. For every challenge, every triumph, and for the love that has carried us through. I place tomorrow in Your hands, knowing that You will guide us as You always have."

When she climbed into bed, her heart was full, her soul at peace. Tomorrow, she would walk down the aisle, not just to marry Don, but to step into the life they had built together—a life filled with love, faith, and the promise of forever.

Chapter 56: The Wedding Day

The long-awaited day had finally arrived, and the Parker and Phillips families awoke to a morning filled with a mix of calm and excitement. The sun shone brightly in a cloudless sky, casting a golden glow over the venue, a lush garden surrounded by tall oaks and vibrant flowers. It was the perfect setting for a union as profound and beautiful as Don and Lisa's love story.

The Morning Preparations

Lisa's side of the house was alive with activity. Her bridesmaids fluttered around her, helping her into her dress while making last-minute adjustments to their own. The room was a blend of laughter, perfume, and the rustling of satin and lace.

Lisa stood before a full-length mirror, her reflection breathtaking. Her dress, a timeless design of soft ivory with delicate lace details, hugged her figure perfectly. A cathedral-length veil cascaded behind her, giving her an air of ethereal elegance. She touched the pendant around her neck—a gift from her late father—and whispered a prayer of gratitude.

Emma approached her soon-to-be stepmother with a soft smile. "You look beautiful, Lisa. My dad... he's going to lose it when he sees you."

Lisa turned, pulling Emma into a gentle hug. "Thank you, sweetheart. You've been such a blessing to me. I'm so glad you're here."

Across town, Don's siblings—Karen, Robert, and Evelyn—kept him company as he prepared. His tuxedo was sharp and classic, a black jacket with satin lapels paired with a crisp white shirt and a black bow tie. Karen fussed over his boutonniere, adjusting it just so, while Robert offered unsolicited advice on keeping his cool during the vows.

"You've got this, Don," Robert teased, clapping him on the back. "Just don't cry too much. No one wants to see a groom blubbering like a baby."

Don rolled his eyes but couldn't hide the nervous grin on his face. "I'm marrying Lisa. How could I not cry?"

The Ceremony Begins

Guests began arriving at the venue, their laughter and chatter filling the air as they took their seats. The garden was transformed into a dreamlike setting, with rows of white chairs adorned with blush ribbons and flower arrangements cascading down the aisle. A soft harp melody played in the background, setting the tone for the momentous occasion.

Don stood at the altar, flanked by Jonathan as his best man and Robert as his groomsman. His heart raced as he scanned the crowd, waiting for the moment he would see Lisa walk down the aisle.

The music shifted, and all eyes turned toward the back of the garden. Emma, carrying a small bouquet of blush roses, walked gracefully down the aisle, her smile radiant. Behind her, the bridesmaids followed, their dresses a soft shade of blush that complemented the garden's natural beauty.

And then, the harpist played the first notes of the bridal march.

Lisa appeared at the end of the aisle, her arm linked with David's. The sight of her took Don's breath away. She looked like a vision, her veil framing her face as her eyes locked onto his. The world seemed to blur around him, leaving only her—a beacon of love and grace.

As Lisa walked toward him, she felt her heart swell with emotion. She saw Don standing at the altar, his face a mixture of awe and devotion. This was the man she had prayed for, the man who had stood by her through every trial. And now, he was waiting to become her husband.

When they reached the altar, David handed Lisa's hand to Don, his voice thick with emotion as he whispered, "Take care of her."

Don nodded, his grip firm but tender. "Always."

The Vows

The pastor began the ceremony, his voice warm and resonant as he spoke of love, faith, and commitment. When it was time for the vows, Don turned to Lisa, his hands trembling slightly as he held hers.

"Lisa," he began, his voice steady despite the emotion in his eyes. "From the moment I met you, I knew there was something special about you. You've shown me what love truly means, what it looks like to have faith even in the hardest times. You've made me a better man, and I promise to spend the rest of my life loving you, honoring you, and standing by your side through every storm and every sunrise."

Lisa's tears spilled freely as she smiled at him. Taking a deep breath, she began her vows. "Don, you've been the answer to prayers I didn't even know I was praying. Your love has been my shelter, your strength my foundation, and your faith in me, my encouragement. I promise to honor you, to support you, and to love you with all that I am, for all the days of my life."

As the pastor pronounced them husband and wife, Don lifted Lisa's veil with trembling hands. Their first kiss as a married couple was met with cheers and applause, sealing their union in the presence of family and friends.

The Reception

The reception was a lively celebration under a canopy of twinkling lights. The Parker and Phillips families mingled, their laughter filling the air as they toasted to the happy couple. David's culinary talents shone in the menu, a fusion of Caribbean and American dishes that delighted every guest.

Emma gave a heartfelt speech, her voice steady despite the tears in her eyes. "Lisa, you've brought so much light into my dad's life, and I can't thank you enough for the love and kindness you've shown to all of us. I'm so happy to welcome you into our family."

Jonathan followed, his words quieter but no less impactful. "Dad, Lisa... I've seen how strong you both are, how you've faced challenges together and never let go of each other. That's the kind of love I hope to find one day."

As the night went on, Don and Lisa shared their first dance as husband and wife, swaying to a soft melody that spoke of forever. The garden seemed to sparkle around them, the stars above bearing witness to their joy.

A Moment of Reflection

Later, as the reception began to wind down, Lisa found a quiet corner to reflect. Don joined her, wrapping his arms around her waist as they watched the twinkling lights.

"We did it," she whispered, leaning into him.

"We did," Don agreed, his voice filled with contentment. "And this is just the beginning."

As they stood together, surrounded by the love of their families and the beauty of the night, they knew that the journey ahead would not be without challenges. But they also knew that with faith, love, and each other, there was nothing they couldn't face.

Their story had only just begun, and it was already the greatest adventure of their lives.

Chapter 57: The Day After Forever

The gentle morning sunlight spilled through the window as Lisa stirred awake, wrapped in the comforting warmth of Don's arm. Memories of the wedding danced through her mind—the vows, the laughter, the love that had surrounded them. It felt like a dream, but as her gaze fell on the golden band on her finger, she smiled, knowing it was real.

Don stirred beside her, his lips curving into a sleepy grin as he opened his eyes. "Good morning, Mrs. Parker," he murmured, his voice still husky with sleep.

Lisa chuckled softly, her heart fluttering at the sound of her new name. "Good morning, Mr. Parker."

Their quiet moment was interrupted by a soft knock at the door. A familiar voice called from the other side. "You two lovebirds decent?"

Lisa laughed, recognizing Bain's teasing tone. "Come in, Bain!"

The door opened to reveal Bain standing there with a mischievous grin, holding a carefully wrapped box. Behind him trailed Weslie, David, Don's daughter Emma, and his siblings—Karen, Robert, and Evelyn—all wearing eager smiles.

"First surprise of the day!" Bain announced, handing the box to Lisa and Don.

Lisa exchanged a curious look with Don before carefully lifting the lid. Inside was an envelope resting atop soft tissue paper. Lisa opened it with trembling hands and gasped, pulling out two first-class tickets to a private Caribbean resort.

Bain grinned broadly. "That's right. A week-long, all-inclusive honeymoon!

From all of us."

Don's eyes widened as he stared at the tickets. "Are you serious? This is amazing!"

Lisa's voice trembled with gratitude. "You didn't have to do this. It's... incredible. Thank you so much."

David stepped forward, his warm smile lighting up the room. "You deserve it, Mom. We wanted you to have the kind of getaway you've always dreamed of."

Bain chuckled. "And don't worry, it's all set. Flights, accommodations, and even a private dinner on the beach. We took care of everything."

The Breakfast Feast

Downstairs, the aroma of freshly baked bread, sizzling bacon, and Grenadian cocoa tea filled the air. David and Weslie had woken early to prepare a lavish breakfast. Plates of fluffy scrambled eggs, golden fishcakes, crispy bacon, and slices of still-warm bread lined the table.

Lisa's eyes widened as she took in the spread. "David, Weslie, this is incredible. You two have outdone yourselves."

Weslie shrugged with a grin. "Just making sure our mom and new dad start their first day of married life right."

Karen grabbed a plate, eyeing the food appreciatively. "This is the best breakfast I've ever seen. David, you should be running a restaurant."

David laughed modestly. "It's nothing, Miss Karen. Just wanted to do something special for Mom and Don."

As everyone sat down to eat, Don leaned over to Lisa, his voice low and filled with warmth. "Your sons are amazing, Lisa. You must be so proud."

Lisa nodded, her heart swelling with emotion. "I am. They've always been my rock."

Gifts of Love

After breakfast, Evelyn brought out a small velvet pouch. "We've got one more surprise," she said, handing it to Lisa.

Lisa untied the ribbon and reached inside, pulling out a delicate necklace with a heart-shaped pendant engraved with the words, *"Forever Yours."* Her eyes filled with tears as she looked up at Evelyn.

"It's beautiful," Lisa whispered. "Thank you so much."

Evelyn hugged her warmly. "We wanted you to have something special to remember this day."

Emma stepped forward next, her eyes sparkling. "I thought you might like a bit of pampering, Lisa, so I arranged for your favorite perfumes and skin creams to be waiting for you at the resort. You're going to be spoiled."

Lisa laughed, shaking her head. "You're all spoiling me already! But thank you, Emma. That's so thoughtful."

Bain chimed in. "And Weslie and I added a little adventure to your trip—a sleek convertible rental. You'll be cruising around the island in style."

Don shook his head in disbelief. "You guys really went all out. You thought of everything."

Karen grinned. "Of course we did. You two deserve every bit of it."

An Outdoor Gathering

That afternoon, the family planned a casual outdoor gathering at a nearby park. The lush greenery and soft breeze set the perfect backdrop for an afternoon of fun and relaxation. Don and Lisa arrived to find picnic blankets spread out, a small barbecue set up, and a cooler filled with drinks.

"Looks like a perfect day," Don said, squeezing Lisa's hand.

Karen was tending the grill, expertly flipping skewers of chicken and vegetables. "We figured after all the excitement yesterday, you two could use a little downtime."

The family spent the afternoon playing games, sharing stories, and enjoying each other's company. Emma and Jonathan joined a lively game of frisbee, their laughter ringing out as they chased the disc across the park. Bain and Robert engaged in a competitive game of dominoes, while Karen organized a scavenger hunt for the younger cousins.

At one point, Robert pulled Don aside, his tone serious yet warm. "Don, I just want you to know how happy I am for you. You've been through a lot, but you've come out stronger. And Lisa—she's incredible. She's exactly what you needed."

Don nodded, his expression softening. "Thanks, Robert. I feel like I've finally found my place. And it's all because of her."

A Moment of Gratitude

As the sun dipped lower, casting golden light over the park, the family gathered together for a toast. Evelyn raised her glass, her voice filled with emotion. "To Don and Lisa—may your love continue to grow, and may this be the start of a beautiful journey."

The family clinked their glasses, the warmth of their love and support filling the air. Lisa looked around at the smiling faces of Don's family, her sons, and their children. She felt an overwhelming sense of gratitude for the life they were building together.

Later that evening, as Don and Lisa walked hand in hand, the cool breeze brushing against their faces, Lisa glanced up at him, her eyes shining with joy. "Can you believe how much love we've been given?"

Don wrapped his arm around her, pulling her close. "It's overwhelming. But you know what? It's just a reflection of how incredible you are, Lisa. You've brought so much joy to all of us."

She smiled, leaning her head against his shoulder. "And you've brought so much joy to me. I can't wait to see what's next for us."

As they walked beneath the starlit sky, they knew they were surrounded by love—love that would carry them through every challenge and triumph ahead. Together, they were ready for whatever the future held.

Chapter 58: A Honeymoon to Remember

L isa and Don's honeymoon began with an air of excitement that had been building since the moment they opened Bain's gift at breakfast. The family had outdone themselves, giving the newlyweds first-class tickets to a Caribbean island and the keys to a sleek convertible for their adventures. After a heartfelt goodbye to their loved ones, Lisa and Don set off on their dream getaway, a trip crafted with love and thoughtfulness by their family.

The Caribbean welcomed them with open arms, the balmy breeze and sunlit shores painting a picture of paradise. Their resort was nestled on a private beach, where the waves gently lapped at the shore, and the swaying palms provided shade and serenity. For days, they explored the island together, laughing as they drove the convertible along winding coastal roads, stopping at quaint villages and secluded beaches. Don took dozens of photos of Lisa, capturing her carefree smiles and the glow of happiness that seemed to radiate from her.

Their days were filled with adventures—snorkeling in turquoise waters, hiking through lush tropical trails, and sampling local cuisine that tantalized their taste buds. But as much as they loved their time exploring, it was the quiet moments they cherished most: holding hands on the beach, watching the sunset paint the sky in brilliant hues, and sharing whispered conversations under the starlit sky.

The Final Night

As their honeymoon drew to a close, Don had one more surprise planned for

Lisa. On their last night at the resort, he had made special arrangements for the private dinner on the beach. A table for two was set under a canopy of fairy lights, the sound of the waves providing a soothing melody. The air was filled with the scent of salt and blossoms, and the soft glow of lanterns created an atmosphere of intimacy and romance.

Lisa gasped when she saw the setup. "Don, this is... incredible."

He took her hand, kissing her knuckles. "Not as incredible as you. I wanted our last night here to be unforgettable."

They enjoyed a decadent meal of fresh seafood, grilled to perfection, paired with tropical fruits and a crisp white wine. Don toasted to their future, his words brimming with love and gratitude. "To the woman who changed my life, who showed me what it means to love and be loved. Lisa, you're everything I've ever wanted and more."

Tears welled in Lisa's eyes as she raised her glass. "And to the man who brought me back to life, who makes every moment feel like a blessing. I love you, Don."

Blissful Intimacy

Later, in their private suite overlooking the ocean, Don led Lisa inside. The room had been prepared with care: candles flickered softly on every surface, casting a golden glow; rose petals were scattered across the bed; and the sound of the waves drifted in through the open balcony doors. The stars above seemed to shine brighter than ever, as if the heavens were blessing their union.

Lisa turned to Don, her eyes shining with love. "You've made this the most amazing trip of my life."

He stepped closer, cupping her face in his hands. "It's only amazing because I'm sharing it with you."

Their lips met in a kiss that was both tender and filled with longing, a kiss that deepened as they let go of everything but each other. Don's hands moved to her shoulders, slipping the straps of her dress down with a slow, deliberate motion. He took his time, as though committing every curve of her body to memory. Lisa felt her breath quicken as his touch ignited a fire within her.

"Lisa," Don whispered, his voice husky with emotion. "You're my everything."

She smiled, her hands moving to unbutton his shirt. "And you're mine."

The night unfolded like a dream, their movements slow and deliberate, a dance of love and devotion. They explored each other with unhurried passion, savoring every touch, every sigh, every whispered word. The world outside their suite faded away, leaving only the two of them, wrapped in each other's arms.

For Lisa, the moment was overwhelming—a culmination of years of longing and a love she had once thought unattainable. Don's touch was gentle yet firm, his kisses leaving her breathless. She felt cherished, adored, and completely free to give herself to him fully. It was the time she had dreamed of, 'to melt in his arms, like ice cream on a sunny day.'

For Don, it was a revelation. Lisa's presence filled every corner of his heart, her love a light that banished the shadows of his past. He took his time, ensuring that every moment was a celebration of the life they had built together, of the love they had fought so hard to protect.

A Perfect Peace

Hours later, they lay entwined in each other's arms, the cool breeze from the ocean caressing their skin. Lisa rested her head on Don's chest, her fingers tracing lazy patterns along his skin. The steady rhythm of his heartbeat was a soothing lullaby, a reminder of the man who had become her home.

She looked up at him, her eyes soft with affection. "I never imagined it could feel like this—so perfect, so right."

Don pressed a kiss to her forehead, his arms tightening around her. "You deserve nothing less, Lisa. This is just the beginning of forever."

They stayed like that, speaking in whispers, sharing their hopes and dreams for the future. The flickering candles cast a warm glow around them, illuminating their shared smiles and the quiet joy that filled the room.

As they drifted off to sleep, their fingers intertwined, Lisa felt an overwhelming sense of gratitude. She had found the love of her life, and together they had created something beautiful—something worth fighting for.

The Journey Home

The next morning, they packed their bags and said goodbye to the resort, their hearts full of memories that would last a lifetime. Driving the convertible along the coastal road to the airport, Lisa turned to Don, her hand resting on his.

"Thank you for this," she said, her voice filled with emotion. "For making me feel loved every second of every day."

Don smiled, lifting her hand to his lips. "Thank you for letting me love you."

As the plane carried them back to New York, Lisa rested her head on Don's shoulder, feeling a sense of peace she had never known before. Their honeymoon had been everything they dreamed of and more, a testament to their love and the life they were building together.

They stepped off the plane hand-in-hand, ready to face the future. Whatever challenges lay ahead, they knew they could conquer them—together.

Chapter 59: Homecoming and New Beginnings

Returning to New York felt like stepping into a fresh chapter of their lives. Don and Lisa arrived home to a warm reception from Don's siblings—Karen, Robert, and Evelyn—and Lisa's sons, David and Weslie. The family had transformed Don's apartment into a cozy haven, with balloons, flowers, and a hand-painted banner reading, *Welcome Home, Mr. and Mrs. Parker!*

"Look who's back!" Robert greeted with a wide grin, pulling Don into a hearty embrace. "How was paradise?"

Lisa laughed as she stepped into Karen's open arms. "It was magical. I don't even have words to describe how perfect it was."

Evelyn nudged Don with a teasing smile. "Well, judging by the glow on both of you, I'd say it was more than perfect."

David handed Lisa and Don a steaming cup of cocoa tea, grinning. "Mom, you look like you've been walking on sunshine. And Don—" he paused, raising an eyebrow, "I see why you've been smiling all this time."

Weslie leaned casually against the counter, watching his mom with an affectionate expression. "So, when do we get to see all the pictures?"

Lisa blushed, and Don chuckled. "We've got plenty to share, but first, we need to sit down. That was a long flight."

Settling into Married Life

As the days passed, Don and Lisa began to settle into their new rhythm as husband and wife. The apartment, once solely Don's domain, now reflected both of their personalities. Lisa's warm touches were everywhere—plush throws on the couch, fresh flowers on the dining table, and a jar of homemade cookies in the kitchen. The place felt more like a home than ever before.

Their evenings were spent planning the next steps of their journey together. With Lisa's sons now on vacation in New York, they were enjoying the rare gift of uninterrupted family time.

One evening, while the family gathered in the living room, Karen brought up the idea of a celebratory dinner to officially welcome Lisa into the Parker family.

"It doesn't have to be anything fancy," she said, her eyes twinkling. "Just a family feast to show you how much we love having you here."

Lisa smiled, deeply touched. "I'd love that, Karen. Thank you."

David and Weslie immediately volunteered to handle the cooking. "Mom taught us well," Weslie said with a wink. "We'll whip up something you'll never forget."

The Feast

The following weekend, the family gathered for the dinner, held in Don and Lisa's apartment. The aroma of Caribbean spices wafted through the air as David and Weslie worked their magic in the kitchen. Macaroni pie, ox tail, stewed chicken, steamed bananas, yams and sweet potatoes sliced, mixed vegetable salad and the now famous lime juice, lined the table.

As the family sat down, Karen raised her glass. "To Lisa and Don—two people who've shown us all what love and resilience look like. We're so glad you found each other."

"Hear, hear!" Robert chimed in, lifting his own glass.

Lisa's eyes glistened with tears as she looked around the table, her heart swelling with gratitude. "I don't even know where to begin. You've all made me feel so welcome, so loved. I'm truly blessed to be part of this family."

"And we're blessed to have you," Evelyn said warmly. "You've brought so much light into Don's life—and ours too."

Bonding Moments

The dinner turned into an evening of shared stories and laughter. Don's siblings reminisced about their childhood antics, making Lisa laugh until her sides ached. David and Weslie teased their mom about her meticulous cooking lessons, while Don shared memories from their honeymoon that left everyone grinning.

Even Emma and Jonathan, who had been cautiously observing Lisa at first, seemed to relax completely. Emma leaned over to Lisa during dessert, whispering, "You really make Dad happy, you know. I'm glad he found you."

Lisa squeezed her hand, her heart brimming. "That means so much to me, Emma. Thank you."

Jonathan, sitting across the table, gave Lisa a small but genuine smile. "I'll admit, I didn't know what to think at first. But after everything you've done for Dad—and for me—I get it now. You're exactly what this family needed."

A Quiet Moment

Later that night, after everyone had left, Don and Lisa sat on the couch, reflecting on the evening. Don's arm was draped around Lisa, and her head rested on his shoulder.

"They really love you," Don said, his voice filled with awe. "I always knew they would, but seeing it tonight... It just makes me love you even more."

Lisa tilted her head to look at him, her smile soft. "And I love them. You have an amazing family, Don. I'm so grateful to be a part of it."

He kissed her forehead, holding her close. "You're not just a part of it, Lisa. You're the heart of it now."

They sat in silence, watching the city lights twinkle outside the window. The world seemed vast and full of possibilities, but in that moment, all they needed was each other and the family they had brought together.

As Lisa drifted off to sleep in Don's arms, she couldn't help but think about how far they had come. Every trial, every tear, had led them to this—this life of love, laughter, and the promise of forever.

Chapter 60: The Gifts of Love and Memories

The golden rays of late afternoon sunlight filtered into their apartment, casting warm shadows across the room. Lisa stood by the window, watching the city bustle below, her heart brimming with gratitude. Every corner of their home was filled with reminders of the love that surrounded them—the gifts, the laughter, the memories they had begun creating as husband and wife.

The soft hum of the doorbell interrupted her thoughts. Lisa opened the door to find another deliveryman with a bright smile. He handed her a carefully wrapped package and a bouquet of lilies. "This just came in for you and Mr. Parker," he announced cheerfully.

Lisa thanked him and set the package on the kitchen counter, marveling at the bouquet's fragrance. The attached card read: *To Don and Lisa Parker, with all our love. May your days be as beautiful as this bloom. – Karen, Robert, and Evelyn.*

Don walked in moments later, his tie loosened, carrying his briefcase. His eyes softened when he saw Lisa standing with the lilies. "Another one?" he asked, grinning.

Lisa held up the card, laughing. "Your siblings are determined to spoil us."

Don kissed her temple and glanced at the package. "Shall we see what's inside?"

They unwrapped the box together, revealing an elegant set of crystal glasses etched with their initials. Nestled alongside was a bottle of aged wine with a note: *A toast to a lifetime of happiness.*

Lisa sighed, her eyes glistening. "They're incredible. I'm so lucky to have married into this family."

Don slipped his arms around her waist. "And I'm lucky they finally get to call you family."

Back to Work and Warm Teasing

Don's first day back at the hotel was a whirlwind of laughter, teasing, and heartfelt congratulations. From the moment he stepped into the lobby, staff members greeted him with knowing smiles, offering sly comments about his honeymoon glow.

"Mr. Parker!" Mark, one of his colleagues, called from across the lobby. "Welcome back, sir. Or should I say, *newlywed extraordinaire?*"

Don chuckled, adjusting his jacket. "Alright, alright. Get it out of your system now."

As he made his way to his office, a small crowd gathered in the staff lounge, where a table was piled high with gifts from his coworkers. A glittery banner hung overhead, boldly proclaiming: *To Mr. and Mrs. Parker!*

Don shook his head, laughing. "You guys didn't have to do all this."

"Oh, but we did," Mark quipped, handing him a large envelope. "Go on, open it!"

Inside was a collection of handwritten notes, each one filled with well-wishes and heartfelt messages. Don read through them, his chest tightening with emotion. One stood out—a simple line from a longtime colleague: *You showed us that love is worth fighting for.*

Later, Don was called into the general manager's office. His boss handed him a small, velvet box and a heartfelt note. "We wanted to give you something special to mark this new chapter in your life."

Don opened the box to reveal a sleek pen with his and Lisa's initials engraved on the side. The note read: *For the chapters you're writing together—here's to a lifetime of happiness.*

An Evening of Reminiscing

That evening, Don returned home to find Lisa curled up on the couch, flipping through their honeymoon photos. She looked up and smiled, patting the spot beside her. "Come join me. I've been reliving our perfect getaway."

Don sat down, pulling her close. "How could I resist?" He shared stories of teasing and gifts from work, making Lisa laugh until her cheeks hurt.

"They're so sweet," Lisa said, resting her head on his shoulder. "It's amazing how much love we've been surrounded by."

Don kissed the top of her head. "That's because you're easy to love."

Lisa blushed, her eyes shining with affection. "And you're impossible not to love."

As they flipped through the album, Don pointed to a photo of Lisa laughing on the beach, her hair windswept and her eyes alight with joy. "That's my favorite," he said softly. "You were so free, so happy."

Lisa smiled, tracing her fingers over the image. "That's how you make me feel, Don. Like I can be myself—free, happy, and loved."

They spent the rest of the evening reminiscing about their honeymoon, recalling the laughter, the quiet moments, and the love that had blossomed even more deeply between them. Every photo, every memory was a testament to the journey they had taken to reach this place of peace and joy.

A Family Toast

The following weekend, Don's siblings—Karen, Robert, and Evelyn—joined them for a small gathering to celebrate the newlyweds' return. David and Weslie were there as promised, filling the apartment with the aroma of a delicious meal.

David emerged from the kitchen with a tray of freshly baked bread, sliced with butter and cheese melted over it, and crunchy coconut tarts which he just took out of the oven, while Weslie carried an ice-cold mug of passion fruit juice. The table was a feast of vibrant dishes, the perfect blend of Caribbean and American flavors.

As everyone gathered, Robert raised his glass. "To Don and Lisa—welcome home. We're so proud of you both and can't wait to see the incredible life you'll build together."

"To Don and Lisa!" the family echoed, their voices ringing with love and support.

Don looked around the table, his heart full. He squeezed Lisa's hand under the table, silently thanking her for being the anchor that held them all together.

Lisa glanced at him, her eyes sparkling. "This is what life is about," she whispered. "Family, love, and moments like this."

Don nodded, his voice soft but sure. "And we'll have so many more of them."

As the evening wound down, the family lingered, sharing stories and laughter late into the night. Don and Lisa watched their loved ones with a shared sense of gratitude, knowing they had been blessed with more than they could have ever dreamed. David and Weslie would be flying back home the next day, after a holiday well spent.

When the last guest left, Don pulled Lisa into his arms, holding her close. "I don't know how we got so lucky," he murmured.

Lisa rested her head against his chest, her voice filled with quiet joy. "It's not luck, Don. It's love. And it's exactly where we're meant to be."

Chapter 61: A Mother's Resolve

The soft rustle of pages and the faint melody of piano keys filled the apartment. Lisa sat at her desk, her hands trembling as she read through the final chapter of her book. Each word on the page felt like a piece of her soul—her pain, her faith, her unwavering hope poured onto her computer screen. The words were more than just a story; they were a battle cry, a declaration that love could conquer even the deepest wounds.

Across the room, her piano waited, a stack of sheet music perched on its edge. Lisa's gaze lingered there, her heart aching as she thought about Lyron. She hadn't seen him in over three years, and the absence of his presence at her wedding had been a silent, gaping void. Margaret's manipulations had been relentless, her interference cutting Lisa off from her son was a cruelty Lisa could hardly fathom. But that chapter of her life wasn't closed yet, and Lisa was determined to rewrite it.

She opened her laptop and navigated to her files. The lyrics to "Prodigal Son" appeared on the screen, a song she had crafted from the depths of her pain. It was raw, unpolished, and filled with every ounce of longing she had for her child. She hummed the melody under her breath, her voice catching on the final line: *"I would never forsake the son of my womb, not now, not ever, not everrr!"*

Tears welled in her eyes, but Lisa didn't let them fall. Instead, she stood, moving to the piano. Her fingers hovered over the keys before pressing down, each note reverberating through the room like a heartbeat. She sang the song from start to finish, her voice steady despite the storm inside her. This was her truth, her unshakable promise to Lyron.

A Plan Takes Shape

Later that evening, Don returned home to find Lisa immersed in her work. Her energy was different—focused, determined, and electric. He leaned against the doorway, watching her with quiet admiration as she reviewed her lyrics and notes.

"Hey, beautiful," he said softly, stepping into the room.

Lisa looked up, her face lighting up at the sight of him. "Hey," she replied, setting her papers aside. "You're just in time."

Don walked over, wrapping his arms around her shoulders from behind and pressing a kiss to her cheek. "In time for what?"

"In time to help me figure out how to make some noise," she said, turning to face him. "It's time the world hears my story—and Lyron's. Margaret has hidden behind her lies for too long, and I'm not going to sit by and let her keep my son away from me. I need to do something bold, something she'd never expect."

Don's brow furrowed as he listened, his protective instincts flaring. "What are you thinking?"

Lisa gestured to her laptop and notebooks. "The book, the album, everything I've been working on—it's all connected. If we can get the media to take notice, to share our story, it might force Margaret's hand. People need to know what's happened, and Lyron needs to hear that I'm still here, waiting for him."

Don's hand tightened on hers. "Lisa, that's a big step. The media can be unpredictable. Are you ready for that kind of attention?"

Her eyes gleamed with determination. "I have to be. This isn't just about me—it's about Lyron. I need him to know that I've never given up on him, that I'll never stop fighting for him."

Don nodded, his chest swelling with pride at her courage. "Alright," he said. "Let's do it. We'll launch the book and album together, just like we planned. And we'll make sure the world listens."

Perfecting the Song

Over the next few days, Lisa poured her energy into completing "Prodigal Son." She refined the melody, adjusted the lyrics, and worked tirelessly to ensure every note carried the weight of her message. Each line was a reflection of her journey—a testament to her love for Lyron and her faith in God's promise.

On a cool autumn morning, she sat at the piano, the final version of the song before her. She played the opening chords, her fingers moving with purpose as her voice filled the room:

Tears filled my sobbing eyes, my heart cries out in pain,
But I know the God who hears my cry,
Would bring my prodigal home someday.
Like the shepherd who leaves the ninety and nine,
To search for the one lamb that went astray,
I would never forsake the son of my womb,
Not now, not ever, not everrr!

As the last note faded, Lisa closed her eyes, a single tear slipping down her cheek. She felt a sense of peace wash over her—a reassurance that this song would be the bridge between her and Lyron.

The Power of Faith and Action

That evening, Don joined Lisa at the dining table as they mapped out their strategy. They contacted a publicist who agreed to help promote the book. Don reached out to a colleague in the music industry, securing a meeting with a producer who could help them release the album.

But the biggest breakthrough came when a national talk show expressed interest in featuring Lisa's story. The producer had heard a demo of "Prodigal Son" and was captivated by its raw emotion and powerful message. It was the same talk show which had reach out earlier through her private investigator. Hearing the song now, has re-invigorated renewed interest.

"This is your moment," Don said, taking her hand. "You're not just sharing your story—you're giving hope to so many others who feel lost and unheard."

Lisa nodded, her heart pounding with a mixture of excitement and nerves. "This is for Lyron," she said softly. "And for every mother who's ever felt the pain of losing a child. This is our chance to make a difference."

A Mother's Prayer

Before they went to bed that night, Lisa knelt by the window, the city lights twinkling like stars beyond the glass. Don joined her, his hands resting on her shoulders as she bowed her head in prayer.

"Lord," Lisa whispered, her voice trembling with emotion, "You've carried me through so many storms, and I know You're with me now. Please guide my words, my music, and my actions. Help me reach Lyron. Help him see the love I have for him, the love You have for him. And Lord, please soften Margaret's heart. Let her see the harm she's caused and find the strength to make it right."

Don's voice joined hers, steady and firm. "We trust You, Lord, with everything. Thank You for bringing us this far, and thank You for what's to come. Amen."

As they rose from their knees, Lisa felt a renewed sense of purpose. The journey ahead wouldn't be easy, but she knew she wasn't walking it alone. With Don by her side, her music as her voice, and her faith as her guide, she was ready to fight for her son and bring him home.

Chapter 62: The Start of Something Big

The golden glow of autumn sunshine poured through the apartment windows as Lisa sat at her desk, staring at her reflection in the dark screen of her laptop. The past few weeks had been a whirlwind of preparation, but this morning felt different. Today marked the beginning of a journey that could bring her closer to Lyron. Her heart raced at the thought. Could her voice, her story, her music, truly make a difference?

Don entered the room, holding two steaming mugs of Grenadian cocoa tea. The rich aroma filled the air as he set one beside her. "For the lady with the voice that's going to change everything," he said with a warm smile.

Lisa chuckled softly, picking up the mug and letting the warmth seep into her hands. "You're too kind, Mr. Parker," she replied, teasingly emphasizing his surname, which still felt new to her lips.

Don sat across from her, his expression turning serious. "Lisa, I mean it. What you're about to do is brave. You're putting your heart out there, your story for the world to see. That's not easy, but it's powerful. I'm proud of you."

She reached out and took his hand. "I couldn't have done it without you, Don. You've been my strength every step of the way."

They sat in silence for a moment, savoring the quiet before the storm. Lisa's laptop pinged with an incoming email, breaking the calm. She opened it, her breath catching as she read.

"It's from the talk show producer," she said, her voice tinged with excitement. "They've confirmed the segment and sent over the schedule. Don, this is really happening."

He moved to her side, looking over her shoulder at the email. "That's amazing. It's all falling into place, Lisa. First the show, then the book, then the album. The world's about to hear your story."

A Mother's Voice

The next few days were a blur of preparations. Lisa and Don practiced interview questions late into the night, balancing the emotional weight of her story with the need to inspire and connect with others. They worked with the record label to finalize the album's artwork, chose excerpts from her book for promotional teasers, and coordinated with the publishing team to align the book launch with the album release.

On the morning of the live show, Lisa stood in front of the mirror, smoothing the fabric of her navy-blue dress. It was simple yet elegant, reflecting the authenticity she wanted to bring to her story. Don appeared behind her, adjusting his tie. "Ready?" he asked, meeting her gaze in the mirror.

She took a deep breath. "As ready as I'll ever be."

The car ride to the studio felt surreal. Lisa held Don's hand tightly, her thoughts a jumble of lyrics, memories, and hopes. She glanced out the window, watching the city blur by, and silently prayed: *Lord, let my words reach Lyron. Let him know how much I love him.*

When they arrived at the studio, the bustling energy hit her immediately. Producers rushed about with headsets, cameras adjusted angles, and crew members gave last-minute instructions. A makeup artist applied a touch of blush to Lisa's cheeks while Don stood by, offering her reassuring smiles.

The host, a kind-eyed woman named Sarah, approached them with a warm smile. "Lisa, Don, thank you for being here. Your story is incredible, and I know our audience will be moved by it. Just be yourselves, and speak from the heart."

Lisa nodded, her nerves easing slightly at Sarah's genuine demeanor. She took Don's hand as they were led to the stage.

The Interview

The bright studio lights were blinding at first, but Lisa quickly adjusted. She sat beside Don on the plush couch, her palms slightly sweaty as the cameras rolled. Sarah introduced them to the audience, her voice smooth and inviting.

"Today, we're joined by Lisa and Don Parker, a couple whose journey of love, resilience, and faith has captured the hearts of many. Lisa's upcoming book, *Beauty Waiting in the Shadows*, and her debut album, *You Can't Cage Love*, tell a story of hope in the face of unimaginable challenges."

The audience applauded, and Lisa smiled, feeling a surge of encouragement.

Sarah turned to her. "Lisa, can you share what inspired you to write this book and create this album?"

Lisa took a steadying breath. "It started with my son, Lyron," she began. "He's been estranged from me for over three years because of circumstances beyond his control. This book and album are my way of reaching out to him, of telling him that no matter what's happened, my love for him hasn't wavered. They're also a message to anyone who's ever felt lost or separated from someone they love: Love can't be caged or silenced. It's a force that transcends everything."

Sarah nodded, her eyes glistening with empathy. "That's incredibly powerful, Lisa. And Don, what has this journey been like for you?"

Don smiled, his hand resting on Lisa's. "It's been humbling. Watching Lisa pour her heart into her music and writing has been inspiring. She's taken her pain and turned it into something beautiful, something that can help others. I'm just grateful to stand by her side."

The audience erupted in applause, moved by their authenticity.

A Song for Lyron

As the interview concluded, Sarah turned to the camera. "We're going to take a short break, but when we return, Lisa will perform her song *Prodigal Son (A Painful Mothers' Day)*, a heartfelt piece that speaks to the bond between a mother and her child."

Lisa's heart pounded as she stepped onto the stage where a grand piano awaited. She glanced at Don, who gave her a reassuring nod, and then at Sarah, who mouthed, "You've got this."

The first notes rang out, soft and haunting, as Lisa's fingers moved across the keys. She closed her eyes, letting the music flow through her, and began to sing:

Tears filled my sobbing eyes, my heart cries out in pain,
But I know the God who hears my cry
Would bring my prodigal home someday.
Like the shepherd who leaves the ninety and nine,
To search for the one lamb that went astray,
I would never forsake the son of my womb,
Not now, not ever, not everrr!

Her voice carried raw emotion, filling the studio with an almost palpable energy. The audience sat in stunned silence, some wiping tears from their eyes. When the final note faded, the room erupted into applause.

Lisa rose from the piano, her chest heaving with the weight of the moment. She glanced at Don, who was standing now, clapping with pride shining in his eyes. Sarah approached her, visibly moved.

"That was extraordinary," Sarah said. "Thank you, Lisa, for sharing your heart with us. I have no doubt that your words and music will resonate deeply with our viewers."

A Ripple Effect

After the show aired, Lisa and Don were inundated with messages from viewers—mothers, fathers, and children who had been touched by Lisa's story. The song *Prodigal Son* began trending online, and the preorders for her book and album skyrocketed.

As they sat in their apartment that evening, Lisa scrolled through the messages, tears streaming down her face. "Don," she whispered, "people are listening. They're really listening."

He wrapped his arms around her, resting his chin on her shoulder. "They are, Lisa. And I have a feeling Lyron is too."

For the first time in years, Lisa felt a glimmer of hope that her voice might reach her son, bridging the gap that had separated them for so long. And with Don by her side, she was ready to keep fighting, one note, one word, one prayer at a time.

Chapter 63: A Flicker of Hope

The days that followed their live performance were a whirlwind of phone calls, emails, and meetings. Lisa and Don had struck a powerful chord with the audience. The story of a mother's unyielding love and the haunting notes of *Prodigal Son* spread like wildfire across social media. Clips of the song were shared thousands of times, with comments pouring in from people who resonated deeply with Lisa's pain and her unshakable hope.

One evening, as they relaxed on the couch, the hum of their humble apartment filling the air with warmth, Don scrolled through his phone. "Lisa, listen to this," he said, his voice tinged with emotion. He read aloud: "'Your song brought me to tears. I've been estranged from my mother for years, but because of your song, I'm calling her today.'"

Lisa's eyes filled with tears. "It's working, Don. People are feeling it. They're understanding the pain of separation and the hope for reconciliation."

Don nodded, setting his phone aside and wrapping an arm around her. "And if it's reaching them, it can reach Lyron too."

The next morning, the phone rang before dawn, pulling Lisa from a light sleep. Groggily, she reached for it, her heart racing when she recognized the voice on the other end. It was a producer from a major news network, requesting an exclusive feature on Lisa's album and book launch.

The producer's voice brimmed with enthusiasm. "Your story is powerful, Lisa. We'd like to film a segment that includes footage from your performances, an interview with you and Don, and a highlight on *Prodigal Son*. We think it could make a real impact."

Lisa could barely contain her excitement as she nudged Don awake, her words tumbling out in an excited rush. "This could be it, Don. This could be the turning point."

Don's sleepy smile turned into a wide grin as he pulled her into his arms. "I knew it would happen," he murmured. "Your story deserves to be heard."

Preparing for the Spotlight

In the weeks leading up to the feature, the apartment buzzed with activity. Lisa and Don worked tirelessly, fine-tuning every detail. Lisa rehearsed her responses for interviews, drawing on her deepest emotions to ensure her message would resonate. Meanwhile, Don reached out to their growing network of contacts, solidifying partnerships and arranging for the perfect visuals to accompany their story.

When the day of filming arrived, Lisa found herself standing in their living room, surrounded by cameras and bright lights. She wore an elegant navy dress that complemented her natural beauty, her hair cascading in soft waves around her shoulders. Don stood by her side in a tailored suit, his reassuring hand resting on her lower back.

The producer, a kind woman named Amanda, guided Lisa through the process with a calm, empathetic demeanor. "Take your time," she said. "Speak from the heart. That's what makes your story so powerful."

During the interview, the host leaned forward, her expression sincere. "Lisa, the story behind *Prodigal Son* has touched so many hearts. Can you tell us about its inspiration?"

Lisa's gaze dropped for a moment, her thoughts drifting to Lyron. When she looked back up, her voice was steady, but the raw emotion in her words was palpable. "It's about a mother's love," she said. "It's about the pain of separation and the hope that one day, love will bring us back together. It's a plea for my son to know that no matter where he is or what he's been through, he'll always have a place in my heart."

The host's eyes glistened. "You've been very open about your struggles, Lisa. What do you hope to achieve with this album and book?"

Lisa glanced at Don, drawing strength from his steady presence. "I want to bring attention to the pain of parental alienation," she said firmly. "I want people to understand the toll it takes on a family. And most of all, I want my son to know that I've never stopped fighting for him."

The segment ended with a performance of *Prodigal Son*, filmed against the backdrop of a dimly lit studio. As Lisa sang, her voice carried the weight of her longing and love, filling the space with a haunting melody that left the crew visibly moved. When she finished, there was a moment of stunned silence before the room erupted into applause.

A Message That Spreads

The feature aired the following evening, reaching millions of viewers across the country. Social media lit up once again, with messages flooding in from strangers, friends, and family. Lisa and Don watched in awe as the story gained momentum, spreading far beyond anything they had imagined.

One afternoon, as Lisa was checking her emails, a new message appeared. It was from an old friend who had known Lyron during his childhood.

Lisa, I saw your segment on the news, and it was incredible. I think I saw Lyron a few weeks ago at a coffee shop. He looked lost and alone. I didn't know what to say to him, but now I wish I had reached out. I thought you should know.

Lisa's heart pounded as she read the email, tears blurring her vision. She turned to Don, her hands trembling. "It's working," she whispered. "People are starting to see him."

Don pulled her into his arms, his voice steady and full of hope. "We're getting closer. He's going to find his way back."

A Glimmer of Hope

They pressed forward with their campaign, determined to keep the momentum going. Every interview, every performance felt like a step closer to reuniting with Lyron. And though the road ahead was uncertain, Lisa felt something she hadn't in a long time—hope.

As they lay in bed that night, Don held her close, his voice a quiet promise in the dark. "We'll find him, Lisa. And when we do, he'll know just how much you've fought for him."

Tears slipped down Lisa's cheeks, but they weren't tears of sorrow. They were tears of hope, of gratitude. "I believe it too," she whispered. "We're going to bring him home."

The journey was far from over, but with Don by her side, Lisa knew they had the strength to see it through. Together, they were ready to face whatever challenges lay ahead, driven by love, faith, and the unshakable belief that Lyron would one day return to them.

Chapter 64: The Return of the Prodigal Son

The studio lights dimmed to a soft glow, illuminating the stage where Lisa and Don Parker sat. The hum of anticipation rippled through the audience, the air thick with the promise of something extraordinary. The host, a woman with a warm smile and an aura of compassion, leaned forward, addressing the audience.

"Today," she began, her voice steady but tinged with emotion, "we have a story that has captivated hearts across the nation—a journey of love, resilience, and unwavering faith. Lisa and Don Parker have shared their extraordinary story with us, and their song *Prodigal Son* has become a universal anthem of hope for parents longing to reunite with their children."

Applause erupted, a tidal wave of support that resonated throughout the studio. Lisa held Don's hand tightly, her heart pounding. She had shared her story countless times, but the ache for her son, Lyron, never lessened. The spotlight shone brighter today, carrying her deepest hope: that her song had reached him, wherever he was.

The host turned her kind gaze to Lisa. "Lisa, *Prodigal Son* is more than a song. It's a raw and emotional plea. Could you share what it truly means to you?"

Lisa took a deep breath, her voice steady but thick with emotion. "It's the cry of a mother's heart," she began. "It's about the pain of separation, the longing for reconciliation, and the unbreakable bond that not even time or distance can sever. It's my message to my son, Lyron, and my hope that he would one day hear it and know that I never gave up on him."

The host's eyes glistened as she nodded. "And today, we are privileged to hear it performed live."

Lisa moved to the grand piano at center stage, her fingers trembling slightly as she began to play. The haunting melody of *Prodigal Son* filled the air, and when she sang, her voice carried years of grief, hope, and unrelenting love.

"Some say forget him, he brought this on himself,
Others shun me and say that's fake love, she never really cared.
Although not said in words, their actions says it loudest
And the pain cuts deeper, piercing through, sharper than a thousand swords,
You'd think your friends would understand and lend a helping hand,
But I've learned long time ago the only friend who stands by you
In times of distress like this, is the One whose body once hung upon the cross,
For sinners such as me..."

The room was silent, the audience captivated by Lisa's raw vulnerability. As the final note faded, there was a moment of stillness before the applause thundered through the studio. Lisa stood, her eyes shimmering, and took a small bow.

"Lisa, that was breathtaking," the host said, stepping back onto the stage. "But we have a surprise for you today."

Lisa turned toward the host, her brow furrowed in confusion. Don leaned forward, his expression equally puzzled. The host smiled knowingly, her voice dropping to a tender tone.

"Ladies and gentlemen, we reached out to someone very special after hearing Lisa's story. We wanted to help make her dream come true. Please join me in welcoming... Lyron!"

The curtains parted, and there he was—Lyron, standing hesitantly at the edge of the stage. Tears streamed down his face as he took a tentative step forward. The audience gasped, then rose to their feet in a wave of cheers and applause.

Lisa's heart stopped. "Lyron?" she whispered, her voice breaking as disbelief gave way to overwhelming emotion.

In an instant, she was running across the stage, her arms outstretched. "Lyron!" she cried, pulling him into a fierce embrace.

"Mom," Lyron sobbed, clutching her as if he would never let go. "I'm so sorry. I didn't know. I thought you hated me. I believed her lies, and I didn't know how to come back."

Lisa held him tighter, her tears soaking into his shirt. "I never stopped loving you," she whispered, her voice trembling. "Every day, I prayed for you. I searched, I fought, I never gave up. You're my son, Lyron. I would go through it all again just to bring you back."

Don joined them, wrapping his arms around both of them. His voice was thick with emotion as he said, "Welcome home, Lyron. We've missed you so much."

Lyron pulled back slightly, his face streaked with tears. He turned to the audience, his voice raw and trembling. "You don't understand what it's like to believe you're forgotten," he said. "But then I saw my mom on TV, and I heard her song. It was like she was reaching through all the lies to pull me back. I realized she never gave up on me. She's the reason I'm here today."

The audience erupted into applause, many wiping away tears. The host dabbed at her own eyes, her voice cracking as she spoke. "This is what love looks like. This is the power of faith and resilience."

A Special Gift

After the show, the producers presented the family with a surprise. "We wanted to give you a chance to reconnect as a family," the host said, beaming. "This weekend, you'll stay in a luxury hotel to catch up on lost times with your son; and there'll something special waiting for you there. And to everyone in the audience." She said, turning to face them, "Each of you will be leaving here today with a copy of Lisa's book *Beauty Waiting in the Shadows*. The crowd roared, rising to their feet as the show concluded.

The hotel suite was stunning, with sweeping views of the city skyline. A large, gift-wrapped box sat in the center of the room. Lyron opened it, his jaw dropping as he revealed a state-of-the-art gaming console, complete with his favorite games.

"This... this is incredible," Lyron stammered, turning to his parents. "You didn't have to do this."

Lisa smiled, her eyes glistening. "It's from the show, sweetheart. They wanted to brighten your day with something special."

Lyron hugged her tightly, his voice breaking. "Thank you, Mom. For everything. For never giving up on me."

Celebration Across Generations

That evening, the suite buzzed with joy as they celebrated Lyron's return. A video call connected Lyron with his brothers, David and Weslie, and his father, Ronald. The screen lit up with their smiling faces, their voices filled with emotion as they expressed their gratitude to Lisa.

"Mom," David said, his voice thick with pride, "you've always been our rock. Lyron's home because of you."

Ronald, his voice cracking, added, "Lisa, you fought for our son when everyone else gave up. You've done what I couldn't. Thank you."

Social media exploded with the news of Lyron's return. Clips from the show went viral, and people across the world celebrated Lisa's triumph. Messages poured in, hailing her as a beacon of hope and resilience.

As the night drew to a close, Lyron sat beside his mother, resting his head on her shoulder. "I'm never letting anyone take me away from you ever again," he vowed.

Lisa kissed his forehead, her heart full. "We're a team now," she said softly. "And nothing will ever break us apart."

The city lights twinkled outside, but the brightest light was the one shining in their hearts—a family reunited, their love unbreakable, their story a testament to the power of hope and faith.

Chapter 65: Lyron's New Beginning

The Parker household buzzed with energy as family members gathered to welcome Lyron into their lives. Don's siblings—Karen, Robert, and Evelyn—had come with their families, eager to meet the young man they had only heard about until now. Lisa stood near the doorway, watching Lyron as he moved through the room, greeting everyone with a quiet confidence and warmth that felt as natural as sunlight.

Lyron didn't need words to make an impression. He smiled easily, shook hands firmly, and laughed in a way that seemed to fill the room with a quiet joy. When he greeted Emma, Don's daughter, it was with an almost brotherly ease.

"So, you're the famous Emma," Lyron said, a playful lilt in his voice. "Jonathan's been hyping you up. Says you've got all the brains in the family."

Emma rolled her eyes but grinned. "Don't believe a word he says. He's just mad I beat him at trivia last week."

"Noted," Lyron replied, his grin widening. "Guess I'd better stay on your good side."

The banter was light, but it made Emma feel immediately at ease. Later, she would tell Don that she felt like she'd known Lyron for years.

A Natural Protector

Jonathan, who had taken an instant liking to Lyron, gestured for him to join him and Emma in the backyard. The three of them ended up tossing a football back and forth, their laughter ringing through the evening air. Jonathan tackled Lyron with playful aggression at one point, but Lyron, quick and agile, dodged him with ease, drawing cheers from the small group of cousins watching on.

Inside, Robert nudged Don with a grin. "That kid of Lisa's—he's got something special. You can see it in the way he carries himself. Strong, kind, and quick on his feet."

Don nodded, his gaze following Lyron with pride. "He reminds me of Lisa," he said softly. "He's got her kindness, her heart for others. I couldn't ask for a better son."

Lisa overheard the conversation and felt her throat tighten. It was true—Lyron was everything she had hoped he would be. As she watched him laugh with Jonathan and Emma, she saw glimpses of the boy she had raised before Margaret's lies had stolen him away. But now, those memories felt less like wounds and more like victories.

A Shared Bond

That evening, as the family gathered around the dinner table, Lyron helped Lisa set the final dishes—a platter of jerk chicken, rice, and beans. He moved with an easy rhythm, anticipating her needs before she could speak them.

"You're a natural," Lisa said with a smile.

Lyron shrugged, his eyes warm. "Learned from the best," he said softly, glancing at her with an expression so full of gratitude it made her heart ache.

When dinner was served, the room was alive with conversation and laughter. Lyron didn't dominate the space, but every time he spoke, his words carried weight. He asked questions about everyone's lives, listening with genuine interest, and when he spoke about his own experiences, he did so with humility.

At one point, Evelyn leaned over to Lisa. "He's wonderful," she whispered. "You've done an incredible job."

Lisa blinked back tears, her heart full. "Thank you," she murmured. "He's everything I prayed for and more."

Guarding What Matters

After dinner, as everyone lingered around the table, Lyron stood, holding up his glass of sparkling cider. "I just want to say thank you," he began, his voice steady. "To Mom, for never giving up on me. To Don, for showing me what a real dad looks like. And to all of you, for welcoming me into your family."

He paused, his gaze moving around the room. "I spent years feeling like

I didn't belong anywhere, believing lies that kept me away from the people who loved me most. But now, being here... it feels like coming home. And I promise, I'm going to do everything I can to protect this family. You've given me a second chance, and I'm not taking it for granted."

The room was silent for a moment, then erupted into applause. Jonathan clapped Lyron on the back, Emma gave him a high-five, and Robert raised his glass with a grin. "Welcome to the family, kid," he said. "You're one of us now."

A Moment with Don

Later that night, Don found Lyron sitting on the back porch, looking up at the stars. He joined him quietly, handing him a mug of cocoa Lisa had prepared.

"You've made quite an impression," Don said, his voice warm. "Everyone's talking about how lucky we are to have you."

Lyron turned, his expression thoughtful. "I'm the lucky one," he said. "You didn't have to welcome me like this. You didn't have to love me like I was your own."

Don placed a hand on Lyron's shoulder, his grip firm but gentle. "You are my own," he said. "From the moment you came into this family, you became one of us. And I'm proud to call you my son."

Lyron's throat tightened, but he managed a small smile. "Thank you, Don. That means more than you know."

Catching Up with Ronald

Later, Lyron excused himself to make a call to his biological father, Ronald. The two spoke often now, sharing stories and laughter as they rebuilt their relationship. Tonight, Lyron told Ronald about the family dinner, about Jonathan's jokes and Emma's quick wit, about the warmth and acceptance he had found.

"Your mom's amazing," Ronald said, his voice thick with emotion. "I hope you know that. She fought for you when no one else could."

"I know, Dad," Lyron replied, his voice quiet but firm. "And I'll never let her forget how grateful I am."

As the night wore on, Lyron returned to the living room, where Lisa and Don waited. He sat between them, leaning back with a contented sigh. He reached for Lisa's hand, holding it tightly.

"Thank you," he said simply, his eyes shining. "For everything."

Lisa smiled, resting her head on his shoulder. "You're worth it, Lyron. You always have been."

And in that moment, surrounded by family, Lyron felt something he hadn't in years—a sense of belonging, of being loved without condition. He was home, and he intended to make the most of every moment.

Chapter 66: A Reckoning in the Spotlight

The studio buzzed with electricity as the crew prepared for what would become one of the most talked-about episodes of the year. Lisa, Don, and Lyron sat backstage, awaiting their cue to step into the spotlight once again. Their story had gripped the nation, and audiences couldn't get enough of the powerful journey of love, loss, and redemption.

But Lisa's heart was heavy with anticipation. This wasn't just another interview. Today held the promise of closure.

Lyron sat beside her, his hand resting protectively over hers. "Mom," he said softly, "you've got this. Whatever happens today, we're here together."

Don nodded, his steady presence grounding both of them. "We've faced worse. This is just one more step toward healing."

Lisa managed a small smile, drawing strength from her husband and son. "Thank you. Both of you. I couldn't have done any of this without you."

The host, a seasoned professional known for her compassionate yet sharp demeanor, introduced them to thunderous applause. As they walked onto the stage, the audience rose to their feet, their cheers a wave of support that washed over Lisa, bringing tears to her eyes.

"Thank you so much for joining us again," the host began, her voice warm but laced with anticipation. "Your story has resonated with millions. Lisa, your song *Prodigal Son* has become a beacon of hope for families everywhere. How does it feel to be here today with your son by your side?"

Lisa glanced at Lyron, her eyes shimmering. "It feels like a dream come true," she said. "For years, I prayed, I hoped, and I believed. And now, having Lyron here, it's more than I ever dared to imagine."

Lyron leaned into the microphone, his voice steady. "I didn't know what I was missing until I found it again," he said simply. "My mom's love is... unshakable. She never stopped fighting for me, even when I didn't believe she loved me. That's something I'll carry with me forever."

The audience erupted into applause, some wiping away tears.

The host leaned forward, her expression turning serious. "Lisa, your journey hasn't been without challenges. And today, we have someone here who wants to address what's been said. Your sister, Margaret, has agreed to come on the show."

Gasps rippled through the audience. Lisa's breath caught in her throat, and she turned to Don, who gave her hand a firm squeeze. Lyron's face hardened, his jaw set in defiance.

Margaret stepped onto the stage, her expression a mix of defiance and nervous energy. The audience's reaction was immediate—a collective murmur, followed by a smattering of boos. Margaret flinched but quickly composed herself, taking a seat opposite Lisa.

"I came here to defend myself," Margaret began, her tone sharp. "Lisa has been painting me as a villain, but she's not the saint everyone thinks she is. I had to step in to protect Lyron—"

"Protect me?" Lyron's voice cut through her words like a blade, his tone incredulous. "You told me my mother hated me. That she didn't want me. You kept me trapped in your house, fed me lies, and made me believe I was better off without her."

The audience fell silent, every eye fixed on the young man who had become the heart of Lisa's story.

"I believed you," Lyron continued, his voice cracking with emotion. "But deep down, I always felt something was wrong. I couldn't remember my mom ever being the way you described her. And when I heard her song... when I saw her fighting for me on TV... I knew the truth. You didn't protect me, Auntie. You stole me."

Margaret's face twisted, her composure slipping. "That's not true! I did what I had to do to—"

The host raised a hand, silencing her. "Margaret, your actions have caused a lot of pain. But we've done our research, and we have someone here today who can shed light on what really happened."

The studio doors opened, and a man stepped onto the stage. Lisa recognized him immediately as Margaret's former boyfriend. The audience gasped, the tension in the room thick enough to cut with a knife.

"I stayed silent for too long," he began, his voice trembling but resolute. "I saw what Margaret did to Lyron, how she manipulated him, isolated him from his family. I wanted to speak out, but I was afraid. She threatened me, made me feel like I couldn't."

Margaret shot to her feet. "You're lying!" she shrieked. "This is all a setup!"

But the audience wasn't buying it. They booed loudly, their disapproval drowning out her protests. Margaret's face contorted with rage as security personnel stepped onto the stage.

"Margaret," one of them said calmly, "we need to speak with you. Please come with us."

Realizing the gravity of the situation, Margaret's bravado crumbled. She was escorted offstage, her cries of protest fading as the doors closed behind her.

The host turned back to Lisa, Don, and Lyron. "Lisa," she said softly, "it seems justice has finally caught up to your sister. How do you feel?"

Lisa took a deep breath, her voice steady but filled with emotion. "I feel free," she said simply. "For years, Margaret's lies controlled my life. But now, the truth is out. And my family can finally heal."

Lyron wrapped his arm around her, his voice firm. "She'll never hurt us again," he said. "We're stronger than that."

The audience erupted into applause, rising to their feet in a show of solidarity.

A New Chapter Begins

The days following the broadcast were a whirlwind. Social media exploded with support for Lisa and her family. Lyron became an instant sensation, praised for his courage and integrity. Media outlets clamored for interviews, eager to share his side of the story.

Back at home, Lisa and Don watched as Lyron flourished. He took every call from family members and old friends with a gracious heart, his kindness and thoughtfulness shining through. Don's siblings welcomed him warmly, and Emma and Jonathan quickly became his biggest cheerleaders.

One evening, Lyron joined Lisa on the back porch, the two of them gazing up at the stars. "Mom," he said softly, "I don't know how you did it—how you kept going all those years."

Lisa smiled, tears glistening in her eyes. "Because you're my son," she said. "And a mother's love doesn't give up. Ever."

Lyron leaned over, wrapping her in a hug. "Thank you," he whispered. "For everything."

As they sat there, the stars above shining brightly, Lisa felt a peace she hadn't known in years. Her family was whole again, and their future was as limitless as the sky.

Chapter 67: The Greatest Feast

The morning sun streamed into the kitchen as Lisa hummed softly, stirring a pot of delicious corn porridge with creamy coconut milk. She had just baked a mouth-watering batch of coconut bakes. She knew that Lyron would have missed his favorite dishes for so long and she wanted to give him back the familiar tastes he'd long for. The aroma of freshly baked goods filled the air. Life in their home had found a new rhythm since Lyron returned, one filled with laughter, warmth, and a sense of completeness. Lyron's presence had brought a light that Lisa hadn't realized she was missing.

Don walked in, carrying two glasses of freshly squeezed lime juice, the tangy citrus scent following him. "Morning, Darlyn," he greeted, handing Lisa a glass.

She smiled, taking a sip and savoring the balance of sweet and tart. "Still perfect, even with white sugar," she teased.

Don grinned. "I told you I've mastered it. This lime juice might just be the highlight of the feast."

Lisa laughed, her eyes twinkling. "Feast? What feast?"

Don raised an eyebrow. "You didn't forget, did you?" he asked, feigning shock. "You promised Lyron the greatest feast, like the father in *The Prodigal Son* story. Or was that just a clever lyric in your song?"

Lisa paused, her smile softening. "Don, I was so caught up in the joy of getting him back that I forgot." She set her glass down, her eyes brimming with gratitude. "You're right. I made a promise, and it's time to keep it."

Don kissed her forehead. "Then let's make it happen. I'll help with the lime juice—of course—and whatever else you need."

Preparing the Feast

The kitchen came alive with activity as Lisa got to work, determined to make Lyron's favorite dishes. The macaroni pie bubbled in the oven, its golden crust glistening with melted cheese. She marinated chicken legs with her signature green seasoning, baking them to tender perfection. Bowls of crisp vegetable salad and golden-crusted potato pudding lined the counter, alongside a platter of coconut buns glistening with a light sugar glaze.

Don, true to his word, focused on the lime juice. He proudly mixed a pitcher, tasting it with exaggerated flair. "This," he declared, "is going to steal the show."

Lyron walked in, catching the end of Don's proclamation. "That lime juice has nothing on Mom's macaroni pie," he teased, his eyes lighting up at the sight of the spread.

Don laughed, clinking his glass with Lyron's. "We'll let the guests decide."

The Gathering

The backyard was transformed into a vibrant celebration. Strings of fairy lights twinkled above tables adorned with colorful tablecloths and fresh flowers. Don's siblings—Karen, Robert, and Evelyn—arrived early, each bringing their infectious energy and heartfelt excitement.

"Lisa," Evelyn said, wrapping her in a warm hug. "You've outdone yourself. The table looks incredible."

Karen added with a wink, "And I see Don's lime juice is front and center."

Lyron set up his phone on a tripod, streaming the event live to his growing social media following. Fans flooded the comments with messages of excitement and support.

"Lyron!" one comment read. "You're the star of the show! What's on the menu?"

He grinned at the camera, gesturing to the feast. "Everything my mom makes best—macaroni pie, baked chicken, coconut buns... and my stepdad's famous lime juice," he added with a playful smirk.

Don leaned into the shot, raising his glass. "Cheers to that!"

The crowd gathered, laughter and conversation filling the air as they settled around the table. Lisa stood at the head, her voice carrying warmth and gratitude.

A Remote Reunion

Though David, Weslie, and Ronald couldn't attend in person, they joined the celebration through a video call from Grenada and Canada. Their faces lit up the large screen that had been set up in the corner of the yard.

"Mom, the table looks amazing!" Weslie exclaimed, his voice filled with admiration.

"And Don," David added, grinning, "I hear you're becoming a very famous Grenadian lime juice expert now."

Don raised his glass to the camera. "That's right! Your mom's been teaching me well."

Ronald's voice, quieter but sincere, cut through the laughter. "Lisa, you've always been the glue holding this family together. Thank you for never giving up on Lyron. I'm proud of you."

Lyron stepped into view, his voice steady as he addressed his father and brothers. "I'm just glad to be back, Dad. And I'll visit soon—I promise, or you can come visit me."

The emotion was palpable, the video call bridging miles and hearts. Lisa wiped a tear from her cheek, her voice trembling. "This is what I prayed for—for all of us to find peace, no matter where we are."

Lisa Tells the Story

"Before we eat," Lisa began, her hands resting gently on Lyron's shoulders, "I want to tell you all the story behind *The Prodigal Son*. It's from the Bible, in Luke 15. A father had two sons, and the younger one demanded his inheritance early. He left home, wasted it all, and found himself in ruin. But when he returned, broken and ashamed, his father welcomed him with open arms and threw him a feast."

Her voice softened, her eyes glistening. "This feast is for my son, Lyron. He may not have squandered his life like the son in the parable, but he was lost to me. Now, by God's grace, he's found. This is my promise fulfilled."

The guests nodded, many wiping their eyes. Lyron hugged his mother tightly. "Thank you, Mom," he whispered. "For never giving up on me."

Then, before sitting to eat, Lyron blasted the Prodigal Son music on his phone. Everyone hummed to the song as they dug in.

A Night of Celebration

The meal began with a toast—Don raised his glass of lime juice high. "To Lisa, for being the heart of this family. And to Lyron, for reminding us all of the power of love and forgiveness."

Karen chimed in, "And to Don's lime juice, because we can't stop talking about it."

The table erupted into laughter as they dug into the feast. Lyron moved through the crowd with quiet charm, helping to serve plates, pouring drinks, and making everyone feel welcome. His gratitude shone in every gesture, his actions speaking louder than words.

As the evening wore on, Lyron's live stream continued to buzz with activity. Fans commented on the food, the decorations, and Lisa's story, their messages of support pouring in.

A Family Reunited

Toward the end of the meal, Lyron took a moment to address the camera. "I'm here today because of my mom," he said, his voice steady but filled with emotion. "She never stopped fighting for me, even when I didn't know it. And now, I'm home."

The guests applauded, their cheers blending with the virtual claps and heart emojis flooding the stream. Lyron smiled, raising his glass. "To my mom, the real MVP."

Lisa wiped her eyes, feeling a surge of pride and love. She leaned into Don, who wrapped an arm around her. "This is what it's all about," he said softly.

A Legacy of Love

As the feast wound down and the laughter faded into the evening breeze,

Lyron stood beside his mother, their eyes fixed on the horizon where the sun dipped below the sea, casting a warm, golden glow. Lisa's expression grew thoughtful, her fingers idly tracing the edge of her plate.

"You know, son," she began softly, her voice steady but filled with determination, "I've been reflecting on everything that happened. The next thing on the agenda is to advocate for a change in the laws. The age limitations that stopped me from helping you—those need to go. People like you, who need help but lack the confidence or the means to ask for it, shouldn't be left stranded."

Lyron turned to her, listening intently. Lisa continued, her gaze distant but her words sharp with resolve. "I tried so many times to get you away from Margaret, but every time, the police's hands were tied. They couldn't do anything because you were an adult. If you had been a minor or elderly, I could have intervened, but being an adult barred me from doing so. Margaret used that loophole to keep you hidden, to maintain control. It's not right, and I'm going to make sure no one else has to go through that."

She paused, then smiled faintly. "And there's one more thing—I want to finish developing the app I prototyped years ago. Do you remember 'ProtectEM?'"

Lyron's face lit up with recognition. "I remember, Mom," he said quietly. "That app could make a real difference for people in abusive or controlling situations. I want to help you with it, and with your advocacy work. Whatever comes next, I'm in. David, Weslie, and I can work on the technical side—research, development, anything you need."

Lisa turned to him, her eyes misty with gratitude. She reached out, pulling him into a warm embrace. "Thank you, Lyron. You're incredible. With your help, we'll make this happen. I'm so proud of you."

Closing the Night

As the first stars began to twinkle in the velvety night sky, the family gathered for a group photo. Laughter and joy radiated from their faces, and at the center stood Lyron, his arm draped protectively around his mother. The way he looked at her spoke volumes—of gratitude, of love, of the unbreakable bond between mother and son.

When the guests began to depart, Don joined Lisa in tidying up, their movements in sync as they cleared plates and folded tablecloths. Picking up the last glass of lime juice, Don took a deliberate sip, savoring the taste.

"Still perfect," he declared with a playful grin.

Lisa chuckled, leaning into him, her smile warm. "You've officially earned the title of Grenadian lime juice expert."

Across the yard, Lyron's voice rose above the murmur of conversations as he chatted animatedly with Karen and Evelyn. His smile was infectious, lighting up the night like a beacon of joy.

Lisa sighed, her heart swelling with contentment. "He's home, Don," she said quietly, her voice tinged with emotion. "That's all I ever prayed for. He's home."

Don wrapped an arm around her shoulders, pressing a tender kiss to her temple. "You brought him back, Lisa. And now he's not just home—he's part of a family that's stronger because of you."

The night deepened, the stars twinkling brighter against the inky sky. As Don and Lisa finally retired for the night, Lisa paused at the doorway, her gaze lingering on the vibrant memories of the evening.

She closed her eyes, whispering a silent prayer of gratitude. Her heart overflowed with love, faith, and hope. Tonight had been more than a feast—it was a celebration of resilience, redemption, and the enduring power of family.

Bottom of Form

Chapter 68: Building a Legacy

The morning air was crisp, and the first rays of sunlight spilled into Lisa and Don's living room, where Lyron sat at the dining table, his laptop open, and a determined look on his face. Across from him, Lisa sifted through a pile of notes, sketches, and old blueprints—remnants of an idea she had held close to her heart for years.

"Mom," Lyron said, glancing up from his screen. "This is amazing work. You were way ahead of your time when you came up with this. I can't believe you didn't push it further."

Lisa smiled, her expression warm but tinged with regret. "I didn't have the resources back then," she admitted. "Or the right skills. I knew what I wanted it to do, but I didn't know how to make it happen. And with everything else going on... it just got left behind."

"Well," Lyron said with a grin, "it's not getting left behind anymore. *ProtectEM* is going to happen. And I'm going to help you make sure of it."

Lisa's heart swelled with pride and gratitude as she reached across the table to squeeze his hand. "You don't know what this means to me, Lyron. If we can get this app out there, we might save lives—give people a way to call for help when they feel trapped."

Lyron nodded, his expression serious. "We're not just doing this for you, Mom. We're doing it for everyone out there who doesn't have a voice. It's about making sure no one else has to go through what we did."

A Shared Mission

The project quickly became a labor of love for both mother and son. Lyron leveraged his connections with social organizations and law enforcement agencies, reaching out to build partnerships and gather insights. He spent hours on calls and video meetings, explaining the vision for ProtectEM and rallying support from advocacy groups and tech developers who were eager to be part of something impactful.

Meanwhile, Lisa focused on the app's design and functionality. She sketched out user interfaces, imagining what features a victim might need in a moment of crisis. The app had to be discreet—something a user could activate without drawing attention. It needed to connect them directly to the authorities or trusted contacts with the tap of a button.

Don, always supportive, kept them fueled with coffee and encouragement, even stepping in to help brainstorm solutions. "What if that app could be embedded into ordinary devices for ease of use and discreteness?"

"That's brilliant, Dad!" Lyron said, quickly typing notes. "We can integrate that as a safety feature."

Lisa smiled, her heart brimming with love. "See, Don? You're part of this team too."

"I wouldn't have it any other way," Don replied, kissing her on the cheek.

Advocacy and Change

As the app development progressed, Lisa and Lyron turned their attention to advocacy. One of the key barriers Lisa had faced in the past was the age limitation on abuse reporting—a limitation that had prevented her from seeking help on behalf of Lyron when he was in Margaret's clutches, and one that Margaret used to her advantage.

"Mom," Lyron said during one of their planning sessions, "we need to push for changes to the law. If ProtectEM is going to work, the system has to work with it. People need to be able to report abuse, regardless of the victim's age. Noone should have to suffer in silence like I did, just because of fear."

Lisa nodded, her resolve hardening. "You're right, Lyron. We need to do more than create a tool—we need to fix the system that failed us in the first place."

Together, they drafted proposals, met with policymakers, and testified at public hearings. Lyron's presence added weight to their arguments; his story, told with raw honesty, was impossible to ignore. He spoke about feeling trapped, about how Margaret had manipulated him into believing lies about his mother. But he also spoke about the power of love and resilience—how his mother's unwavering faith had saved him in the end.

"Abuse isn't always physical," Lyron told a captivated audience at one hearing. "It's control, manipulation, isolation. And it doesn't stop just because someone turns eighteen. We need to protect everyone, regardless of their age."

His words moved lawmakers and advocates alike, sparking a wave of support for their cause. Slowly but surely, they began to see progress. Policies were revised, and new protections were introduced, removing the barriers that had once hindered families like theirs.

Bringing ProtectEM to Life

After months of hard work, the first version of ProtectEM was ready to launch. The app was sleek, intuitive, and packed with features: an emergency alert button, GPS tracking and even resources for victims seeking shelter or legal aid. It was everything Lisa had dreamed of—and more.

To mark the occasion, they hosted a small gathering at their home, inviting friends, family, and some of the key partners who had helped make the project a reality. Lyron stood at the center of the room, his laptop connected to a large screen as he demonstrated the app's features.

"And here's the best part," he said, pulling up the emergency contact screen. "When someone uses ProtectEM to call for help, it doesn't just alert authorities—it also sends a message to their trusted contacts, letting them know what's happening and where to find them."

The room erupted into applause, and Lisa felt tears prick her eyes as she looked at her son. "You've done so much, Lyron," she said softly, her voice trembling with pride. "You've turned my dream into a reality, my pain int pride."

He turned to her, his expression warm. "We did it together, Mom. And we're just getting started."

A Legacy of Hope

As ProtectEM went live, it quickly gained traction, drawing praise from advocacy groups, law enforcement agencies, and users who hailed it as a groundbreaking tool for empowering victims. Lyron, now a passionate advocate for the cause, continued to work closely with his mother, attending conferences and sharing their story with audiences around the world.

One evening, as they prepared for a major presentation, Lisa paused to look at her son. "Lyron," she said, her voice thick with emotion, "I couldn't be prouder of the man you've become. You've taken our pain and turned it into something beautiful—something that will help so many people."

He smiled, pulling her into a hug. "I learned from the best, Mom. You taught me to never give up, no matter how hard it gets. And now, we're making a difference—together."

As they stepped onto the stage that night, Lisa felt a profound sense of fulfillment. ProtectEM wasn't just an app—it was a symbol of resilience, a testament to the power of love and faith. And with Lyron by her side, she knew they were creating a legacy that would endure for generations to come.

Chapter 69: God Meant It for Good

The golden hues of the setting sun bathed Lisa and Don's home in a warm, tranquil light. Lisa stood by the window, gazing out at the city skyline as the evening breeze rustled the curtains. Her heart was full, yet peaceful—a deep, abiding peace that could only come from a place of unwavering faith. Behind her, Don sat on the couch, flipping through a photo album filled with memories of their journey together.

"Do you ever think about how we got here?" Lisa asked softly, her voice carrying a tone of reflection.

Don looked up, his eyes meeting hers with a tender smile. "Every single day," he replied. "Sometimes I can't believe it, Lisa. Everything we've been through, everything you've faced—and yet, here we are."

Lisa moved to sit beside him, her fingers tracing the edge of the photo album. "I was thinking about the verse in Genesis 50:20," she said, her voice thoughtful. "'What was meant for evil, God meant for good.' I see it so clearly now. My divorce, the pain of losing Lyron, and even the people who turned their backs on me without a cause—it was all part of God's plan."

Don nodded, listening intently. Lisa continued, her gaze distant as she recounted their journey. "If my family hadn't been disrupted, I wouldn't have been pushed to my knees, crying out to God. If everyone had helped me, I wouldn't have had the drive to write the book, create the music, or develop the app. And if none of that had happened..." She paused, turning to Don with a smile. "I wouldn't have met you."

Don reached out, taking her hand in his. "I've thought about that a lot," he said, his voice low and filled with emotion. "If things hadn't fallen apart for both of us, we wouldn't have crossed paths. Lisa, you've changed my life. Watching you move through everything with such grace and faith... it's made me see the world differently. You've shown me what it means to trust God, even when everything feels hopeless."

Lisa's eyes glistened with an assured look. "I couldn't have done it alone, Don. God was with me every step of the way. And so were you."

Don took a deep breath, his hand tightening around hers. "I've been thinking about something," he said, his voice trembling slightly. "Watching you live out your faith, seeing how it's carried you through—I've realized that's what's been missing in my life. I've always believed in you, Lisa, but now... I believe in Him too. I want to live for Christ, just like you do."

Lisa's breath caught, her heart swelling with emotion. "Don... that's the most beautiful thing you could ever say to me."

He smiled, his eyes filled with sincerity. "It's the truth. I want to follow Him, Lisa. I want us to build our lives on faith, together. And I promise to love you, no matter what."

Tears streamed down Lisa's face as she leaned in to kiss him, her heart overwhelmed with gratitude. "Welcome home, Don," she whispered. "This is just the beginning of a new chapter for us."

Forgiveness and Redemption

In the days that followed, their family grew even closer. Lyron, David, and Weslie kept in constant contact, sharing updates and laughter over video calls. Ronald, who had moved back into the family home with David, their eldest son, had found a new sense of peace. He called Lisa one afternoon, his voice steady and filled with humility.

"Lisa," he said, "I've been thinking about everything that's happened. I want you to know that I've made peace with it all. I've made peace with myself. I see now how much you've done for our sons, and I'm grateful. You're an amazing woman, and Don is lucky to have you. I give you both my blessings."

Lisa smiled, her heart warm with forgiveness. "Thank you, Ronald," she said. "That means more than you know. And I want you to know that I've forgiven you, a long time ago. I encourage the boys to check on you, to make sure you're doing well. We're still family, and we will always be."

Ronald chuckled softly. "You've always had the biggest heart, Lisa. I wish you nothing but happiness."

As the call ended, Lisa felt a sense of closure wash over her. Forgiveness had come full circle, and the wounds of the past had finally begun to heal.

A United Family

Their home became a hub of love and laughter. Lyron had fully embraced his role in their new family, bonding with Don's children, Emma and Jonathan, as if they had known each other their entire lives. Don often remarked on how much Lyron resembled his mother—not just in appearance, but in his kindness, thoughtfulness, and determination to help others.

One evening, as the family gathered around the dinner table, Don raised a glass of Lisa's freshly made Grenadian lime juice—now a staple in their home. "To Lisa," he said, his voice filled with pride. "The woman who brought us all together, who never gave up, and who shows us every day what love and faith truly mean."

The room erupted into cheers, and Lisa laughed, her cheeks flushing with happiness. Lyron grinned at her from across the table, his eyes shining with gratitude. "To Mom," he said. "The strongest person I know."

As they clinked glasses and shared stories, the warmth of their love filled every corner of the room. It was a picture of unity, a testament to the power of forgiveness and the beauty of a family rebuilt on faith.

A New Legacy

Lisa's work continued to thrive. Her book and album had become bestsellers, her app ProtectEM was saving lives, and her advocacy work was making a tangible impact. But more than any of her accomplishments, Lisa treasured the love that surrounded her—the family she had fought so hard to rebuild, the husband who had found his faith, and the sons who had grown into kind, loving men.

One quiet evening, as she sat on the porch with Don, watching the stars, Lisa leaned against his shoulder, her heart full. "Looking back," she said softly, "I see it all so clearly now. Everything we went through—it wasn't random. God had a plan. What was meant for evil, He turned into good."

Don kissed the top of her head, his voice a tender whisper. "And I'm so thankful for that plan. Because it brought me to you."

They sat in peaceful silence, holding hands, as the sounds of their family's laughter drifted through the open window. The shadows of the past had finally faded, leaving only the light of a love that had triumphed over every obstacle. In the silence of the evening, Lisa began humming the song she had written, and saw how well it had summarized their journey of love:

"You Can't Cage Love"

(Verse 1)

You can't cage love, no you can't tie it down
It's like the wind, it moves all around
No walls can stop what the heart truly feels
When love is real, yeah, it's gonna heal

(Pre-Chorus)

Through every storm, through every fight
Love will find its way, like stars in the night

(Chorus)

You can't cage love, it's wild and free
It will break through chains and fly to where it's meant to be
You can't stop hearts from finding their place
Love will break free and win the race
Oh, you can't cage love, no, no you can't cage love

(Verse 2)

Don't try to limit what two hearts share
When love's alive, it's always there
It whispers softly, it fights so loud
Love will rise up, it's never bowed

(Pre-Chorus)

Through every tear, through all the pain
Love will find the sun, after the rain

Lisa and Don closed their eyes, as Don led in a simple prayer of gratitude. "Thank you, God," he began. "For everything you have led us through, and for this song, and the impact it will have on those who hear it. Thank you so much Lord, for your perfect plan for our lives, and for bringing us all together in perfect love. Amen!"

And as the stars twinkled above, Lisa and Don embraced the promise of a future filled with faith, love, and the unshakable bond of a family that had been made whole once more.

The End.

Bottom of Form